TSAR'S WOMAN

By the same author

THE DEVIL OF ASKE
WHITTON'S FOLLY
HEATHERTON HERITAGE
NORAH
THE GREEN SALAMANDER
STRANGER'S FOREST
DANECLERE
FIRE OPAL
A PLACE OF RAVENS
THE HOUSE OF CRAY
BRIDE OF AE

TSAR'S WOMAN

A NEW HISTORICAL NOVEL BY THE AUTHOR OF *Bride of Ae*

Pamela Hill

St. Martin's Press
New York

TSAR'S WOMAN. Copyright © 1977 by Pamela Hill. All rights reserved. Printed in the United States of America. No part of this book may be used or reproduced in any manner whatsoever without written permission except in the case of brief quotations embodied in critical articles or reviews. For information, address St. Martin's Press, 175 Fifth Avenue, New York, N.Y. 10010.

Library of Congress Cataloging in Publication Data

Hill, Pamela.
  Tsar's woman.
    1. Catherine I, Empress of Russia, 1684-1727—Fiction. I. Title.
  PR6058.I446T7   1985   823'.914   85-2664
  ISBN 0-312-82192-1

First published in Great Britain by Robert Hale Ltd.

First U.S. Edition

10 9 8 7 6 5 4 3 2 1

AUTHOR'S NOTE

Perhaps it would be as well to state here that Marfa Skavronskaya, Marfa Vassilievka, Ekaterina Vassilievka, and Ekaterina Alexievna were, for reasons to be explained, the same remarkable woman whom we barely remember in history as Catherine I of Russia, widow of Peter the Great.

CONTENTS

1	God's Fair	9
2	Elizabeth Petrovna's Tale	45
3	The Empress: Drumbeat	54
4	The Pieman's Tale	79
5	The Empress: The Island of Hares	106
6	I, Alexis	138
7	The Empress: Absalom	162
8	The Cap of Monomakh	192

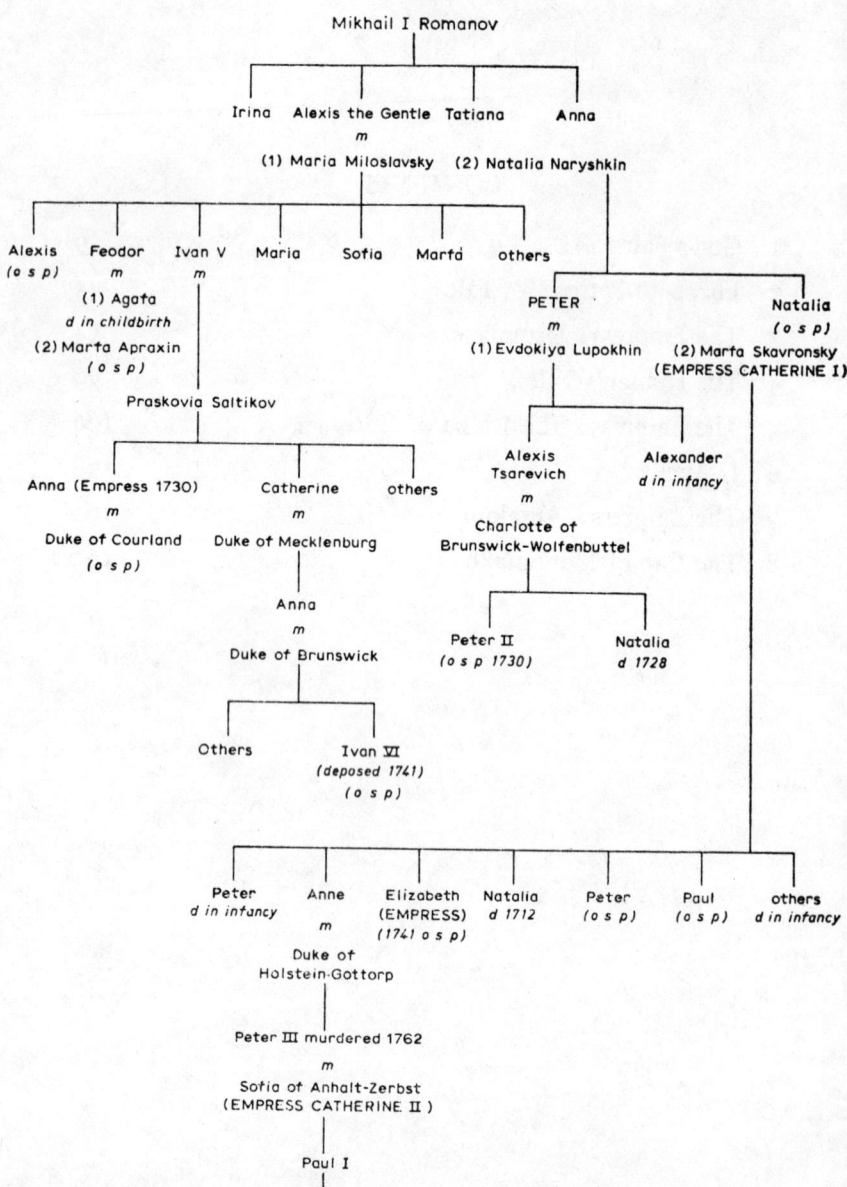

The Romanov dynasty, ending in Nicholas II and his son Alexis, murdered 1918.

ONE

GOD'S FAIR

"Get beer, and plenty of it. See that it's iced."

I turn then to the place where on the linen-hung wall, away from the window giving on to the garden with its roses and lime trees, hangs a Venetian mirror shattered by my husband in course of our last quarrel. I have never had it mended; there are still enough fragments of glass left for me to see myself. I am wearing, today, the purple velvet cloak and the regalia. They will be laughing outside, maybe even as far as the kitchens, because I have chosen to dress up to receive my daughter Elizabeth and, with her, my husband's two grandchildren. "She will have herself painted and bejewelled to receive certain persons, then let her hair down so that the servants see her drunk in a morning-wrapper." That is what they will be saying and it is true. But Elizabeth Petrovna and the children are not ordinary persons. It is probable that young Peter Alexievich will reign after I am dead, in spite of everything the late Tsar decided. In any case it is my fancy to receive my guests formally, and have the beer as well. Why tell me I am Autocrat of all the Russias if I cannot do as I wish?

I have been some good to them, when all's said. Only the other day I opened the Academy of Sciences, now it is finished, and a bookshop on what used to be a marsh. That for me, who cannot read or write, is something. So besides being myself, what am I? What do they say that I am? The most high, most potent, most serene—bah—Great Lady and Grand Duchess of all the Greater, Lesser and White Russias; Self-Upholder and Autocrat; Ruler of Muscovy, Kiev, Vladimir, Novgorod; of Kazan and Astrakhan; of Siberia; Lady of Plesco (where is that? We never went there)—Grand Duchess of Smolensk, Ugoria, Permia, Vatkia, Bulgaria; Lady and Great Duchess of the Lower Countries, of Czernichov, Rezan, Rostov, Yaroslav, Belozersky, Adorsky, Obdorsky, and Condinsky; Commander of all the Northern Coasts (ay, they may well say so, after the trouble we had), Lady of the Lands of Tveria and Grudzinia; Ruler of the Lands of Cabardinia, Circassia, and Duchess of the Mountains and of many other dominions and countries, east, west, and north. That means Cossacks and Tartars and Bashkirs and Muscovites and God knows who else. And there was nobody but me left to govern them.

The broken mirror shows me my face, on which the red and white paint is beginning to run. I've had to paint a lot lately. Underneath, my skin is still brown and smooth, though I sag a bit; but after all I've borne twelve children. My hair is still plentiful, and before putting on the crown today I had them freshen it up with black dye, for the roots were showing grey. And they painted my eyebrows. These are my best feature, and I'm as proud of them as I'm ashamed of my big hands and feet, a peasant's. But my brows are like a bird's wings, a questing and curious bird about to take flight. They arch over dark eyes which are not a bad pair, although that young madam Wilhelmina of Prussia once described me as pop-eyed. I have a short nose and good-tempered mouth and cleft chin and my teeth are sound. There is nothing about me—is there?—which should have attracted Peter Alexievich to me above all other women, from whom he returned to me always. As he used to say, it was my good-nature he liked; he found it restful. What I say is that there's enough trouble in the world without adding to it, and most of the trouble comes from folk who are idle. I never was; I used to be a washerwoman, and no one could launder and iron fine linen better. If they turned me out tomorrow I could keep myself, doing that. I always did the Tsar's shirts to the end, though he let them get very dirty. And I darned his hose, because he wouldn't wear the new ones I knitted for him when we were on campaign—dear God, how I remember that bitter winter the year of Poltava—and the hot summers in the south, and the Tsar and I shaved our heads and wore helmets and were fired at, but never hit. It was like a miracle, the way he escaped, and so did I. I was often beside him in the front line.

Strange now having nobody to please but myself, no one to take orders from. The guard outside still call me Katia, but they don't know I know it.

He is dead, my own man, all that fierce thrusting energy and purpose that struck fear into weaker hearts, stilled in a moment and changed to dust. But I was with him to the last there, too. I closed his eyes.

At least, nowadays, I can have the children brought to me, his son's children. He would never permit them, for the sake of their father whose death he took on himself, to be brought to Court. Soon they will come shyly in, not yet having quite lost the fear in which they were made to exist till now: it must have been all about them, always, and it's difficult to shake off a thing like that. I want to do as much as I can for those children. It's a good thing Elizabeth gets on with them; she's nearer their age than I am, after all. But they cling together, those two, as if for protection. When I asked young Peter Alexievich the other day what he wanted most in the world, he said, "If it please your Imperial Majesty, never to be parted from Natalia." The mother's dead, it's true; they never knew her. And Alexis while he lived cared nothing for them. As for the Tsar, some fool of a servant told them—I had this from Elizabeth—that if their grandfather once set eyes on them, it would cause him to fall into one of his terrible fits, when he used to do things he regretted afterwards. And the fits themselves came of Peter's own fear. I knew that, though I'm an uneducated person.

The beer has come. It tastes good; this has been a hot day, although the shadows are beginning to come in now over the sea. How many shadows there are! I can almost see them creeping past between me and the painted window-shutters. So many dead; some in battle, that is to be expected. Thousands and thousands in battle, and thousands more in the marshes here, digging the earth with their bare hands and carrying it in their coats when the sacks wore out; hungry and thirsty, and fevered often, and not kept warm. A hundred and thirty thousand dead to build Petersburg. Well, it's a fine city. And the others, who were tortured; I can still hear them screaming. I try not to put a face to the screams, but sometimes it comes in spite of me; young men's faces, gentle-featured; like Alexis the Tsarevich, or William Mons.

Mons was lucky. Although he'd been my lover he wasn't knouted to ribbons or roasted over a slow fire before they killed him. The Tsar gave out that his crime had been taking bribes, everything kept polite. Peter could be merciful in his own strange way. Why otherwise didn't he kill his wife Evdokiya or his sister Sofia or William's sister Anna? Why, for that matter, didn't he kill me? But the screams of the tortured are not few; they have echoed in the city's streets here and in Moscow, sounding as far as Novodevichi, as Suzdal Pokrovsky, where the nun Helen, the nun Susanna, heard them. Helen; Peter's first wife Evdokiya, mother of Alexis, whom he didn't love. I never saw Evdokiya. And I couldn't have seen Sofia, for she died while I was still following the army up and down Livonia and the Swedish provinces. She died in her convent cell, but she'd been a clever woman; she ruled as Regent all Peter's youth, when he and the half-wit Ivan were twin Tsars. I often think about Sofia, and what she'd have done or said when certain decisions are brought to me. They think I don't rule, that Alexasha Menshikov does it all for me, but I keep an eye on Alexasha, as the Tsar always did. He's a slippery customer at lining his own pockets, is Menshikov. If I were younger I'd do without him more. But I go out very little now. Sometimes they carry me in a chair through the suburbs and villages, and behind the orderly double ranks of the guards I see gaunt faces peering. If, again, I were younger I'd have the chair set down, and get out and see for myself the way the peasants live. After all, I used to know. Have they enough to eat? Do the landowners work them too harshly, without a fair share in the harvest afterwards? Are there warm clothes for the children and the old folk? I should find out all these things, for they are my people now and Alexasha only tells me what he thinks I should hear. But I seem to have grown old, quite suddenly. It is perhaps better not to know.

The children have come and gone, although Elizabeth stayed

with me for a little while afterwards, chatting and yawning. She's lazy, which neither I nor her father ever were: since the disappointment about her French marriage I swear she amuses herself with lovers. She is like her father in height, very tall for a woman; and in her round forehead and clearly marked brows and level gaze. They say she's handsome, but what good is that? Everyone is better to have some purpose in life. I will say Elizabeth doesn't complain about the way she must pass her days in her own palace in Petersburg, and that's helpful. But it's sad, if you think of it; almost as sad as the lot of women used to be when they all lived in a Terem, a separate quarter, and knew nothing of what was going on, or if they did they kept it to themselves. Peter altered all that. They say he ripped the veils from women's faces and the beards from the men's. Everything was different in Russia before he came; nothing in Russia will be the same again, now that he has come and gone like a whirlwind. There was never a man like him anywhere. Even the older nobility would agree with that, though they resented the things he did; what they wanted, and didn't get, was a Tsar like a puppet in a silver robe and golden crown, doing nothing, except crossing himself with the proper number of fingers and falling flat before the ikons. Someone told me that Peter's father used to make one hundred prostrations every day. Peter was different, even to the widow he left who still enjoys her beer. Well, they can all get on with their business and leave me to mine. I've got good advisers and a few friends, and my brothers if one can include them. I made counts of the Empire of them after Peter died, so that they would have an income and position. He'd found them again for me in 1722; Karl was a groom somewhere and I don't know what Feodor was doing. They'll be all right now when I die.

The children. I wish they hadn't gone so soon, but their tutors keep them at lessons. Young Peter is good to look at, tall and straight as a young tree. He doesn't cringe like his father Alexis used to. He reminds me of an eaglet. I said to him today, "The late Tsar was a giant of a man, seven feet tall. You will resemble him when you're grown." Then I cursed my clumsy tongue, remembering their terror of their grandfather. But it doesn't do any good not to speak of him. "You have more toys than Tsar Peter Alexievich ever had," I told them, for it has been my particular care that a chest full of playthings is placed ready for them wherever they want it. "When he was your age he only had a rocking horse that had belonged to his father, with a copper bridle."

"He had wooden cannon later on, and play regiments, and as soon as he was old enough he asked for the cannon to be of metal and the regiments to be issued with carbines," said Elizabeth, whose knowledge often surprises me; perhaps she isn't as lazy as she looks. Young Peter said, "I shall not make any wars," and his fair cheeks flushed a little so that he resembled more than ever his poor young German mother, except that she was marked with the smallpox and, praise God, Peter Alexievich has so far escaped it. "No, peace is better than war," I agreed with him, and he nodded and looked at me.

"That's what you told the English, isn't it, grandmother?" I was pleased; I didn't know he would have heard of what was only a commonsense letter dictated on my part, telling the English they might patrol the Baltic as much as they pleased, but it takes two to make a war. There has been too much war and the country is exhausted, and I said so when they showed me the map at the Academy of Sciences. I may not be able to fathom letters, but I can read a map. My husband's conquests were marked in red. There were enough of them and I do not intend to try to make any more. Why do rulers despise peace? It's the only sane condition for a country to develop, especially a country like ours where there are thousands of square miles of forest and untilled marsh, and mouths to feed everywhere. There are enough families without fathers. So I smiled at young Peter Alexievich and he smiled back at me, still shyly. After they had gone away I wondered who had told him he would rule, for the late Tsar issued a ukase saying the successor must be chosen. But I would choose young Peter in any case, especially when he has grown older. He is of the line of Romanov and will have a good education.

Little Natalia—she is a sweet child—said to me, "Did

you have toys, Imperial Majesty?" and I laughed; she would mean no harm by it. "No," I said, "it was lucky if I got enough to eat. Toys weren't thought of where I came from."

Everyone looked abashed and I cheered them up and had them laughing before they went away. It won't take long to make reasonable, happy children of them, if I'm spared to do it.

Natalia's innocent question has stayed in my mind, and now I am alone again I can take time to remember the years when I was without toys and most other things.

Memory goes a long way in distance and time. The earliest I have is of dust. We lived in a hut where the floor was made of trodden black earth, and there were a great many of us and in summer it would get dry, and fly up into our clothing in the same way as it churned into clouds behind the horses and carts of passers-by. Hardly anyone stopped in Ringen, Livonia.

I used to play on the floor, near my mother. I stirred the dust with my fingers into patterns and shapes. They had no meaning, in the way the flat grey-green distances, beyond which no one ventured, had none either. That they might hold danger I knew from the day a party of shouting soldiers came and passed roistering through the village, and my mother said they were Danes. The Danes had come from nowhere and went no one knew where, and they might come back. The only safe place was near my mother's skirts.

I would look up from time to time, from where I played, to see her face. I can remember it still. She was a broad-cheeked woman with patient eyes of a grey-green colour, like the distances, and her hair was lint-white like all Livonian women's. She must have been pretty when she was young, and although besides my brothers and sisters there lived with us, in the hut, a set-faced peasant named Samuel Skavronsky, who was my mother's husband, I always knew that he was not my father. Many have tried to tell me since that a nobleman sired me, and although it makes no difference to me I think it may not be unlikely.

Women of my mother's class who are occupied with childbearing and the care of a poor household do not take casual lovers from their own kind. It must have been someone with leisure for patronage, perhaps money, though I do not recall that we ever received that or food from anyone. I do not know how we lived, though Skavronsky would return at night from the fields and my elder brothers worked with him. But we were often hungry. In winter the dust turned to black mud and then froze over, and merchants, or sometimes students, from the nearby town of Dorpat came to drink in the tavern or to try to sell goods by sledge now that the roads were hard: but we could buy nothing.

One thing which makes me curious is that I have always been able to ride. The awareness of a horse's back between my thighs is so familiar that I do not know when I was first mounted. Skavronsky himself would have nothing to do with me and would kick me out of his way when I got in it. But my brother Karl liked to hold horses' heads when by chance a traveller stopped at Ringen for water, and he would bring home coins which he hid in a secret place, for he wanted to leave home and become a groom in some great household. It may have been through Karl that I learned to ride. But I do not remember.

When I was three years old my mother died, and I can recall a desolation which held more kicks than tears. Now I had no refuge, and this for a child is the worst thing of all. I must have made a nuisance of myself in some fashion, for my next memory is of being in a larger house with more than one room, which belonged to the local pastor. Perhaps my unknown father had paid him to look after me. I still saw my sisters and my second brother Feodor at a distance, but not Karl; he must have gone. I expect I mentioned it; I was a child who prattled a lot, especially now that there was no Skavronsky. I remember the pastor taking me on his knees. He was a kindly man with a round body, despite the fact that like everywhere else here there was not enough to eat. He and his wife had many children of their own and were poor. He talked to me of God. I was more interested in why Karl had gone away.

"God will watch over Karl, for he is a willing boy and a

good worker. You also, Marfa, must learn to work and to say your prayers. Only so can you live; those who do no work starve, and those who do not pray might as well be dead in their bodies as in their souls." But this was too much for me.

I was taught simple household tasks and took to them well enough. I have always preferred doing something to doing nothing. I also, I remember, even at that early time, knew that to do anything at all, one must do it well. It was not that I was whipped or punished for lack of success, for these folk were kindly. But the task would only have to be done again and so it was better not to waste one's time in the first place. The only occasion for doing nothing else was when we had prayers, and this happened morning and evening and when everyone sat down to food, which was nearly always buck-wheat gruel. We thanked God for the thin stuff and scraped the wooden hollows in the table so hard that the wood had long ago taken on a greasy look, as though it had been polished. Sometimes there was a change: the parish folk would bring a lean fowl or a cabbage or some eggs to the pastor, and then we would eat well and thank God even more. Whether by reason of gruel or cabbage soup I grew taller and stronger, and sometimes I would surprise a worried look on the face of the pastor's wife, especially when she was nursing her baby; there were two more babies during the time I spent there. She would watch me, I know, without thinking that I saw her; if our eyes met she would look away. I knew without being told what she was thinking, that if I were not there it would be one less mouth to feed. But there was nothing I could do about it. I tried my best to help and to be no trouble to anyone. I can remember going to watch the women break the ice on the frozen well and taking a hand to bring up the bucket and someone said, "She will fall in and be drowned; she should not be here," which made me ashamed. I wanted to help to wash the family linen with the water and tread it with my feet and wring it with my hands. I knew already that these were too big; I used to sit on them to hide them.

The winter deepened and the ground grew hard and there were no more fowls or cabbages. Most of the men, except the pastor, had been taken away to the Danish war. This left no one but the women to till the ground and take in such harvest as there was by the year's end. One day everything was worse than usual, for we were expecting a guest and he would have to be fed. His name was Glück and he was pastor of Marienburg, a fortress town, and was passing through Ringen. Of course he must stay with us, because parsons are too poor to pay the bill at an inn, and hospitality is sacred. I was sent out to try to scrabble up some late roots to lend flavour to Pastor Glück's soup, and later watched clean linen being unfolded for his bed, which he would share with the two eldest boys of the house. We were all of us scrubbed and washed and told to be on our best behaviour, and the only garments we had were looked over carefully to see that they were darned in the worn places. Nobody ever had new clothes. Mine were handed down from the younger daughters and by the time I had finished with them they would be ready for the eldest baby. By this time they were frail as spiders' webs and did not keep out the cold, so one kept moving.

Pastor Glück arrived and instead of going to bed early after his travels, stayed up late talking with the Ringen pastor and his wife. Part of it was about me and I heard my name, Marfa Skavronskaya, mentioned many times, but the rest of it was in whispers. Next day the pastor and his wife took me aside and kissed me and said goodbye, as I was to travel with Pastor Glück to Marienburg. I did not cry as I knew there was no help for it, but I felt almost as I had done when my mother had died. Children get used to one thing and don't like to be changed to another.

However, there was the horse. It was brown with a white fetlock and its nose was pink, which meant it had been sold cheaply. Pastor Glück hoisted me up beside him and wrapped me in a corner of his cloak, as the journey would be cold.

So I left Ringen.

I have said already that Marienburg was a fort. The tower stood up in the middle among huddled houses mostly made of wood. From it a flag waved and when I asked Pastor Glück whose it was, he said it was Swedish. Pastor Glück seemed happy to be home. There were advantages to living in a town, as he had tried to make clear to me on the journey. For one thing it is not so cold, as the houses are built close together for warmth; he did not add that when there is a fire they are all burnt down. For another thing, there are no wolves in the streets, though I had heard them howling often enough beyond Ringen. Also, there is a market-place and even when one has no money, there are things to be seen; bright apples, coloured ribbons and men selling gingerbread, and in time of peace great sides of meat hanging ready for sale. But this was not peacetime. However nothing should happen amiss to Marienburg, as I heard many people say by the time I had lived there a year. It had always been able to defend itself; it had a strong fort and a good garrison. I remember the last saying because the person who made it, whose face I forget, gave me an apple bought in the market. I bit into the white flesh and thought it delicious. It was the first I had ever eaten.

For a long time, from my fifth year till I was almost seventeen, nothing did happen. Pastor Glück's family was like the one I had left behind at Ringen; kindly, large, devout, and poor. However a town holds more parish folk than a village and the pastor accordingly received more money and more gifts; often a new-baked loaf made from flour milled almost under our noses, so that the whole of life seemed filled with the fresh smell of bread. Or it might be part of a bale of cloth left over from clothing a family, the stuff itself having come in the first place from Dresden or even Amsterdam. Once I got hold of a tiny scrap of velvet, too small even to make a head-kerchief, but I treasured it for its rich feel and tried to imagine what it must be like to be clad in it. For years I kept it by me in the narrow place where I slept side by side with the pastor's daughters. I was, of course, a servant; but in many ways Pastor Glück treated me like a child of his own, and would no doubt have taught me to read and write if I had shown myself apt. He himself was a scholar and loved books. He said to me one day—it was before he hired a tutor for his increasing family—"Marfa, you are clever and able at your tasks, and you help my wife a great deal. I think that we should give you some education." He was, I may say, ahead of his time; he did not think of women as brood-mares or unpaid household drudges.

After that, for a few painful weeks, I went to his study and made blots with a quill on paper. I tried to master the difficult letters, but it was useless. God had not given me that kind of mind. One day I laid down the writing-things and said, "Pastor, I will never be a learned woman. We are wasting time and paper, and I'd rather be helping the mistress to iron the house-linen." He looked sad and said, "Marfa Skavronskaya, if you would learn you could. There is nothing you cannot do if you set your mind to it. It grieves me to see you end as a maidservant, a laundress. There are those who can wash and iron, but certain others are worth more, much more." And he looked at me as if he could see me, not as I was then, a strong scrubby girl with flaxen hair well hidden under a round laundered coif, but someone else I could neither see nor imagine.

However he agreed to stop the lessons, and after that I worked in the house.

My mistress was pleased with me. "You eat work, Marfa," she said, "and your behaviour is decorous." I was glad of the praise, because firstly it still brings joy to me to see a floor well polished, a table well scrubbed, fresh food and fresh linen. As for luxury, I knew nothing about it then; nowadays, I am too fond of it, though I still wear a darned kirtle when there's no company. Regarding decorum, I had not then seen indecorous manners, and I only copied what I saw. So I deserved no praise for that.

The centre and the core of all our ironing and cleaning and darning and scrubbing was, in fact, church twice on Sundays. Every other day of the week led up to that, and for it we wore the best we had, though nobody in a Lutheran church dresses other than plainly. Pastor Glück came into his own then; during the week he was quiet in his study and only appeared for meals. But in church he was different. A light seemed to shine in him; he hammered out his well-prepared sermons as though he spoke to other scholars, of which there were few. The congregation was made up of miners, millers, housewives, children, lacemakers; such folk. Half of what the pastor said went over their heads, and mine. But he was happy. I am glad that I was able to secure him a well-paid state post before he died.

However, in those days I was too young to doze through the service, as many did. I would steal glances about me behind my fingers during the prayers, and sometimes during the sermon. People have always interested me, and the sleepy familiar folk of the parish were often varied by others; the soldiers of the garrison, some of whom were billeted in the town. These fascinated me particularly because of the great mustachios which half hid their faces, and their boastful gait—they were not always quiet in church—and the uniforms they wore, the officers gay in shining braid and the men clad in green, often mud-splashed if they had been beyond the town. When it was time for the psalm to be sung they would raise their voices lustily. One in particular often returned my stare; he had bright blue eyes above his fair moustache.

As a rule I would look away, not daring to giggle or to make myself a cause of scandal in the pastor's pew. However instead of listening to the sermons and prayers I gradually began to think of myself and the soldier. I knew my body had changed and was now strong and full-breasted, and that men liked to look at me. I was not very tall, but my mouth was shapely and red and if anyone wanted to kiss it. . . .

Such thoughts in church were not seemly.

The sergeant of dragoons—he was a sergeant—came to Pastor Glück soon and asked if he might marry me. It was an honest offer and I was lucky to attract it with no dowry. Pastor Glück told him I was a foundling and my suitor said he did not mind. The good pastor then asked questions about the sergeant's own prospects. He—his name was Vassiliev—made no great boast about himself, which pleased the pastor. Vassiliev's parents were poor and lived in Sweden. On his marriage, he said, his commanding officer had promised to promote him to corporal. "Well, we must not delay your promotion, eh, Marfa?" said the pastor, when he found out that I was willing.

"I made haste to ask because it is not certain how long the regiment will be in Marienburg," said the sergeant, chewing his moustache. He fell silent then, being a man of few words. It was only that he had seen me in church and liked the look of me. He told me so later. He said nothing about my looking about and catching his eye in return, and this loyalty made me pleased with him.

"You must not take her away to follow the camp," said Pastor Glück. "She will stay here, where she has a good home, and you may come to visit her." If the pastor had been less unworldly I would have said he did not want to lose a good servant. But he was concerned only with my welfare.

My wedding to the sergeant of dragoons was a quiet affair. The simple vows I made then have been overlaid with others now, colourful, richer, more enduring. But at that time I was sincere enough. Pastor Glück himself conducted the service and I can recall being as much aware of his presence as of the man I was marrying. Afterwards everyone kissed me including the sergeant, and his fair moustache scraped my neck. I was aware of great gratitude to Pastor Glück and to God and altogether had a feeling which I have often known since after drinking too much wine. But in those days I had drunk none. I remember thanking the pastor for being so good to me. "If I ever have the chance I'll be good to you in return," I said, and he replied in the words my mistress had already used and said that I had always been hard-working and had behaved with decorum. Years later when I enabled Pastor Glück to open the first school in St. Petersburg I reminded him of that conversation, because by then certain of my enemies had spread about the tale that the pastor had had to marry me off to the first bridegroom he could, as my ways were so wild. The pastor took note of it and, in his quiet way, saw to it that the truth of the matter was put down in writing by Gottfried Würm, who by then had a government appointment in Hanover. I should have mentioned that Gottfried Würm was the tutor who came to teach Pastor Glück's children.

One or two of my husband's comrades in arms had been in church to see us married, but afterwards we were left for a little while alone. The town's street was full of the sounds of shouted orders and of clanking spurs and the stamping of officers' horses from the changing garrison. My husband grasped me about the waist and held me up shoulder-high and said almost the only words he ever uttered to me. "You are Marfa Vassilievka now," he said. "I know of a barn where we can be left in peace. Best be quick."

So we were quick. The barn was a part of the flour-mill which had been used lately for storing hay for the horses, and as we lay down I was aware of the smells of flour and hay and damp, for the roof was leaking. I saw the callouses on Vassiliev's big hands as he lifted my dress. There was not much time now before he had to march and I did not know if I would ever see him again. So I lost my virginity in mouldy hay, in too much haste because the regiment was marching. To this day I never did hear whether or not they promoted my husband corporal, because I never saw him again. He must have been killed at Hümmelshof. When the sound of marching boots had died away in the street and I had collected myself, I went back to the parson's house and got on with the ironing. Everybody was glad that the war had moved on.

I have said little till now about the war. For one thing, it had been going on for the whole of my life; one war led into the next. In the second place, it has been my lot to live close to one person who for his own reasons waged the war, and one loses sight of reality in terms of glory or defeat; bursting fireworks when we had won, gloomy silences when the others had. But for ordinary people it is not like that. It is nothing to them who wins or loses, unless they have sons who have gone away to fight. Even then, whatever happens, they will be taxed more heavily, their breadwinners taken, their women ravished or carried off, their homes burned along with their harvests and cattle. This is what happened in Livonia; not a single blade of corn or living thing was to be left to feed the enemy. The Bible speaks of the abomination of desolation; this is what Livonia was like, when the

Cossacks had finished with it. Sometimes—I must have grown used to this sight very early—there would be nothing to see but column upon column of enlisted men, bearing their heavy equipment through leagues of mud and slush left behind by the cavalry. Sometimes they would have wounds with only the cold to stanch them, there being no bandages: and their feet would be padded with tied straw because there were no shoes. The faces of those men are to me the face of Russia, Livonia, Sweden; it does not matter which side they are on. Nor does it matter why the Tsar of Muscovy makes war, or the King of Sweden. They meant nothing to us in the days when the Russian army came at last to besiege Marienburg after their defeat at Narva by Charles XII. The town held out for a week, a month, longer; there was nothing left to eat because the Swedish army had requisitioned all the food before leaving. But the fort held out. It held out till in the end there was nothing to be done but blow it up.

The foe was encamped with his cannon half a mile from the town's wall. Ah, that firing! The first time one hears it it is as if both ears would burst. After that one gets used to it. They say the Tsar took great pride in his cannon and so did Charles of Sweden. Such men are still children playing with toys, maybe. I was not afraid of the firing after the first. The poor careworn pastor's wife, pregnant again and with no food in the larder, looked at me one day almost with enmity.

"You have no fear in you," she said, as though I was different from the rest. I could not help it. I tried to comfort the children. These clustered about us with their heads hidden in our skirts, trying to keep out the pounding of the mortars and to close their eyes and nostrils against the powdered stone-dust that lay on everything, floors, tables, clothes, hair. "They say the Tsar of Muscovy is Antichrist," screamed the parson's wife. "His own people say it. He has melted down the bells of his churches to make more cannon. Ah, dear God, let the noise only cease!"

As she raised her fists to her ears the din stopped, so that it was as if the poor woman's prayer had been heard. At that moment the pastor and Gottfried Würm, the latter with his face chalk-white beneath the dust, stumbled in. Pastor Glück looked at his wife and children and went into his study. After a moment Würm came to me and told me to go to our master, quickly. They must have made the plan before entering the house.

I put aside the children's sticky clutch and went in. The pastor was standing with a Slavonic Bible in his hands. I remember thinking, "What use is that?" In a short time, I supposed, the Russian fire would begin again; it had only stopped because they are lazy and sleep after their meal at midday. Charles of Sweden had known as much when he defeated them in the snow at Narva. At the same time I was wondering why the pastor wanted me. He looked up from his Bible.

"Marfa," he said, "I want you to get together what is needful for us to take into the Russian camp. My wife is hardly able to help."

"The Russian camp?" I repeated; I had never before questioned an order, but it sounded as though he had gone mad. The Russians were bears and wolves, I knew, and especially to women.

"Do as I say," he said gently; I have never seen him lose his temper. "I have had word from the commander here—you will be discreet—that it is no longer possible to hold Marienburg against the besiegers. He will blow up the fort. If I ask to be taken to the Russian commander and offer myself as an interpreter to the Tsar and his generals, there may be hope for us. Otherwise there is none," and his face crumpled and I remembered that he was a quiet man leaving the home he had known for years and the people whose shepherd he had tried to be. I went and did as I was told and got together the children's warm clothing and a shawl for the baby who was soon to be born, though it was unlikely to live if we had to stay in the open. When the bundles were ready I brought them to the house-door. The parson was there already with his wife and children and Gottfried Würm. He still carried his Bible.

Outside it had begun to grow dark. I remember our silent journey through the deserted streets. The cannon were still dumb, but everyone except ourselves stayed indoors. As we went a thought came to me and I told myself that the fort's commander had told Pastor Glück of this secretly in friendship, so that there would be no panic in the town. It was the first time I had experienced this cool separate thinking in danger, and it explained the fact that the sentry let us out through the gate.

Before us lay an expanse of flat ground which in the half-dark was slippery, but I could not yet tell why. Then I saw corpses lying about unburied. They did not stink as it was too cold. In the near distance torches were being lit and soon, as we made our way across the slippery places, they shone on our faces as we approached the enemy camp. I tell the truth when I say that I was not afraid. I had no feeling at all.

The flares grew bright enough to dazzle. At that moment I was aware of the looks of our poor stumbling party, shivering and thin and ill-clad as they were, and the children beginning to cry as they always do when no one will explain what is happening. Only Pastor Glück bore himself upright, as though he were the God he stood for. At any moment they might have struck him down. I have known popes and patriarchs and archimandrites since, but he is still my image of a man of God. I believe God loves simple people and that is why His Son was a carpenter. I followed the pastor and held my head high as he was doing. To cower before an enemy does not pay.

Pastor Glück came to a halt before the camp, and called out in Russian. I had known that he knew many languages but before it had not mattered. A shout answered, and a sentry with a brutish face, the eyes slanting above a flaring nose and flat cheeks, held up a torch and surveyed us. This was the first Muscovite I ever saw, and I think now he was a Great Russian because they look different from the rest. He wore a peaked cap lined with fur and had a carbine slung against his belt, and his slant eyes glittered in the torchlight. He surveyed us insolently, then shouted words I did not understand. Out of the night other men appeared, and surrounded us. The pastor's wife began to pray aloud. "Hush," I said to her. "They will take us to the commander." I knew that if they had been going to kill or rape us, they would have done it by now. I felt, God forgive me, impatient with the poor woman.

They marched us through the sprawling camp to a tent outside which were more guards. Although I was dazed with hunger and weariness like all the rest, I could not help noticing the wild figures which sprang to life beneath the torches as we passed by. Some were slumbering about fires; I saw women among them, and one was combing her hair as though nothing else mattered. I found my eyes fed with strangeness for the first time in my life. There were small men with yellow faces and bow legs and slit eyes like our guard, and they were Tartars smelling of goat-curd. There were others in tunics that could have stood by themselves with the embroidery upon them, and their filth. These were Kalmucks and Cossacks and Bashkirs, the last adept at despoiling a countryside which was why they had been brought to Livonia. They could not be trusted not to change sides and the commander, Sheremetev, kept them under his especial eye. Others were tall as giants, and all were beardless. I noticed to my surprise that many of the Muscovites were dressed like our own folk, in German coat and breeches. Later I was told this was a reform of the Tsar. "Go and make garters of your old sleeves, they dip in the sauce," he had said to a boyar at a banquet, and had taken scissors and cut off a broad band of the sleeve in the same way as he cut off beards. But anyone could keep his beard if he wore a label on it to show as a receipt for tax. I did not know this then or it might have made me laugh.

But none of us were laughing, or anywhere near laughter, as we entered the commander's tent. I felt the children's little hands grip me tightly; I had them and the bundles, and the tutor carried other bundles and the pastor his Bible. Inside the tent were men in German uniform and heavy perukes. The air was thick with smoke from their clay pipes. I suddenly felt miserable and alone and wondered if life were worth keeping, a thought that has never occurred to me before or since.

The commander, General Field Marshal Sheremetev—I soon learned to call him by his full title—sat at a table. He was a big man with a big belly. The table cut into it, and on his breast was pinned a glistening order. This was the man who was laying waste Livonia by order of the Tsar. He had won many victories over small towns such as ours. Even as I stared at him out of eyes already watering with the smoke, I heard in the distance the dull booming sound of the explosion of our fort of Marienburg. Sheremetev heard it too and threw back his head in a bout of boisterous laughter. He said something to an officer by him, who laughed also and slapped his thigh.

Pastor Glück stepped forward and made his errand clear. It says something for his presence that he was able to make those animals listen to him. Discussion broke out noisily among the Russian high command, as if to make up for the time they had spent listening. I was to find out before long that a Russian talks almost all of the time, and when he does not talk he sings. Even now, after the sound of the explosion of the doomed town, drunken singing floated to us from the camp-fires. I wondered what had happened to the market and the neighbours and the church and the remaining garrison and the cat who used to call on us before the siege and eat scraps. At the same time I was aware of a surge of new feeling. It was as though, at this moment which ought to have been sad and dreadful, I had broken out of confinement into life. I felt a stirring within myself as much as to say "That man singing by the camp-fire has a wife and children at home whom he may never see again, and yet he sings. We are not the only ones badly off," and then I looked at Sheremetev, to find that he was looking at me. It was, in a way, like the time the sergeant had looked at me in church, only not so respectfully. The General Field Marshal looked first at my bosom, then at my face, then back again. Presently he began to speak to the pastor in broken German.

"You may go, as you can make yourself useful, with my officer, who will take care of you. Ekaterina here stays with me." His eyes still assessed me in a way I did not care for. Green as I still was, despite the brief tumble in the hay with my Swedish dragoon, I occupied my mind with wondering why he had called me Ekaterina. I did not know then that it is the Russian soldier's name for any woman he may call after in the street.

Pastor Glück was protesting. "This girl is my maid, a foundling, in my care," he was saying, and added, "She is married to a Swedish officer," as if that would help.

"That does not matter," said the General Field Marshal. "She stays with me."

I felt his thick fingers close about my wrist, and the children's clasp was pulled away. I watched the colourless little group taken out into the night which by now had fallen. Last to go was the pastor himself. I was near tears, which does not often happen. When I saw the trouble he was in, I blinked them back and smiled. I knew it was important to smile. Pastor Glück must be allowed to go in safety.

"Marfa," he was beginning, "you do not know how rough, how brutal a camp-follower's life——" But I forestalled him. I must make him think I didn't care. Only so would he go willingly to the new task of interpreter, and forget me; he must do that.

"I'll fare well enough, never fear," I said, smiling. "Go with God, pastor."

I did not look at him as he went out. I knew I must not. The General Field Marshal's hands had already left my wrist and were thrusting inside my bodice.

They say I made a good whore. At the beginning I did not take to it. Sheremetev was dirty and gross, and in addition used to flog me, after the first, before making love. I had never been flogged even by Samuel Skavronsky in the old days, and I did not understand the reason; the first time it happened I raised a yell fit to shake the tent. The General Field Marshal slapped me across the mouth.

"Shut up, you slut. I do as I please."

By then, it will be seen, I had picked up a few words of Russian. This made it easier for me to be on friendly terms with the other women. Most of these had followed the army from Wenden, Wolmar, Valk, Dorpat, Pernau, Riga; some even from Moscow. The last were mostly soldiers' wives, many of them widowed. One, whose name was Anisa, had had a husband killed at Erestfer and had followed the men ever since. She spoke some German, as they mostly did, and was able to tell me things. Seeing my bruises, she explained to me about Sheremetev.

"He is a good enough commander except at Narva, but a bad lover. He has exhausted himself and often couldn't do anything if it weren't that he beats the women before sleeping with them. Who says you're the only one?" and she showed me an upper arm whose thin flesh carried a long weal, greenish black and partly healed. In return I showed her my right breast, on which the Order of St. Andrew left an imprint which never had the chance to disappear with Sheremetev bouncing up and down on me almost nightly. "One day we will show the Tsar our orders of merit," said Anisa. "It will make him laugh."

"Does he laugh easily? I thought the Tsars of Muscovy were grave, like your ikons." I had already seen these among the Russian baggage when Sheremetev, as he sometimes did to tame me, gave me to the men. I didn't mind them so much. One talked about his children in Novgorod and another talked about how to plant cabbages. A third had shown me his ikon. Anisa herself laughed now, showing discoloured teeth.

"Some say Peter Alexievich laughs too much. But he cut two hundred heads off in a week, in Moscow. That was after his household guard, the streltsi, rebelled. It was the second time, and Tsar Peter said there would not be a third. I was younger then, with my husband in Moscow. Lord, the blood! And he dragged old Miloslavsky's coffin up out of the ground and showed them the corpse all eaten with worms, and left it where the blood would run down into it because he said they worshipped Miloslavsky, and there was his altar."

I did not know who Miloslavsky might be and instead of asking yawned, for I was weary and needed a good night's sleep. But Anisa seemed inclined to talk; her voice had taken on a dreamy quality and she used Russian again which I did not altogether understand. Since then I have found out what she meant. Maria Miloslavsky was the first wife of Tsar Alexis, the father of Tsar Peter, and she bore many sons and daughters. After she died Tsar Alexis fell in love with a beautiful girl named Natalia Naryshkina and married her, and she bore a son who was to be Tsar Peter. This happened because of the first family only three sons grew up, and one, the cleverest, died on reaching manhood. Of the rest,

Feodor, the eldest, was delicate and died on his wedding night. Ivan, the last, was half-witted and tongue-tied and could not keep his eyes open. Nevertheless the supporters of Miloslavsky wanted him for their Tsar rather than Peter, who was tall and quick-witted, and they knew that if he came to power there would be trouble for them, There was a lot more of it from Anisa, and then as she often did she started bewailing Narva, where two of her favourite lovers had been killed, one with the snow whirling in his face and the other while swimming the river.

"That Sheremetev and his orders! I'd give him marching ones. He was enough of a fool to let the men turn and slaughter their own officers in the snow, mistaking them for the foreigner; and afterwards he was the first to get away and swim the river himself, though it drowned a thousand men. Eight thousand dead on the field as well; you'd think even Boris Mikhailovich could have done better."

Her voice was becoming shrill and I feared we would be overheard, so I asked her where I could borrow a flat-iron.

Anisa screeched with sudden laughter. "Listen to the child; one minute corpses, the next flat-irons. If it isn't to hit our friend over the head with, I'll ask one of the men. They can pick up anything they like in the towns. "Ivan!" She hailed a passing soldier, who came and stood before us. He knew me very well, and grinned. "Good day, Katinka."

"It isn't to hit him with, but to make his linen decent," I said. "If I have to sleep with a man I don't like him to live like a pig." In this I was hard on pigs, who are clean animals. Sheremetev, like many Russians, would rather relieve himself on the spot than go and look for a latrine, and pigs are particular on this point.

I had to become his laundress quite soon. One night he made ready to flog me, as usual, and suddenly I was sick of it and raised my knee and kicked him hard in the balls. He screamed and called on God and the saints and said he would brand me with a red-hot pike. "Who do you think you are? Any lint-haired good-for-nothing Swede can be bought nowadays for five groschen in the market-places," and he cuffed and beat me again and threw me out of the tent. When I am angry it is like a slow fire and I stuck my head back round the tent-flap. I had seen the children for sale in the market-places because there wasn't enough for them to eat, and it was better to follow the army, even with Sheremetev, than not. Besides, he mustn't think he had made me afraid of him. "I'm not any lint-haired good-for-nothing," I said, mimicking his accent as best I could. "Give me the filthy shirt off your back and I'll wash it clean." I nearly added provided he had another, but thought it best not to go too far. He roared at me for a whore and a bitch and stripped the thing off his back and threw it at me. "Come back with it clean and dry tomorrow or it will be the worse for you," he said, and went away rubbing his sore place. I made my way down to the river with the shirt, greasy and smelling of he-goat as it was, and scrubbed and trod it repeatedly in the ice-cold water till it was clean. Then I brought it back and spread it out and dried it on whatever stunted bushes remained beyond camp, but I couldn't iron it. After that I was given all Sheremetev's linen and was less his whore than his laundress, which was better.

Anisa's Ivan strode off now. "He can get anything," she said again. "He'd find beer in the cannon's mouth." Her rather hard grey eyes softened as they dwelt on my bruises, which still showed. "I'll give you butter to rub on; it's rancid, but it'll do," she said. "It's hard on you, I know, young Marfa."

"This is not my name now. I'm Ekaterina the whore."

In some way it was true; I was no longer Marfa. Ivan returned soon with a flat-iron red with rust from an exploded town, and I rubbed it clean and used it to iron the General Field Marshal's linen. The iron might also have been the same that had always sat at the right hand side of the stove in Pastor Glück's house, but by now we were a long way from Marienburg.

Pastor Glück and his family I had already heard had been sent to Moscow. Perhaps they would meet this young Tsar who chopped off heads. By degrees I heard more about Tsar Peter Alexievich. He had deserted his wife almost immediately on marrying her and had gone away to build boats, which he preferred, although he had got a son on the poor woman before parting. I had even seen his portrait in

Sheremetev's tent; a young face with great lustrous eyes and short curling hair of a chestnut colour.

Next day I said to Anisa, "Get your Ivan to fetch me some black hair-dye."

"Get him yourself. He'll do as much for you as for me. But I can make better from the bark of trees with some of your iron-rust. What do you want black hair for? Mind, with your brown skin it might be pretty."

I said nothing. I did not yet know enough Russian to explain that because I was no longer Marfa the decorous serving-maid in a Lutheran parsonage, and because I had been called a lint-haired Swede by a man I disliked, I wanted black hair. In the end Anisa made me the dye and I put it on thick as soot, and on my eyebrows as well, using a brush made of tied horse-hair by way of the cavalry. Soon I tried to look at myself in a flat pool where I did the washing, and a different person met me in that water.

When Sheremetev next sent for me I sidled in. I saw his mouth fall open and his pig's eyes stare and heard him shout, "Why, what's this? We have a Circassian whore tonight!"

"No, you have a black-haired laundress," I quipped, evading him.

It worked. The men liked it, and they always liked me anyway. When I went past they would whistle and call out "Katia, Katinka," and other things, and I tossed my newly-blacked mane and swung my hips and cared for nothing, not even Sheremetev.

But it was not an easy life. If Alexasha Menshikov had not come soon and rescued me from General Field Marshal Boris Mikhailovich and his stinking linen and his beer-heavy breath and the Order of St. Andrew, I might have been no more heard of and have died in a ditch, sometime when the winter quarters were a field full of snow and the ice lay thick as a Russian skull on the black water of Livonia.

Friendly Anisa is still with me, as one of my ladies of the bedchamber. I don't forget friends. Few now except Alexasha himself know how far we have all travelled together, and even he doesn't know everything.

The war was not over but we were going home. This for most of us meant Moscow. I myself was as well prepared to go and live there as anywhere else. By this time I rode in Sheremetev's own household following. Since I had dyed my hair black and washed his linen white I had become worth keeping. The men and I jested as we rode. They told me about a serf named Kurbatov, who had belonged to the General Field Marshal and had been promoted by the Tsar to be a government servant. "Perhaps the Tsar will promote our Katia also." I laughed. The man Kurbatov had invented stamped paper. It is a simple thing when one thinks of it, but it took Kurbatov to think of it first. I forgot about him and stared ahead over the backs of the ponies and mules with their bundles. A large amount of baggage collects in a camp and a good many of them would hold plunder worth selling. The rest Sheremetev would keep, to embellish his house in the foreign quarter of Moscow. Everyone lived there now because the Tsar would not willingly go into the city.

That journey was like other journeys since; endless, bleak and cold. Now and then we would rest at inns, some of them part roofless. The Kalmucks who had been let loose with fire and sword had done well. It was as impossible for us to feed ourselves as for the conquered people. I felt myself no longer one of them; such as we met looked at me with the same indifference as they kept for the rest of the army. The men shot duck in the marshes and we ate that, and Sheremetev seemed to have plenty of wine, which he kept to himself. He drank deep and boasted and then wept, for he felt that the Tsar had not rewarded him enough for his Swedish victories.

"Who saved the rearguard at Narva? None but I!" (He had already forgotten about turning tail and swimming the river and drowning the men; a commander like Sheremetev will always believe the stories he tells himself. No doubt the Tsar knew this also.) "Who reconnoitred along the Reval road and braved the Swedish guns while the Tsar went hurrying off to Moscow to raise twelve more regiments? Who but I, yet does Peter Alexievich call me his heart's child, his little brother? Never! It is all for Menshikov, who is a nobody, a groom's son. Tsar Peter Alexievich prefers those of low birth." And the great fist would crash down on the littered wine-flasks while tears ran down Sheremetev's cheeks.

My first sight of Moscow was like magic in a dark world. She arose in the distance with the setting sun lingering on her towers, differently painted and gilded as they were, in shape each like a sturdy bud rising on its stem. Nearer at hand the squalor became visible. Beyond the earth wall fires burned to warm the naked beggars, many of them women, who stood about. (You must learn to work, Marfa, or you will starve or be a beggar. Who had said that, long ago?) They ran out to clutch our stirrups and beg for coins, clinging though the men tried to kick them away. Sheremetev's guard rode back along the line then cracking long whips, and the horde fell back screaming and cursing.

Presently a white wall arose, then a third, the Kremlin wall itself beyond which we did not pass. There was still a smell of burnt wood from the great fire there had already been that winter, destroying whole streets in the town and much of the old palace. Muscovites are used to fires. We did not stop in the town, but rode eastwards. Sheremetev's house was in the Nemenskaya Sloboda, the German quarter beyond the wall. All of Tsar Peter's boon companions, of whom Sheremetev even yet hoped to become one, lived there among not only Germans, but Scots and Dutch as well. The Tsar's great friend, who had told him many things about modern warfare, had been a Swiss named Lefort, but he was dead. The men told me of him and of how handsome he had been. "Now Menshikov takes his place," they muttered, and I noted both that that name had been spoken of twice lately and, also, that the men themselves seemed to have no liking for Menshikov. Perhaps, as he was a man of the people like themselves, they grudged his favour with the Tsar. I felt a stirring of curiosity to see him, and the Tsar also, and the other wonders this Sloboda held; the stone houses, the gardens seen in the flare of torchlight by the doors and in our company, and even a fountain, splashing water in the night; I had never seen one before. There were shops, with their shutters closed at this hour, and a little market with the booths all empty. I hoped Sheremetev would let me shop for him. I had been used to bargain in Marienburg before the war came to us there, and the pastor's wife had always sent me to buy our vegetables, especially when she was ailing.

Had we passed the house where Pastor Glück and his family lived in Moscow? I felt the blood stain my cheeks. I did not want them to meet me as I was now. It was better to stay here, in the foreign quarter. They would not be able to afford to live here.

Sheremetev must have made haste to report his arrival to the Tsar, but no one at all came to visit him for several days. I had been clearing chests and presses for linen, for the General Field Marshal had sent for me and told me that I was now his housekeeper. I was anxious to do well at this, and so I did not take time, as the other servants did, to stop work and gape at the sudden arrival of a great personage. "It is Alexander Danilovich Menshikov," said the scullery-maid. She giggled, and I looked up from what I was doing. "Oh, Katia, he has a curled wig on his head all powdered, as they wear 'em now, and a blue coat braided to the eyes. He's a pretty sight, our Alexasha."

"He knows it, too," called out another maid, and I laughed and told them to get on with their work. I have always found that if one laughs with servants, they will carry out orders quickly. "Perhaps we will see him when they all dine," I said, "and you'd better be sure there is plenty to eat." There had been some scrawny chickens running about the yard whose necks would be better drawn, as I had already found that they laid no eggs. Sheremetev had told me to give my own orders to the servants and I did it. The chickens were soon drawn and plucked and roasting over the fire, and I was hot and dishevelled with my hair falling into my eyes, when my master sent for me. I was to bring up more wine. Why the devil, I thought as I toiled to the cellar and then upstairs, can't one of the men bring it? I have enough to do, and those stupid girls will burn the chickens and then Sheremetev will beat me.

But Sheremetev had sat down to drink with the smoothest

face I had ever seen on him. Beside him sat the beauty in the blue coat, powdered curls and all, and having been warned by the girls of this vision I did not betray my astonishment. Both men stared at me and Menshikov said in Russian, "Now I see why you are so proud of your clean shirts, Boris Mikhailovich. You are fortunate to have so good and handsome a laundress." And he raised his wine-cup to me, and winked. I smiled and set down the bottles I had brought, saying nothing because it was not my place, but noticing a good deal; Menshikov might be Sheremetev's guest, but the General Field Marshal was eyeing him now, despite his smiles, as a bear might eye a baiting hound. I could tell at once that not only did the two men dislike one another's company, but that there was another reason for rivalry, possibly the war.

As if to render this state of things more amusing Menshikov lifted his wine-cup so that the rich lace fell back from his wrist and his jewelled buttons sparkled more brightly than the wine. "To your good health, Boris Mikhailovich, and may the next campaign bring better fortune."

"The last did not come to any ill through lack of my effort," growled Sheremetev, as if to bid this puppy lie down. "Your own health, Alexander Danilovich, and may fortune not look back for you."

Menshikov laughed outright. He never minded any dig at his past or reminders that he had once sold hot pies in the Moscow streets. I liked him, ridiculous as he seemed; I wished that I could stay and listen. I had done as I was bid and merely moved about tidying the room of its empty bottles, stacking them near the door. I heard Menshikov say suddenly, after a silence in which I knew they were both watching me,

"I should like to borrow your laundress, Boris Mikhailovich. See how dirty my lace is! Can you iron lace, young woman?"

I answered and did not look at Sheremetev's face. "I can iron anything if I have washed it first. I would take care of fine lace, I can tell you that."

"Hi! Katia! Take your bottles and go," thundered Sheremetev. "I regret it, Alexander Danilovich, but the wench is not for lending. Get back to your duties, woman; bring us some dinner."

"She is not a serf, is she?"

"No, she is a Livonian picked up in the campaign. I will not part with her, Alexander Danilovich; no, not for many roubles! She is a good worker. You may not have her, I say. Otherwise, my house is yours." He looked glum and as if he did not mean a word of the last sentence. Menshikov was smiling broadly. The other had no power against him and he knew it.

"Then if she is free she may choose for herself. Will you come with me, Ekaterina Vassilievka, or stay with him? Mine is a fine house, with everything clean and new. You will find life easy if you come."

I was astonished to find that he already knew my name; he must have ways of finding out whatever he wanted. Such a man was not to be refused; something in my mind said to me, "If you let this chance go, you will never more be heard of, except as Sheremetev's Livonian whore." I do not know why I expected to be heard of in any case. I only know that I thought quickly and then nodded and smiled and said "If it pleases you, sir, I will go with you." And I did not look at Sheremetev's face, which I knew would be turning purple.

"Then collect your bundle of gear, and be ready after dinner."

After dinner would be many hours. I served at it and watched Sheremetev's scowls and Menshikov's gaiety, and kept myself too busy to show my joy that shortly I should be free of my old bear with his Order of St. Andrew. Things had been better lately, but they would be better still elsewhere. I also reflected that it showed the humble birth of Alexander Menshikov that he even remembered that servants had gear to be bundled. Few others in his position would have thought of it.

I was still not clear what his position was, but could see that it was higher than Sheremetev's, perhaps than anyone else's about the Tsar. That Menshikov could sit and impudently relish his dinner, and get drunk with the General Field Marshal afterwards, might have meant he was brutal and not important. But I knew, myself, that Menshikov was important and not brutal, though cunning. It would be a pleasure to live with a man who was not a brute.

Dear God! We are still the best of friends, Alexasha and I.

I must say a word about the Nemenskaya Sloboda, for it arose in the first place by reason of happenings in the world beyond Muscovy. Some time before, the English had cut off the head of their king. Those who were on his side and opposed the dictator, Cromwell, came to Moscow to be out of Cromwell's reach, and having made fortunes by trading they stayed on, and married and bred. Most of them were Scots and not English, and nearly all were Catholic, which in any case meant that they could not live inside Moscow because the Orthodox popes forbade it. So they built the foreign quarter with its own Catholic church. They found some countrymen already there; these had come to Muscovy as traders before the time of Ivan the Terrible. Scots are shrewd bargainers and, having but a poor country at home, they leave it to get rich and, if they are pleased and left in freedom where they are, they stay. This also happened with the Jacobites, who left England and Scotland in large numbers when the Dutch King William displaced their James II. Oddly enough the Dutch and the Scots Jacobites were not enemies when they met in the Sloboda, for the Hollanders were there as well, and the Germans, all for the same reason; trade and a fortune to be won and made greater. They had, most of them, unless they were born in the Sloboda, seen the great world beyond Muscovy and knew the many things Russia needed and had not got. This is partly why they came to the notice of the Tsar. But I shall speak of him later. Meantime the Quarter resounded with the jabber of Dutch, German, English and Russian. As I had seen on my arrival, the houses were neat and prosperous; so were the women. They wore such high fashion that at first it made me laugh. Their gowns were of brocade or velvet (what had become of my little scrap of long ago?) and their bodies were pinched with whalebone stays and on their heads, making them much taller, were stiffened lace and ribbon pinners over which it was difficult to place a hood, and made them tower over the men beside whom they walked, even though the latter wore high perukes. Yes, I enjoyed my first weeks in the Sloboda, especially now that I was in the house of Menshikov.

Of course he became my lover: that was expected. He taught me many things about the body that I had not known, for he was expert in the ways of love as not all men are. Perhaps he taught me enough by the end to make the Tsar love me, or perhaps again that would have happened by itself. Menshikov had two sisters who stayed in his house, and they were friendly with me, which I had not expected. Besides all this, Menshikov never beat me, and I looked after his linen and his lace as he had asked. Much of it was very fine, having come from Holland, and I was pleased when everyone began to compliment Menshikov on its fresh and clean appearance.

I did not know who did Sheremetev's washing after I left him, or carried his bottles of wine or was his mistress. Sometimes he would come to Menshikov's house as a guest and we would greet one another. I am not one to hold grudges and if Sheremetev was prepared to forget certain things, so was I.

Also I found a much better hair-dye in the shops in the Sloboda, and still buy it there.

I have spoken of Menshikov's two sisters, Maria and Anna. They were wild young women and I think he secretly feared that they might hinder him in his rise in the world. If one or the other could be married, the other would go with her to her new home. Then Menshikov would be free to marry his gently bred sweetheart, Daria Arsenieva, who with her sisters Barbara and Aksinia had posts at Court about the Tsar's own sister, Natalia. But it would not be possible to cram Daria in beside such hoydens. So Menshikov waited and tried to interest worthwhile suitors in Maria and Anna.

He told me all this; very early I became his friend. There was also the question of his name and how it was to be used between us. At the beginning I called him sir, count, master; anything but the familiar Alexander Danilovich, for I had not yet accustomed myself to the fact that in

Russia, even a serf addresses his master by his birth-name and the name of his father, as his friends do. Menshikov laughed at me and said, "Those who love me call me Alexasha. The Tsar uses no other name except when he is drunk, and then he calls me the pieman."

"How can I love you and be your washerwoman, and speak to you like the Tsar?" I asked. "We are master and servant," I added, which was a fact; Alexasha paid me and ordered my days and nights. I had spent some of the money on new shifts and hair-dye and slippers made of calf's leather, but I still wore the same gown, which was my only one and had been through all the campaign in Livonia. Some day, perhaps, I thought, Menshikov would notice how shabby I was and give me money to buy a new one. But it had not happened.

He frowned a little. "I am no better than you," he said. "You know where I came from, and that it is only because I have won the Tsar's favour that I have this rich house, and my position."

"You have also fought in the war. When will this Tsar come here? I have heard talk of him since ever I joined the army, but that is all." I ran my fingers through my new-blacked hair; it had been washed with birch bark lately and was soft to the touch.

"Peter Alexievich is no spirit; you will meet him soon. He stays here mostly when he is in Moscow, for he will not sleep at the Kremlin."

"Why not?"

Menshikov lifted his richly-clad shoulders and spread out his hands. "It would take too long to tell you now, Ekaterina Vassilievka. Perhaps Peter Alexievich—he likes better to be known as Peter Mikhailov, the bombardier—will tell you himself when he comes back from Novgorod and his meeting with the King of Poland."

I laughed loudly. It sounded hardly likely that this would happen.

One day I was returning from the small market where I had been buying lemons. With me was young Maria Menshikova and an acquaintance of my own from the days of Sheremetev. This was the ex-serf Kurbatov, the one who had invented stamped paper. He was now a collector of revenue, and very tiresome. He cringed before great folk and was discourteous to plain ones if they let him be so. I had given him the rough side of my tongue a while back and since then he had stayed civil. He had met us in the market and walked with us now part of the way back to the house.

We were gossiping together when a carriage drove past, splashing the bystanders with mud and snow. Inside were two people; a very beautiful golden-haired woman dressed in the latest mode, and beside her a foppish little man in violet brocade and hair-powder. I said to Kurbatov, "Who is she? She is very beautiful," and Maria gaped after the carriage.

"That is Anna Mons, the Tsar's mistress," said Kurbatov, in hushed tones as one might speak of the saints. "Some say her father was a German goldsmith and others a wine-merchant."

"She used to belong to Lefort, and the Tsar took her over," interrupted Maria, using a term I would not have let her use had she been in my charge to correct. They had run wild indeed, these two sisters, and Alexasha's rise in the world had gone to their heads. "I do not know, I do not know," said Kurbatov, terrified lest he seem to offend the proprieties and lose his new position. He took leave of us, scurrying away through the crowds on the street as though all he wished was to remain unnoticed. We went home.

Later I told Alexasha about seeing the Tsar's mistress. He always enjoyed the slightest titbit of news; it helped him in his ambition to know everything about everybody, and to make use of it. I was no longer surprised that he had made sure of my name before coming to drink wine at Shere-metev's. I still did not know, however, what use he hoped to make of me. When the bride Daria came it was possible I should have to find other quarters. The future was like a shadow in my mind, but why allow the future to darken the present? So I shrugged, and laughed, and told my master about Kurbatov and how he either cringed or strutted, and also of the foppish man in powder who had been in the carriage with Anna Mons. I went on to describe their attendant, a gaily clad dwarf who had stood outside at the back, showing off his stunted ugliness against Anna Mons' beauty. But I saw that Menshikov was not listening to me about the dwarf and that his eyes had narrowed. He spoke of dwarfs all the same.

"Those creatures are popular everywhere, because the Tsar likes monsters. Two-headed men, twins joined together, hunchbacks, giants, dwarfs, buffoons without number, these amuse him," he said, and then added, "Tell me more of this man you saw with Anna Mons. Yes! she is beautiful, and has made good use of her beauty; the Tsar has given her estates, jewellery, a small palace of her own; she ought to be content."

I described the man's violet coat. "It sounds like Kaiserling, the Prussian envoy," Menshikov told me. "You are discreet, Katia, and I can say many things to you which I would not to any other woman," and I wondered if he included his dear Daria. "You keep your own counsel, do you not?" he said.

"I learnt to hold my tongue before I could talk. What is this great matter?" He was right in thinking that I would not betray him; I have never betrayed anyone.

"Why, that the woman Mons is a fool and a bitch, and I hope to bring about her downfall. If she is known to be taking lovers in the Tsar's absence——"

"There was Lefort." I liked to air my knowledge. Menshikov looked at me with a bright enquiring gaze, like a monkey.

"Lefort was the Tsar's friend, and he is dead. Peter Alexievich would have shared anything with Lefort, even Anna. But now—well, we will see. I have a plan already, I think. That woman, you see, is not my friend; if she can she will act against me. So it is a question of who is first, eh? I am grateful for your news, Katia. Keep your ears open and your tongue still."

A few days later the men were by themselves at dinner— we still dined separately in Alexasha's house—when there was a great roaring above stairs as if the place were on fire.

Afterwards it was as though a god or a giant had come in and was throwing the bottles about like ninepins, or cracking heads.

I knew without being told that the Tsar was here.

TWO

ELIZABETH PETROVNA'S TALE

1727

I said goodbye to my mother the Empress today earlier than I thought I should, not that time means anything to me nowadays; but I saw her fingers plucking again at the wine-cup, and knew that what she wanted was to be left alone to fill it to the brim, a fourth and a fifth time, as many times as it takes to empty a flagon, then send for more. I do not think Her Imperial Majesty, whom I love dearly, has been fully sober since her reign began, but she never walks unsteadily or makes a fool of herself in any way in public. At all such times—such as at the late opening of my father's Academy of Sciences, where we were all present—her demeanour is simple and dignified, and gives rise to no gossip. She drinks so much nowadays, I do believe, because despite everything she feels herself to be incomplete without my father. I can watch and understand this, as many other things, without myself being able to feel the lack of such a completeness of my own. I have known from the beginning, from the years when I was a child running about with my sisters, or grandly dressed to watch my mother's public wedding to the Tsar, or her coronation, that there are times when I must retreat within myself, much as my father used to go off alone to work with wood and saws in his house in the lime-tree. I am too lazy to work, but I need my solitude.

I'm not a spinster, in that sense. It isn't that I do not need, and do not take, lovers; I've done so since I was sixteen years old. My parents should have been the last to try and stop me, knowing their own inclinations. Nobody protested much but my sister Anne. "But, Elizabeth, it will spoil you for the marriage market!" she said fearfully; Anne is always fearful. She and I differ totally from one another except in that we are both young women born of the same parents. Anne was made to be a wife and mother, to do as she is told by some man. All she can think of nowadays is having married her Holsteiner now the difficulties over the Swedish interest have at last been settled. Charles Frederick seems a poor creature to me, and likely to father witless children if any; but perhaps I am being unkind to Anne, who dotes on him. The marriage took place quite lately. Anne is delicate, like our younger sister Natalia who died. I hope she will have no difficulties in childbirth.

I once had a Holsteiner of my own to whom I was engaged for the Swedish reason. He came to St. Petersburg, correct in powder, bowing and scraping and making sheep's eyes. Shortly he fell ill and died and I made pretence of mourning him for a long time. It left me in peace from other offers. I do not intend leaving Russia.

I rose from my curtsy to the Empress today and for a moment saw myself reflected in the shattered mirror she won't let them take away. My round high forehead and bright gaze stared back at me, and they are my father's. I have his height also, which is why all other men seem unimportant and small to me, now he is gone. The glass breaks off where the lower part of my face ought to have been, but I know it well enough. I look a great deal in mirrors. They tell me I am beautiful—I think I am handsome, no more—and that they sent this report of my looks to France at the time they hoped Louis XV would marry me. They said then also that I am the best dancer in Europe, which is true. They did not add that I can ride any man out of the saddle and shoot straight, for that would have been tactless and have made the French feel inferior. I was glad when my mother's low birth caused them to refuse me for Louis XV, though after that there was talk instead of the Duc de Chartres, the Regent's son, and that we were to be made king and queen of Poland. Poland is constantly changing its kings and I am better where I am. It is not in me to be subservient to any man, even His Most Christian Majesty who is younger than I am and cuts at his courtiers with a cane sometimes in pale imitation of my father's *doubina*. No, I never feared the Tsar even in his rages and he never beat me or Anne, though he was constantly belabouring poor Alexis who by then was usually too drunk to care.

I cannot take second place now, though I may pretend to. This means that I am a hypocrite. However it may save my life, even though it was the end of Alexis'. It is better to let Menshikov and the rest who are about my mother think of me as no obstacle to their plans, which means that they will end by not thinking of me at all. If they see only an idle, somewhat lecherous, frivolous, feather-brained princess who lives only for her horses and lovers, that will do very well. They do not think of me as having any thoughts, nor do they know what I am told. I am told many things, mostly by the common people, whom my father thought of only as soldiers or mothers of soldiers. I know them better, and know the things they need more than carbines, more than swords.

How do I know them? Why, that is easy; I follow my father's way and learn more than he did. From time to time I slip out of my Petersburg palace and take the road to some shrine with peasants and their children, my head bound about with a kerchief like theirs, my feet bare. They know me, and do not betray me; they call me the North Star. This makes me feel humble. When I can I will try to deserve it, and their trust.

I cling to the memory of a certain day, a day when I was free of Menshikov's spies whom he has placed about my mother so that every word we exchange together is reported to him. I went out into the streets, and there was a pilgrimage —the old forms of religion are permitted again since my father's death, and there were crucifixes and chanting and the smell of incense and the rub of people close-packed in the street. I followed the crowds for a long time till we were out in the suburbs, where the wooden houses still lean crazily to remind one that this city was built on a marsh, at my father's order. I had begun to talk to some of the women, who showed me their babies. One of them asked me to come home with her and meet her grandmother.

"No one knows how old she is," she said. "She is more than a hundred years old."

I marvelled; so old a woman must remember the Troubled Years, before they had anyone to rule them and found Mikhail Romanov for Tsar, and robber hordes spoiled the land. I went with the young woman, whose name was Katia like my mother's. She led me to one of the wooden houses on the marsh. The walls inside were plastered with clay against the wet, and the fire smoked badly, making the room dim. It must have been such a house as my mother knew in Livonia when she was a small child. By the fire sat an old creature who was no more than a bundle of evil-smelling rags; the people are too poor to afford enough clothing and keep what they have, never washing or taking it off, summer or winter. Below her kerchief sloe-black eyes looked at me. She crossed herself and mumbled something.

"She can tell the future," said Katia. "If your Highness"—they always know who I am—"would not be angry, would not tell of it, or get her into trouble for witchcraft? She is harmless, and only says what she sees; she uses no spells."

I knelt by the old woman, who had commenced to stare at the fire. The yellowish smoke curled up into patterns. Suddenly she reached out an aged claw and I knew what she wanted; I had heard of such things. I took a pin from my bodice and put it into her hand. The claws closed over it. Presently she began to speak.

"I see only the dark," she said. "It will come, the great blackness, as it was before."

"Before our rulers?" I tried to help her speak; she was gazing at the smoke, and seemed to have forgotten me.

"I cannot tell. There is the blackness for long and then there is starlight, and I see a tall woman stand by a door, and there are many who are glad, and will follow."

The eyes in their wrinkled flesh turned towards me, and I felt a creeping of my skin. "Is it myself?" I asked. "Am I the woman?"

"Well you will know what you are, and can be. You will wear the crown, but you will not gain happiness; and afterwards another will reap all you have sown."

"I care nothing for that," I said harshly. What is happiness? I have comfort and ease now, and my horses and my lovers. There will come a time when these are not enough.

I do not expect to be content, like other women. I shall never bear children. I may die alone. But the crown; that is different. If I may wear it, nothing else troubles me, not the darkness before nor the loneliness after. I gave the old woman a silver coin and bade her keep the pin she had had from my bodice. I have other pins. But she had told me something that has been in my own mind for as long as I can remember, as long in fact as my mind has been capable of forming words, images.

Yes, I cling to the memory of that day the old woman told me that I should reign. That, even if it is only for a year, a moment, will be worth everything I must pay to gain it. I know that death forms a part of the pattern. At present my nephew Peter Alexievich is healthy, and should make a good Tsar, they say, when he is grown. He does not cringe like his father; he has the look of a young eagle, and besides being proud he is open and gay. I know my mother and her advisers intend him to succeed her, thus avoiding a long regency such as would have been necessary had young Peter come to the throne at once when my father died. Oh, they have it all planned fairly enough, to suit themselves. But somehow, in what exact fashion I know not, their plans will miscarry. Perhaps young Peter himself will die, of fever or an accident. I shall grieve when this happens, for I love the boy and his sister, one of the many Natalias of the imperial family. But what has been promised me out of the future will surely be, and such a future cannot contain young Peter Alexievich as well as myself. I will take no hand in his end; that I know.

The right course is for me to do nothing meantime, except to prepare myself inwardly. When my time is come I shall know what to do. I think that I shall appeal in the first place to the guard, as my mother did. I shall summon them to me in my father's name.

This may not be soon. I have a feeling that many years lie between me and the consummation, and that as the old woman said there will be much darkness between, much suffering, though not for me. I pray to God that the darkness does not mean another war. The land is sick of it. My mother was right in what she said the other day, when they showed her a map of my father's conquests marked in red. "By now we are big enough. The country needs a long rest. Wars cost too much."

She is a wise creature, my mother, for everyone except herself. Also, she is the kindest soul on earth. There is nothing she will not do to ease the lot of anyone brought to her notice; the trouble is that Menshikov and Osterman and the rest shield sights from her that she ought to be shown. I, who am not yet twenty, know more of the life of the people than she does, from my secret wanderings. The knowledge will be useful.

Menshikov's spies hide in passages and behind curtains. They are paid well, no doubt, out of the riches that man amassed in the reign of my father. Alexasha the pieman is beginning to shed such caution as he ever possessed; there was a ridiculous story I heard that he intended my mother to marry him once she had gained the throne, but mother sent him to the rightabout. Menshikov might have been her lover long ago, before she met my father. Things are different now, and Ekaterina Alexievna is the greatest lady in Russia and would not ally herself with an adviser of low birth. So Alexasha, who can take defeat gracefully, hatched a plot instead to marry his daughter Maria to young Peter Alexievich. But the boy is aware of such things, and said roundly to me the other day, as we played with his toys, "I won't marry Menshikova, and when I am Tsar I'll send her father to Siberia."

"He has been a good servant."

"He feathers his own nest."

I knew that others must have been talking to him, and I warned him not to speak too loudly, although as long as his sister Natalia guards him little harm will come. That child is like an angel, older than her years. Yet what do even I know of good or harm? I can only await the will of God, and reassure myself that God has enough justice not to permit the marriage of a Romanov with a pieman's daughter.

I have not, of course, spoken to young Peter Alexievich or anyone else of what the wise old woman told me. That is a secret wrapped in my own heart. I will not spoil what those two children have left of childhood; they have endured enough. The Empress treats them kindly, and I need not pretend the love I feel. They are charming, and moreover defenceless against what life may bring; but are not we all? Also, my mother has seen to it that Peter Alexievich has good tutors, which neither she nor my father ever had for themselves. It seems incredible now, watching the grave and learned men about Peter Alexievich, to think that my father turned his tutor Zotov into court fool, saying it was all the man was fit for. Such things do not happen any more. The boy is well taught, and so could I have been had I not been idle. The only thing I did well at was the speaking of correct French, because when it was expected that I might become Louis' queen not even my laziness was allowed to prevail. This French will be useful. Also, I think that situation saved my mother's life at the time: the William Mons affair (Oh, yes, I have heard of that, though it isn't public knowledge) they say made my father think of executing her; after all, a man who has destroyed his son and heir may do likewise with his wife, particularly if she is low-born and unfaithful. But it was not considered expedient to execute the possible mother-in-law of the King of France. I daresay there were other reasons for her escape from judgment. In fact, the Tsar loved and needed her.

How different I am from her! She cares nothing about how she looks, except in the regalia which she wears often. I, on the other hand, love to study fashions, and when I can I spend all I have, and more, on new gowns and hats from Paris, and I look at myself in a glass that is not broken. I know however that I can charm men with a raised eyebrow, even though I am dressed only in a smock. To say this is vanity and not to say it would be hypocrisy. One falls between the two evils, and I do not trouble my head.

There is a great deal to think about and I can think all day if I choose, having made myself unimportant. I lie on my sofa with its gilded legs and satin covering, and look out beyond the Nevsky Prospekt to the water. Again, remembrance comes of my father; he is never far away. I can remember when he compelled each citizen to have his own boat, to keep it well tarred and lit and to appear in it, with his wife and family, suitably dressed of an evening. All of St. Petersburg used to meet and pass, there on the water all jewelled with the reflections of the lights, and I sailed with my father in our boat among the rest. His huge figure was known to everyone and now that I am older I marvel that there was never a single attempt made on his life, for anyone might come near him, especially at such times. He always wore an old shovel hat and a coat my mother had mended and a waistcoat she had knitted, and he used to sit at the tiller. I recall once, when I was quite small, getting my hand on it and steering; I felt the powerful thrust of the prow against the water. It must have been a moment when the Tsar was hailing a citizen and had turned aside. Presently I felt his big calloused hand lay itself over mine and heard his voice roaring, "Ho! Ho! A woman at the helm!"

Why not? He had, after all, his sister Sofia's reign to remember if he chose. I do not know how he would have taken to the notion that it is my mother now who steers, and that well enough. He made a law before he died that the reigning Tsar must choose his own successor, and then failed to do it; so they had to manage as best they could.

He was more than a Romanov, my father. He was a peasant on his mother's side. They may say what they like about my grandmother Natalia Naryshkina and how beautiful and high-born she was. Beautiful she may have been, but her name was Yarishkin till Tsar Alexis discovered her and married her, and her father tilled his own field though his sons forsook the land. I like to feel the strong peasant blood run in me, and when I am Autocrat I shall see to it that no field is ever left idle and full of tares because all the men have been sent to war. The rolling black acres, from Archangel to the Georgian plain, could feed every family in Russia. My mother cannot fully understand this, though she has lightened the people's taxes and they bless her for it. I shall do more; I shall take away the fear of death from them. A man cannot work or trade well with the sight of a gallows at every market-place, and the possibility that he may be the next to swing from it. There is too much bribery among officials and too little justice for the poor people, yet they are the salt of the earth.

Ah, this Russia! I feel myself a part of her, as my mother can never do although she has turned herself as nearly into a Russian as any foreigner I know. She understands the fighting men and they love her and put her in power. But I have it in my very blood and bones to love the black soil and the grey, and I treasure the memory of how our ancestors made Novgorod a great trading centre hundreds of years before my father opened his window on the west. If God gives me life I shall make our land a safe one to live in so that its great riches may not be squandered against foreign foes or its blood spilt any more for foreign wars. Then everyone may laugh and talk freely and sing if they will, and dance if they can, and so shall I. I can wait in patience till my time comes, like a woman in travail. I, Peter the Great's daughter, know I have the seed of power in me and that it will grow; I, the true heir of Peter, the North Star.

THREE

THE EMPRESS: DRUMBEAT

How can I remember when our glance first met? I didn't see him at all that first time; everyone was running about fetching salt pork up from the cellars and getting more wine, and loaves, and pickled cabbage; he didn't like fancy food. Nevertheless they ate and drank far into the night, and by the end I was sitting on the stairs listening to the cook, who was drunk.

"Our master will be wild with joy to see the Tsar again. They will have embraced each other and called one another heart's child, little father, little brother." I had heard some of that already, from Sheremetev.

After the party ended I got off my pallet where I slept and went to look out of the window at the waning moon. Under it figures were groping home. One walked swiftly, with great strides, lurching from side to side of the street. He was taller than anyone, almost a giant. His right arm moved swiftly, rhythmically as he walked. He carried a cane. I could not see his face.

Next time, there were more guests home from the war and Alexasha asked me if I would mind waiting at table. "Maria and Anna will come also," he said, as if I needed taking care of. Then he started to talk about the King of Poland who had just been visited; his name was Augustus the Strong and he was Peter's candidate for the throne, but not everyone's. Poland is unusual in that she has an elected king and that her landowners in any case are of more importance. Since the Troubled Years, every Russian hates every Pole and we take care that our country is not overrun again; some say it was worse than the time of the Golden Horde. I speak now as a Russian. It is many years since I thought of myself as anything else.

The main thing I remembered about Augustus the Strong

was that he had so many mistresses he did not know all their names, and as many natural children as there are days in the year. He and the Tsar were physically matched and used to wrestle and have contests of strength, and perhaps for this reason the Tsar always liked Augustus although he could never rely on him as an ally.

I helped lay out the platters for the feast. I had never seen as much food in my life and even the eggs were disguised as part of a great jelly which had sliced cucumbers in a pattern. Since then I have seen many banquets and feasts but this was the first time and it impressed me. The occasion was to celebrate the retreat of the Swedish army from their planned advance on Archangel, but nobody remembered, after dinner, what it was for.

This time I saw the Tsar plainly. He had grown older since the time of the portrait seen in Sheremetev's tent. His hair still curled thickly and his great eyes were full of dark fire, but his face was thinner and harder and he had the commanding manner of a man much older than he in truth was. During the dinner he thumped a fat boyar over the back with a cane he carried. Everyone laughed boisterously, including the victim himself who was a big gross man named Golovin. He later became Alexasha's brother-in-law. Perhaps he saw his bride that evening for the first time. Whether the Tsar noticed me at all, serving food with the rest, I do not know. If he did he made no sign then.

The third time he came I knew what was the matter. Alexasha had brought off his plan regarding Anna Mons. She was never more heard of and I do not know if the Prussian envoy ever married her, but I think not. The Tsar was wild that evening, almost as though it were a meeting of the Society of All-Drunken Mirth which he had already founded in Moscow because he always liked to give names to everything. I heard more later on about the Anna Mons affair. Alexasha had got her to put down in writing that she wished to marry Kaiserling. He told the Tsar who immediately said, "No, no, I have proof that she loves me more than any other." Alexasha took the letter from his pocket and showed it, and that was the end of Anna Mons. I did not think of her often and only mention her now because I am certain that was why Peter Alexievich was crazy with drink that night and called for a woman. Alexasha beckoned me and took me by the elbows as I was, hot with serving food, and thrust me in front of the Tsar.

"Ekaterina Vassilievka is good in bed," he said.

After that I had no more choice but to be propelled forward to a place where there was a couch, and someone jerked a curtain across; I expect it was Alexasha. All around us guests were doing the same thing with the other servants, but not in privacy. Peter Alexievich's dark eyes stared at me. He said nothing. He was still in his sullens, and very drunk. I myself was sober. Had it been any other man I would have said gently, "What troubles you?" For I could see a red gleam at the back of the brilliant eyes, like a bear shows when it has been burnt or bitten. He was hurt in the way big boorish men can be, like schoolboys, and for the sake of their pride dare not show it. But I was only a Livonian servant, and he was the Tsar. So I said nothing. Suddenly he spoke.

"How much are you worth?" he said. "A ducat? No woman is worth more," and then I was certain Anna Mons had hurt him. I cannot say how women know these things but they do. For the last time her beautiful face flashed across my mind, then I forgot her. I have never possessed beauty, and have never needed it.

He was bitter and angry with himself, and like an angry man who cares nothing he took me, there on the couch. It was no worse than submitting to Sheremetev. The face so close to mine was still the face of youth, despite everything. I could see the mole or wart on Peter's left cheek, and I began stroking his hair. This soothing motion pleased him, I think, and presently the grimacing and twitching of his face, which was a habit, grew still. He muttered once, through the fumes of the wine, that he was Peter Mikhailov the bombardier and also a sailor.

Suddenly he sat up and said, "My head, ah, God, my head!" He pretended to blame the wine, but I knew Menshikov and the rest had no such punishment from theirs.

I knew what to say, in Russian, and I said, speaking softly, "Lay it here, child," and, still gently, pulled his head down so that it lay on my bare breasts. I continued to stroke his hair and his temples. He gave a kind of shudder and shortly fell asleep. I remained without moving for a long time, never ceasing the stroking except once, and then he began to move and murmur of a bad dream. So I kept on soothing him, while about us the noisy sounds of the feasting slid at last into silence. I could hear Menshikov snoring, very faintly, from beyond the curtain; he had taken his pleasure with one of the cookmaids.

Presently I myself slept. In the morning when I awoke Peter Alexievich was gone. He had left a ducat by me. I took it and twisted it into my stocking-top to keep it safe. I would not spend it, I knew.

There was one thing I had noticed in this first night of ours together and I will speak of it now, and not again unless I have to. I had seen, in the half-light of the drawn curtain, that the Tsar had a sore on his genitals. I knew what it was; every whore knows, and it is our greatest fear and when we know a man has it we do not, if we can help it, sleep with him. I had known in time. Had I called out "No, Peter Alexievich," he would have left me alone and gone to some other. The Tsar has forced many people to do many things, but he would never have forced an unwilling woman. But I kept silent, saying to myself that I was young and healthy and that it might not prevail in me. But in the years since then I have seen all my children die except three daughters. Would the rest perhaps have lived if the Tsar had not given me the pox?

I believe, that first night of ours together when he slept, he thought that he lay within the white bosom of his mother who was dead. He told me afterwards that she used to calm him and stroke his hair.

After that, when the Tsar came to Alexasha Menshikov's house, he would ask for me by name instead of for any woman. Even at Menshikov's wedding, he stayed by my side. For the first time I saw one or two courtiers eyeing me not in the usual way, but with hope, as if I could get them something they wanted.

Although he probably knew it already as he knew most things, I told Alexasha Danilovich about the Tsar's disease. It occurred to me that if Alexasha himself was to catch it from me, he might lose his sweetheart Daria. He listened and at the end, kissed me on the mouth.

"You are a brave girl, Katia," he said. "It is well known, and we think he caught it either in the Quarter here, or at Amsterdam. The Russians call it the German disease and the Germans call it the French disease and the French blame the Italians, but anyway there it is." Menshikov changed the subject and said he was happy to say that Golovin seemed likely to make an offer for one of the sisters. I felt sorry for whichever it was as Golovin was so gross he reminded me of Sheremetev. Boyars are proud of their girth.

"Soon Daria can come here from Preobrazhenskoe," said Alexasha cheerfully. "She could never have endured my sisters in the house."

I was suddenly concerned with my own fate. "Your bride may not want me in it either," I said. Alexasha laughed, and put his arm about me.

"Would I part so easily with a good cook, a good laundress and a good comrade?" he said. "Daria will learn housekeeping from you; she knows nothing at all except embroidery."

So I said I would stay. After that there were the two weddings and much feasting and in the end Daria Arsenieva brought her sister, Barbara, to live in Menshikov's house and Menshikov's two sisters went to Golovin's. It made less difference to me than I had feared. The bride did not, as I had expected, look down on me as coarse and low-born, a servant and a whore. In fact she was too innocent to think of it, having spent her days, with Barbara and Aksinia, in the Kremlin Terem in winter and at Preobrazhenskoe, where Peter's mother had formerly lived, in the summers, with the Tsar's sister Natalia Alexievna. They had met few men and had kept to themselves among their ikons and embroidery, though at Preobrazhenskoe there was more freedom. At first after she came to Alexasha's, Daria still sat stitching in the upper part of the house and did no work. It was supposed to be a great honour on the part of her family to permit her marriage with the former groom and pieman.

Barbara was different. She used to talk to me often about the life at Court, and the two widowed Tsaritsas Marfa and Praskovia. These were the wives of Tsar Alexis' elder sons, and one had five daughters and the other was a virgin. The last-named, who was Marfa, had the more interesting story. In the days of Miloslavsky, the great enemy of Peter and his mother, Miloslavsky himself had taken the ailing Tsar Feodor out on one of his good days to hunt. When they stopped in the forest for a meal it was, by custom, at a priest's house. Inside was a very beautiful young girl named Marfa Apraxin. Tsar Feodor did as was expected and fell in love, and wished to marry Marfa as his first wife, Agafa, had lately died in childbirth of a dead baby. It was arranged, but on the wedding night Tsar Feodor's physcians gave him so many love-potions that he became very ill and could do nothing, and died soon after. So the Tsaritsa Marfa remained at the Kremlin even though her marriage had never been consummated, and she was very virtuous and given to religion. With her lived Praskovia, Tsar Ivan's widow who was of high birth and ate a great deal, and Natalia Naryshkina, Peter's mother, while she lived, and Peter's own wife Evdokiya who by now he had, of course, put in a convent, taking away their little son Alexis from her and leaving the boy to be brought up by his aunt Natalia Alexievna.

I may add, for I shall forget about it later, that when after many years the virtuous Tsaritsa Marfa died, my husband swore that he would find out if she was still a virgin after all and went and examined her dead body. He came back to me exclaiming "Extraordinary! She was indeed a virgin. Sometimes rumour speaks truth. Think of it! Extraordinary!"

"Well, your curiosity is satisfied," I said comfortably. I had learned long since by then that Peter Alexievich had no notions of propriety, for if he had had them he would not have married me.

Alexasha meantime had ridden back to the war. He was a good officer—shortly after the time of which I speak, the Tsar made him supreme commander of the army—and a clever engineer. Perhaps I have said enough to show that Menshikov could turn his hand to anything. I shall have more to say of that later. Meanwhile, Daria was not to be exposed to the roughness of camp life and so she and I and Barbara stayed on in the house outside Moscow.

It was dull without the men. The time seemed to pass slowly. I wondered what the Tsar was doing and if he was ordering the men or jumping into ditches to help dig them or fixing nailed boards in a boat or sinking foundations in water to make a fort, all of which he had boasted to me that he had done. In the meantime word came that his sister, Tsarevna Natalia, was anxious to visit Daria and see her house in the Sloboda.

A great cleaning and cooking took place, almost as if the men were at home. On the morning of the visit, Barbara Arsenieva brought down a dark-blue dress she said she had no further use for. It had embroidery on the bodice and sleeves, and I was delighted. I had never had such a dress before.

The Tsarevna arrived at last in a litter which was screened from the street by gently swaying curtains woven of palm leaves dried in the sun. "Some of the old ones must have insisted on that," Barbara said, adding that none of the Tsar's family, sons or daughters, ever used to go out unless shuttered in this manner. In fact, as I learned afterwards, the royal women spent their entire lives in the Terem except for certain religious processions, when they wore veils as well as having the palm screens to hide them from the people. Tsarevna Sofia, the rebel Regent, was the first to break with this custom. But I will not speak yet of Sofia as she has her own place.

Tsarevna Natalia had brought the third Arseniev girl, Aksinia, with her, and Aksinia helped her out of the litter and held her train. "Little Alexis Petrovich has not come," murmured Barbara, disappointed.

"The Tsarevich?" I knew Tsar Peter had a young son by his wife Evdokiya, but nothing more concerning them. Barbara had turned away from the window where we all watched and was following Daria out to the door. The sisters always acted in unison, having been so long together in the Terem. I used to wonder if it mattered to Alexasha Menshikov which one he married.

The Tsarevna entered the house and we all made our obeisances. She was a big young woman in her twenties, shy yet noisy. Her height and colouring reminded one of the Tsar, but though Natalia's curiosity was almost as great as her brother's, her manner was less abrupt. No doubt she welcomed this visit as a break in the cloistered life of the Kremlin. She went round the room fingering hangings and ornaments, and then our clothes, while Daria kept up polite talk. I said nothing as it was not my place, and made ready to serve the food when they should want it. It was possible to do without some of the ceremony when the house was only full of women, and we ate downstairs.

The friends chatted together as young women will. "Why didn't Alexis Petrovich come today, the love?" asked Barbara. I saw Natalia Alexievna's cheeks redden a little and she replied rather shortly, "My nephew doesn't like to come out. He is happier with a holy book, like a monk. He says he wants to read through the whole of the Bible, and he's not yet nine years old."

Daria started talking about something else, to cover the embarrassment. Presently I heard the Tsar mentioned. Everyone by now was laughing again as though nothing had gone wrong.

"I wrote to him to be careful of cannon-balls, that time at Azov," Natalia was saying. "Do you know what he sent by way of answer? He said 'I do not go to them, they come to me. Write and tell them to stop it.' He has no fear in the firing-line at all. Perhaps he should be more careful; after all, he is the Tsar." She looked down at her fingers and I was left in doubt as to whether it was a good thing or not for a Tsar to expose himself to danger. But there would be no choice for Peter Alexievich: I could not picture him as afraid except for bad dreams. I leaned against a wall, for my tasks were done, and for moments heard his voice in my ears as it had sounded last time we made love.

"Picture to yourself a city whose streets are all of water, all canals, filled with boats like Amsterdam or Venice." I had said I knew nothing of Venice. "Neither do I," he said, "for the streltsi brought me back again too soon," and I did not know what he was talking about. He had frowned and then laughed and said, "One day I will have built myself such a city and you will come and live there with me, Katia, and we will go everywhere by water and I shall steer the boat." He was never done talking of boats, especially the old one he had first discovered rotting on a lake at Yaroslavl where it had been left since the days of his great-uncle. "I learned to sail it when I had mended it," he said proudly. I thought again how much he seemed like a small boy in some ways and not in others. This sister of his was fond of him, as I could tell from the way she talked. She would not know or care that her brother had been my lover. That there would have been many others like me I knew; servants at the houses in the Sloboda when the Tsar visited his foreign friends, peasant women in the countryside when he passed through with his armies; bought whores when there was no one else. Do not think that you are particularly favoured, Ekaterina Vassilievka, because he talked to you of boats. No doubt every woman he sleeps with hears of water and sailing upon it with him. You must not expect too much. Yet I could see myself well enough in a boat, with Peter Alexievich at the tiller as he'd said, wearing his plain grubby sailor's dress when everyone else wore lace. I wondered if next time he came he would like my blue gown or if, as was more likely, he would be in too much of a hurry to get it off to notice it. Meantime the talk had come to a standstill and soon the Tsarevna said that she must go. As she passed by me she paused and I was aware of her height.

"That was a good meal," she said. "You must come with the rest when they visit me in my rooms in the Terem." Turning to the others she said, "It's pleasanter at the Kremlin now my old great-aunt Irina Mikhailova is dead, and Anna who copied her in everything. We have more freedom in our apartments, everyone comes in and out, and we talk."

After she had gone away Daria yawned and said that she was going upstairs to rest. When Barbara and I were alone we spoke of the Tsarevna's visit. "She was very gracious," I said.

"Goodness, yes. That Terem is very dull. Being in the Sloboda is like coming out into life, but being a woman she can't do it yet, except that in summer, at Preobrazhenskoe, it is not so bad. The Tsar's parents used to have a theatre there, but it's never used now because Peter Alexievich hasn't time."

"Does he take time to see his son?" I asked, not seeming to pry. I had been touched by the story of the little boy who liked reading his Bible. It reminded me of Pastor Glück.

Barbara looked back over her shoulder, as if someone might be listening. "It isn't safe to say much," she told me. "The Tsarevich was taken from his mother at eight years old or less. Evdokiya Lupokhina minded that far more than going into the convent; she was a religious woman anyway. She wearied the Tsar: almost as soon as they were married he left her and went back to his boat-building at Yaroslavl, and wouldn't come back or write. Evdokiya wasn't a bad creature, but she was his mother's choice and not his. That isn't always a good thing. Little Alexis has never forgotten her, I believe, though he doesn't speak of her now even if Natalia Alexievna is out of hearing. I don't think he likes his aunt much. He was put in her charge because she is the Tsar's favourite sister, but she doesn't understand a boy who only wants to read. Neither Natalia nor the Tsar has much time for book-learning for themselves. Sofia, the half-sister who became Regent, was different; they say she had read everything there was. It's not safe to speak of her now, you know."

I was not for the moment interested in Sofia. "The Tsar's mother was very beautiful, they say." I wanted to know about her.

"Natalia Naryshkina? Very, and with as little sense as a goose. She had a great horde of male relations, who all clamoured for Court appointments exactly like the Lupokhini, who didn't get them. But the Naryshkins——" Barbara turned her head away. "There was a massacre," she said, "when the Tsar was a child."

"Tell me of it." I had forgotten that I was a servant; more than anything I wanted to hear of this thing that had happened in the Tsar's childhood. Barbara raised her brows a little, then smiled good-naturedly.

"It wasn't a pretty story," she said. "I don't remember, of course, but I heard of it from the older women in the Terem. You know that no Tsarevna can marry? They stay on there, growing old and sour like Irina, who was Tsar Mikhail's daughter and a beauty in her day. No commoner can marry them, and foreign princes won't ally themselves with Muscovy. So they stay single. The massacre? it was a revolt of the streltsi, the palace bodyguard. Sofia planned it, they say, to make herself Regent; *she* wasn't going to rot in the Terem. They rose and slaughtered all the Naryshkin men they could find, and Tsar Peter and his half-brother Tsar Ivan, who was feeble-minded, had to watch Peter's favourite uncle Ivan Naryshkin thrown to the mob in the square and torn to pieces. Natalia Naryshkina made a priest give him the Last Sacraments first. They'd killed all the others they could lay hands on."

I thought of a small boy, witnessing all of it; it wouldn't matter to the half-wit brother. Perhaps that was why Tsar Peter grimaced now and had nightmares. I knew by this time that he always had to have someone to hold on to, at night, when he had his bad dreams.

Barbara went on talking as though now she had begun, she could not stop. "The Tsar never forgave his half-sister Sofia, but he bided his time. He won in the end; Sofia was made to be a nun till she died, by the time he'd done, and he killed her lovers and hung three corpses of men who'd risen in her favour, later on after his return from his travels in Europe, outside Sofia's cell with their hands thrusting through the bars and holding a petition saying, 'Come back and rule us.' They were left there for five months. The Tsar was angry because, you see, it was the second time the streltsi had risen, and they chose to do it just when he was about to travel on to Venice, and so he had to come home instead. He didn't leave a single one of them alive. When he needed men for the war with Sweden, he had to start training raw recruits. But he's made an army out of those, in the end."

I reflected that it would be as well not to offend Peter Alexievich. His revenges seemed harsh.

I was still astonished at the courtesy of Natalia Alexievna in inviting me to the Kremlin with the rest, even though I could now be called Daria's housekeeper and perhaps companion. But in fact I think that anyone who was foreign, and therefore different, was interesting to those cloistered ladies, who seized at every chance to make the hours pass less slowly.

However it occurred, I found myself with Daria and Barbara in the Menshikov carriage, wearing my blue dress with the embroidery. We had turned westward to Moscow, while Daria, who had started a baby, looked pallid and clutched her stomach every time the carriage lurched. As at any other season, the roads were as bad as they can be except in winter, when the snow hardens them.

I had already glimpsed the budding Kremlin spires on my earlier journey with Sheremetev. Now we drew up by a fretted side-door in the great wall. The fire which had lately destroyed most of the ancient part of the palace had left the Terem alone. After five minutes inside I thought this a pity. The place was completely airless, smelling of incense and female sweat and food. There were ikons everywhere and we made swift obeisance to them in passing; to have done it properly would have left no time to visit Tsarevna Natalia. Dwarfs scuttled about; in this place they called them God's fools and gave them victuals and houseroom. All of the windows were barred, as though the royal ladies were kept like prisoners; indeed, I understand they used to be so. I began to feel faint, as I had often felt lately. I took hold of myself in time to receive the greetings of the Tsarevna, who today was dressed in the customary robes of the Terem, straight and fur-trimmed and with a heart-shaped headdress that was much bejewelled. A brazier burned in the room and from time to time one of the dwarfs threw in herbs from a basket to perfume the air. Others carried dishes of sweetmeats to Tsaritsa Praskovia, who sat with her fat silent young daughters some way off. She was too high-born to greet us and went on munching sweets and gossiping with her ladies. The children said nothing, and I wondered if they were half-witted like their father, Tsar Ivan. If they were not, it must be a weary life for them in here, but perhaps they didn't know it.

I kept away from the brazier's heat, while Daria and Barbara and Aksinia, who had joined them, clustered about it to admire Tsarevna Natalia's own needlework. All about the walls, in the rooms and corridors between ikons, hung such work, signifying the passing of hours, days, years and generations to these women who had no other tasks to occupy them, and grew like flowers in the heavy air, then withered, as flowers do.

A small pale-faced boy crept by presently and Natalia Alexievna in her boisterous way threw a ball to him made of sewn leather. The child fumbled in catching it and let it fall at his feet. I glimpsed an expression of terror and dislike in his eyes as his young aunt mocked him. "Little boys should know how to catch a ball without dropping it," said Natalia. "When your father was your age he was learning to be a drummer, and a fine one he is now, the best in the army. Alexis never plays at anything," she said, turning away to the women again as though the boy could not hear. The daughters of Tsaritsa Praskovia still sat about idly, not playing either. A dwarf brought their mother a dish of hot pancakes, which she began to gobble greedily. Further back in a corner was Tsaritsa Marfa, sewing for the poor.

I turned my eyes away, longing for fresh air from an opened window. By a curtain, alone, sat an old richly-dressed woman, the twin patches of rouge standing out brightly on her wrinkled cheeks. She had frowned a little at the exchanges over Alexis and the frown still lingered. "All children are different," she murmured, and as I happened to be near her the remark was addressed to me as well as to herself. She went on talking, with her eyes fixed not on me, not on the room, but on something much further away, perhaps no longer here at all. I learned later that she was the Tsarevna Tatiana, third daughter of Tsar Mikhail, who had founded the dynasty.

She brought herself back. "Peter Alexievich used to be a very naughty little boy," she said, smiling. "I can remember his mother standing listening behind a door to the Tsar and his advisers talking in the next room; that's nothing, we all used to do it. But Peter gave her a push and ran away laughing, and Natalia staggered through the doorway into the council-chamber and the advisers were scandalised. It was the first time a Tsaritsa had ever been seen unveiled in public. Afterwards, in Sofia's time, we all came out more often. *She* was so much alive, she was like a flame. To end as she did——" The hooded eyes, bright as a hawk's, peered up at me as if the old lady had realised suddenly that she was talking to someone from outside, perhaps an enemy. "Do you read much?" she asked courteously; a change of subject made everything safe.

I explained that I could neither read nor write. "That is the lot of most women, and it is sad," exclaimed the Tsarevna forthrightly. As if she could not long speak of anything else she returned to the forbidden subject of Sofia. "I loved her," she said. "Everything she read she used to discuss with me. I saw to it that her father gave her good tutors, the same as the men. He wouldn't have thought of it for himself. My sister Irina was against it, but I always said, why not let the young women advance in knowledge? Change comes, whether anyone likes it or not. Sofia had the best mind of her generation; she would soak up information like a sponge. And she ruled well, whatever they say now; and was never seen drunk in public."

I had drawn a breath of warning at first, but decided by now that no doubt this very old princess could say whatever she chose. It was also possible that her own mind had grown clouded as old people's do, and that she confused past with present. "Sofia spoke four languages," said Sofia's aunt proudly. "It served her well when she had to deal with ambassadors from the Porte, and from France, and even England where of course they all speak French. The common people still love her dearly and pray for her, they tell me;

I never go out now. The last time was at that procession in honour of Our Lady of Kazan"—the hawk's eyes gleamed with enjoyment—"when Tsar Peter tried to order his half-sister and all the rest of us back inside the Kremlin, but Sofia wouldn't go and we stood solid behind her. In the end *he* went, calling for a horse and leaping on it and riding hard out of the city in spite of the solemn feast-day. That was the first time the people called him Antichrist."

Beside us the little boy Alexis had crept up and was listening. I was certain the talk had become dangerous and tried to think of some matter that would not offend the old lady and might perhaps draw her back from the dead Sofia to the present day. "What pretty curls the Tsarevich has!" I said, and my words sounded foolish and she took no heed of them. Silence fell between us and I could see that the eldest Tsarevna was far back again in her past, thinking of the days when Sofia was Regent of Muscovy and had not yet been shut up in her convent and later on had corpses hung outside her cell. As if to prove me right Tatiana Mikhailova nodded suddenly. "I am glad the Tsar allows her sister Marfa to be with her now; they took the veil together. And, when all is said, Sofia has lived. She had lovers and chose them herself. She has had her hour. As for the present Tsar, I don't know what he will do next. It may be a good thing and it may not that Ivan, who was co-ruler but hadn't all his wits, died and left Peter in sole control. Even when they were boys and had to make their prepared speeches together to foreigners Peter was always finished long before poor Ivan, and the ambassadors preferred him; they said he looked more like sixteen than ten. Of course, that was some years ago now." The eyes focused themselves again on the present, on the whey-faced child staring at the floor, at myself, a stranger, and by the fire the women prattling of the things women talk of always. "I will rest now," said Tatiana Mikhailova, and suddenly looked very old. Shortly Daria and Barbara beckoned me to take our leave, and I had to leave the eldest Tsarevna alone, still murmuring to herself beside the drawn curtain. "She grows foolish now she is old," called Tsarevna Natalia gaily, and I suddenly felt dislike for the Tsar's sister and wondered whether she would resent it when someone said one day of her in her hearing what she had just said in Tatiana's.

The talk we had had fired my brain, and I began to wonder what Tatiana Mikhailova would have said had I replied that Antichrist was my lover and that I was probably pregnant by him. I was glad to go out into the street again after the scented warmth of the brazier. I hadn't tried to get rid of the baby. I wanted it, and felt certain something would happen soon to make it all worthwhile. Perhaps Peter Alexievich would come home.

Something happened indeed, but not as I had expected it. I suppose that by now I should have been ready to expect anything. When we reached the house again a line of recruits was drawn up beyond the gate and inside, everything was in turmoil because Menshikov's provisioning officer, who had a hare-lip so that one didn't know what he was saying, was running about shouting to the servants to get together my gear if I had any. When he saw me he called out, "Katia Vassilievka, where have you been? The Tsar's Majesty requires your presence in camp," and the recruits all laughed. The officer drew himself up. "There has been a great victory," he managed to say, adding that he hadn't had time to collect many details and would I kindly hurry, or Alexander Danilovich would beat him when we got back. I asked if he had had a meal. "Never mind that," he said, "make haste, there's a good woman, and let us be off within the hour. We have a long journey to make to——"

I think he had said it was a place called Noteburg. I gave up arguing and said farewell to Daria and Barbara and the cook and the household serfs, and got my cloak and left with the contingent before night.

Marsh and forest broke the line of the sky on our northward journey; little more. The rains had not yet begun to fall and instead of mud, the rutted ways were carved out of a brittle grey dust which settled on our mounts, ourselves, our baggage, and the provisioning officer's gold braid. He himself had little to say to me, being occupied for the greater part of the time with riding back and forth in harassed fashion to see to the swaying stores and the straggling, weary, bewildered, half-equipped men he had recruited in Moscow. They trudged on in bleak acceptance of their lot and next to no understanding of what the war was about or whom they were supposed to fight. Looking at them, I felt compassion and tried to joke with them when I could. Their own question began to trouble me, though I seldom ask such questions: what was it all about? Why were we—I myself of somewhat more importance now than I had been, for I was the Tsar's woman and had been personally sent for—and the men, and the stores and guns and horses and mules, journeying ever farther from home? I reflected also that I was more a Swede than a Russian, but had no clear thoughts that might belong to either. I heard the men mutter uncertainly, "Narva, they beat us easily at Narva." This fact had not been allowed to be made public, but had leaked out. I saw the officer approaching, his wig awry, his hare-lip streaked with dust and sweat. Poor man, I thought, it is like herding angry cattle.

It seemed to me that if I knew more I could cheer the men more readily. One cannot say, "Soon you will be in camp, boys, and then there will be vodka for everyone," unless it is certain. A man needs more in any case than food in his belly and drink in his cup, though this helps if it has been provided. I could not say as to that. I knew nothing. The supply carts were behind us, moving like humped monsters against the day. Among them might be casks to be drunk for victory, or else not. But it is before the fight that a man needs his guts warmed. I thought how the Tsar, with all his new-fangled notions of more cannon and a navy, took little account of hunger, cold and despair. He would not have cared about them for himself, except the last.

Perhaps, I thought, if Peter Alexievich let me stay with him at the war, there were things I could say and do to make him understand all this. Perhaps not; he was set in his ways, and this itself was shown by the news which was brought us by riders cantering up from the brown horizon with its flat starved grasses and sullen sky. The officer conferred with the riding-party and then came to me. His face was the same as usual, neither elated nor downcast.

"The Tsar's Majesty has retaken Narva, and also Dorpat and Ivangorod." A murmur rose along the column and I turned and said, "There, boys, what did you say about Narva? Push on, and there will be other victories and you'll help win 'em." They cheered, and the hare-lipped officer looked as if something had taken place that was not according to the orders of the day.

"There will be official rejoicing and triumphal arches when the army returns to Moscow," he said. Rejoicing which was not official was, it was evident, out of place. I dug him in the ribs and said, "Get along, you're as pleased as anyone. Let the men have a bit of cheer. Most of 'em need it, now they've said goodbye to their mothers." For to me they seemed only boys. The Tsar had combed the cities and provinces for men and more men for his army and navy, and still would not be satisfied.

Looking back at it all I seem to see clearly scenes I could not have witnessed. At the time of Petersburg's first founding the Tsar had not met me. Yet I see and hear through the voice of Alexasha, who was there; the Tsar, being sometimes religious, choosing the Feast of the Trinity to lay the foundation-stone. There are nineteen islands about the mouth of the Neva and one was shaped like a hazel-nut and another, the Island of Hares, still had the wild things leaping and running about at that time in the marshy grasses. All of the islands were flat and easily flooded; a marsh is not a good place on which to build a city. At first the men's feet squelched in mud and they sank knee-deep: piles had to be sunk as at the foundations of Venice. When they had dug and made earth ramparts, Peter took a bayonet from one of the men and cut two turves and placed them across one another. Above in the pale-blue sky was an eagle, hovering. Later they shot it and the Tsar sailed down the Neva with the dead bird tied to his wrist and everyone feasted till two in the morning. The Tsar had laid a stone on the ramparts and the priests, whom he sent for at such times, came to sprinkle it with holy water. The bones of St.

Andrew had been brought north in their reliquary, and were placed on the stone. Later a hundred and thirty thousand men died of fevers, chills, starvation and accidents in the making of Petersburg. But now there is a city where nobody thought one could ever be, and it is like no other city in the world, except possibly Venice itself which neither the Tsar nor I have seen even yet.

Alexasha told me all this in the days before he grew old and too yellow and thin and cunning, as he is now. At that time he was fresh from making great boxes out of sawn pine trees to hold up the new fortifications at Cronstadt, across the water. This fort and a foundry the Tsar made were necessary lest the Swedes try to cut off supplies; they would not tamely submit to our occupation of the nineteen islands.

As I say, Alexasha was portly then, because the Tsar held that a man's manhood is proved by the amount of drink he can hold, and Menshikov was a prodigious drinker. But already, by that time, Peter Alexievich himself was taking less wine and secretly pouring half his own glass on the floor.

They made the young Tsarevich Alexis drink deep, however. They brought him to camp and took him by the hair of his curly head and held it back and forced wine down his throat while he spluttered and wept. They did this again and again until Alexis could hold his drink. By the time that boy was fourteen, he was a drunkard. Why did Peter do it? I think that perhaps he disliked the fact that his son, his heir, did not want to be a soldier, a military commander and organiser, a sailor, one who takes readily to something new. Alexis liked to read and to go to church, and make his confessions. He was beaten, like the rest, constantly by Peter's *doubina*, the gold-topped stick the Tsar carried always and used when the mood took him.

But on my own arrival Peter Alexievich welcomed me warmly. He took me in his arms in front of everyone and kissed me hard and often, so that the skin of my face was sore afterwards. He held me back and looked at me and said, "At any rate, you've lived through siege before. This won't be any worse than Marienburg. Sheremetev——" and he started to tell me of some island Sheremetev had shelled that held out for twelve hours with its tiny garrison and put paid to five hundred of our men. "We will build the permanent fort on that, and the town's centre where the hares live now on their island. It can be joined by bridges."

I did not yet understand about the hares, the town, the bridges. Then Alexasha, who was there also, laughed and said, "It is the first time she has seen the sea," and I looked at the great flat unending stretch of cold water with its dotted islands and earthworks and guns. Later when the Tsar had gone off to see to the fort-digging Alexasha said, in a low voice as though he were still my lover, "The Tsar needs you, Katia. No one else can bring him comfort and free him from his evil dreams. While you are there he wants no other. We are all glad you have come."

The new town—even Peter Alexievich did not know yet that it was to be a city, the capital, outdoing Moscow—was to be built for the following reasons. The Tsar needed seaports other than Archangel, and the Black Sea ports he had captured on the Azov campaign before he met me. He needed a trading-place and government centre nearer to the coast than Moscow, which in any case was not close enough to the war. The war was fought because of the seaboard, which for some years now had belonged to Sweden. After the town's foundations were laid the huge toiling figure of the Tsar took its turn with the men. "His presence gives them confidence," said Menshikov. "And makes them work," said I.

Alexasha then began to growl about Sheremetev, whom he never liked and who never, as I have said already, liked him. Sheremetev was a boyar and Menshikov was a groom's son whom the other thought beneath him. Nevertheless, the General Field Marshal had lately cast his eyes down to notice a young bootblack, whose name was Yaguzhinsky and who was amusing and clever and a fool. He introduced him to the Tsar, who took to Yaguzhinsky as he always did to such folk. I came to like the bootblack very well and so, in the end, did Menshikov. We still work together, all three. But at that time, as Sheremetev had had his successes,

Alexasha began to boast of his own, not forgetting to mention in the recital the sorry figure the General Field Marshal had cut when he swam the river after Narva. "If the Tsar himself had been with them, they would not have been defeated," said Menshikov. "He would have seen to it that they were not placed with the blizzard blowing in their faces. Charles of Sweden noticed it at once, and though his numbers were by far smaller than ours he won the victory, by common sense. They say he does not always show it."

I looked sideways at Alexasha. "Why was the Tsar not at Narva?" I said. Menshikov began to evade the matter and wave his hands about.

"Peter Alexievich is no coward, as everyone knows."

"I never said he was one."

"It was—foresight—on his part. He needed additional men and went to Moscow to recruit them. He left an able commander in charge and he himself had just concluded a nine years' peace with Turkey. Peter Alexievich is too wily to wage two wars at once. The day after news of peace in the south came, he turned on Sweden."

"And Sweden turned on him." I had heard of the mad young Swedish king, Charles XII, who lived and slept in the saddle and never washed or shaved while on campaign. He had no other interest than in war; strange that there should be two such men in the same place in the same century, though Peter's interests were wide. "No one can say," continued Alexasha, as if he had to defend the Tsar to me, "that Peter Alexievich took no part in the fighting about Azov. That was a triumph, for without the ships we could never have done it. And without Peter Alexievich we would not have had the ships. He's made every boyar in the land work, I tell you, felling trees on the estates and having them hammered and sawn into hulks and keels and masts."

"He is a great man. Has he ever in his life been afraid?" The Tsar himself was out of earshot and I asked because I wanted to know, and nobody but Menshikov would have told me the truth. We have always spoken truth to one another in the end. He dropped his voice, out of prudence.

"Once he was very much afraid, when he fled in his

nightshirt from a supposed plot of the Regent Sofia on his life. No one to this day knows if it was true, but Peter Alexievich believed it. So he fled, like that, and galloped on horseback into the woods where they brought him clothing; then on a further twelve leagues to the Troitsa Monastery to muster men. There the Patriarch joined him, and the army. It was a triumph for Tsar Peter; he was still only a young man, untried in many ways, including power. Last of all, with Moscow emptying itself, the Regent Sofia thought that she had best get to the Troitsa like everyone else, and set out in her carriage. But the Tsar had the soldiers turn Sofia back on the road and drive her home to Moscow, where she was arrested. The rest you know. That is the only time I have heard of fear in the Tsar."

"Surely if Sofia meant him harm, she could have done away with him when he was a small boy."

"You are too shrewd, Ekaterina Vassilievka. Put a bridle on your tongue."

I laughed, and crinkled my eyes against the last of the sun, seen redly and clear above the trees on our left. Soon it would be night. I said to Alexasha, "So he was glad of his friends. Where were you, my man?" For I knew well enough Alexasha had not been there on that long ago ride to the Troitsa.

"I was there and not there, only a dentschnik, a houseboy. I was of no importance except to get drunk with, till the night I warned the Tsar of poison in his food and we fed it to a dog and the dog died. You will see"—he smiled—"Peter Alexievich beat me with his stick, kick me, strike me across the face or over the head with his fists. You will hear him swear by everything that is holy—and at times, despite all he has done to the Patriarch and the popes and their beards and believers, he himself believes—that he will rid himself of Menshikov the pieman, put him in prison, send him to Siberia, break him on the wheel, cut off his head. But he never will, unless I myself forget what I once was." The handsome face had taken on a sad brooding quality, as though it looked into the future. Alexasha Menshikov was among Peter's best servants, and he knew it. He was also my friend. "I will serve him and you," he said now. "Why do you think I made you go to him that first night, and not another? Why did you think he made me marry Daria, saying our betrothal had lasted too long? Do not forget, Ekaterina Vassilievka; do not ever forget."

Was he threatening, or cajoling me? At that time I did not even know such words. I was a simple person, lately a servant myself. It was the first time I knew that the Tsar had made Menshikov marry Daria. If it was true it flattered me. I smiled and said nothing, which I was beginning to learn is always the right answer, and before my smile had died there was a sight to be seen against the dying sun. It sank at last into the sheet of darkly moving water which was the sea: out of the busy detachments of digging and hammering men a giant figure, its face grimed with earth and gunpowder, came up and put its arms about me. "Are you happy, my Katia?" asked Peter. "Look at the sea. I remember the first time I saw it. Now I cannot do without it, or yourself."

We looked together at the dark Baltic and although there was still firing to be heard in the distance, for the Swedes were by no means yet resigned to letting us keep even those places we had won, I was content. Desperate resistances, losses of hundreds and thousands of men, lowered flags over smoking towns, the Russian fleet on its maiden voyage down the Neva stuck fast in ice; the capture of this forest, that marshy island, meant less than two things to me. One was the city which was to have streets made of water. I believed in it already. The other was the big calloused shipwright's hand which cupped my breast. The hand has gone, but the city lives and will outlast me.

"What next, Peter Alexievich?" Everyone had begun to say that instead of "Where next?" as formerly. We had stayed on at the place of islands and soon, Peter would have finished a wooden house where I was to live with him. It was to be a copy of the one he had stayed in at Zaandam, in Holland, when he went there in his youth to learn about shipbuilding, and it would be plain and have low doors and ceilings because the Tsar liked simplicity and also liked to duck his head on entering.

"What next? What next? Why do they ask me? Would I let God's opportunity slip? You will not know, Katinka, that these places were ours in the days of Novgorod the Great, when trade with the West flourished. We are only taking back our own." He would stare over towards the muddled skyline of one of the first places he had taken in this war, and murmur "Schlüsselburg now, the Key City." This had been built on the island shaped like a hazel nut, which Sheremetev had taken. "Then out to sea, to beat them there. How many of you called me a fool for spending my youth in dockyards in Zaandam, more dockyards in London? When I think of the forgotten hulk which was all they had left me for a fleet in Yaroslavl—all honour to it, it's the ancestor, and as I say taught me to sail when I'd plugged it—but you will see, all of you, when spring comes, what we can do at sea."

Spring came, and the ice melted and released the ships frozen hard in the Neva, and it was no longer so bitterly cold, and green growth was already thrusting up through the melting snow. I lay in a tent, for the little house was not yet completed, and listened to the now familiar sounds of war; it felt strange if there was silence. Sooner or later all the flat swampy lands became ours, and the Tsar won a victory also at sea as he had said he would do. It happened overnight when he was on board one of his ships which carried no cannon. Four great Swedish vessels came up and were soon overpowered with their cannon still idle, for the crews were so surprised at the sight of a Russian fleet which could sail that they hadn't time to man them. Thirty small boats Peter had filled with his own crack infantrymen who had been with him from boyhood in the days when he drilled them and drummed for them at Preobrazhenskoe. Two of the Swedish ships were brought in as prizes, and the other two retreated in the end with heavy damage. Later I saw the prisoners brought back, big fair men with sullen faces. I did not say to myself that they were my countrymen. I was a Muscovite now. They would be made to help dig foundations for Petersburg. Later, when there was enough labour, we would not keep prisoners always. Meanwhile the Tsar rejoiced and dug the earth as usual and then sailed out to the empty sea in his boat and thought of the days when Novgorod and Kiev had traded with the West in slaves and furs and honey and wax. "The window on the West is open again and must never be allowed to close," he said when he came back. I laughed when he and Menshikov decorated themselves with the Order of St. Andrew, but would not tell them why.

There was a sadness for me about this time. My baby was born and was a boy, and he lived for a little while and then he died. But I knew I must go on smiling and listening and keeping Peter Alexievich as contented as he could ever be. He still had terrors by night. "Only a bad dream, little father; now it is gone." And I would hold him close and stroke his hair and temples in the way he liked, against my breast. Without anyone to hold him so in sleep he would be full of jerking fear, but nobody else was supposed to know about it and I said nothing, even to Alexasha.

FOUR

THE PIEMAN'S TALE

I saw the Empress yesterday. She is firm in her resolve to send a written protest to the English about their naval exercises in the Baltic. "To do so may mean war," I said, remembering their unpleasant German king and his interest in obtaining the port of Wismar for the benefit of Hanover.

"Not unless we say so," she answered, looking at me steadily with her bold eyes beneath their preposterous dyed eyebrows, which make Ekaterina look as if she would at any instant take flight, like a bird, mocking her solid body. There is an unquenchable life about Ekaterina: I have noted it these many years, twenty-odd of which have been spent, for myself, with my genteel Daria. But Ekaterina, Catherine as she is now, is no longer the same woman I took from Sheremetev to his chagrin. Royalty has laid its mantle upon her; she might have been born in the purple. Peter the Great could have had a less worthy successor, though God knows the trouble I took at the time to bribe the army and those elsewhere to ensure Catherine's election, as Peter had left no will. That she sits firm on her throne now, despite her drinking, is part due to me and part to herself. Who would have thought a camp-follower could become Autocrat? It is like a fairy-tale, or something one imagines after too much wine. As regards that last, I have as good a head as any man in Russia, but I have always been temperate except when in the company of the late Tsar. Then it was of benefit to me to make myself drunk, as he did. All my life I have perforce followed the likely chance, the better prospect. Others have done the same and do not admit it to themselves. It has paid me well enough, when all's said; Prince Menshikov, chief adviser to Our Lady of All the Russias, when once I sold hot pies in Moscow streets and later mucked out stables behind the Kremlin with a brush made of twigs. Tsar Peter never allowed me to forget the past. His widow is more compassionate. We two might never have known one another in the old days, for all we ever say of it. The business of the hour is transacted, and that is all.

I remember the pies. They were all that was warm in a frozen world, and I could not recall a time when I had been other than cold. The pies used to be heated on a charcoal brazier in a cellar within the Moscow earth wall, and it was my task to haul them off with tongs when they were ready and run out with them, piping hot, on a tray into the cold streets. An old devil of a woman baked them and hired me to sell them for her. If I came back with too many unsold, she beat me. If I took one for myself to eat, she cuffed my ears. I was a fairly small boy, and often hungry.

Standing now on the upper floor of my ridiculous palace on the Island of Hares—well I know its foundations are insecure, as are the foundations of all my neighbours, but who except Peter Alexievich Romanov would elect to build a city on a marsh?—wrapped as I am in a satin bedgown, looking out over the dark water of what to me is a foreign place, I think of Moscow. I do not think that it will be permitted me to end my days there; it is no longer the capital and nowadays everyone looks towards the West. But no other city, however magnificent, can ever hold a candle to that great heart. When I think of it I seem to see a thousand ikons and many churches painted red and black and gold, all gleaming. They say I am a hypocrite because despite the worldly life I lead I never miss a church service. But I love, and have always loved, the ritual and the feeling it gives me that I, as a man, as myself, am not important; that nobody is as important as God. Perhaps one could come to the same conclusion in immense solitudes. However it was impossible to be solitary in Moscow, in the days when I hawked the pies barefoot and watched my toes turn blue against the frozen snow. All about me were countless beggars, always those, of whom I might have been one; following me for the good smell of the pies and trying to grab them, so that I had to learn to be nimble and kick out and even bite. Now and again some customer came by on foot and bought a couple, or by luck someone in a litter, who would buy several to take home for supper. Muscovites are great eaters. I knew what I knew, which was that the pies were made of cat's meat with a thin watery crust round them, but I would not have refused one myself except for the old woman. I grew used early to beatings. It was to serve me well, in later years, with Peter Alexievich and his *doubina*, which he was often quick to wield.

At the time of which I speak, Peter Alexievich was himself a small fatherless boy, seldom heard of and never seen. He lived within the Kremlin. His half-brother Ivan had after a fashion come to the throne, but no one often saw Ivan either. I heard the gossip and the mutterings about it. The Naryshkin family, kin of the late Tsar Alexis' second wife, were said to be keeping Tsar Ivan prisoner away from his people. Every evil was blamed on the Naryshkins, except for those few who blamed the Miloslavsky, the family of the late Tsar's first wife, instead. Whoever might be to blame, it was nothing to do with me and my frozen toes. But I listened and kept my ears open.

When the chance for action came I was not ready. There was a press of crowds in the streets and for once all my pies were sold, and through the milling pressing people a party of horsemen thrust its way. Foremost among these was a handsome young man, perhaps twenty-three years old, with hair the colour of honey beneath his boyar's cap, a round forehead, and clothes made of gold-threaded brocade with great fur sleeves, and high boots of finely tanned leather. I had never seen so goodly a sight, and as yet have not, though much has come between.

The picture he made that day is clear in my mind yet. Perhaps that is because he had an air of innocence, as though evil could not touch him. The crowds cared nothing for this or perhaps did not see it; they fell silent and sullen except for a few of the beggars, who continued to call for alms. In the midst of this half-silence the young rider's horse reared as he flung coins, and I saw terror in the whites of its eyes and in the foaming of its mouth against the bit. The young man almost lost his balance and the reins swung out of his grasp and hung slack, a moment, and I shot forward and grabbed them. I did not let go. The maddened horse dragged me for some distance along the way, bruising me against the pressing people. I do not know what made me guess it, but I am quick of wit and my father was a groom: I knew something had been done to the horse to make him as he was, no doubt with the intent that he should throw his rider. Perhaps there was a nail under his saddle; so small a thing can make a horse run mad. I did not know, but I knew that I must hold on, and this I did.

At last the young rider regained his balance. He looked down at me and smiled. He took back the reins and held out a silver piece from his purse. I took it and whispered "Look under his saddle, and do not ride him any more today." I saw his fair brows fly up in surprise and then frown a little. He raised a hand to stop the following and the little party drew to a halt. Still about us were the waiting hostile folk.

"What do you know of this?" the young man, whose name I soon found was Ivan Naryshkin, asked me. I looked him in the eyes—his eyes were hazel, almost the colour of his honey-gold hair but with green in them—and I told him the truth, which was that I knew nothing except that anyone who couldn't guess such a horse had been tampered with before leaving the stables didn't know his left hand from his right. Naryshkin nodded, unsmiling, and slid down out of the saddle, while I marvelled at how brave he was in thinking nothing of the crowd, who in the meantime had drawn back a little, still scowling and in silence.

Naryshkin beckoned one of his servants who rode with him. The saddle was removed while I held the tossing, rearing head. Sure enough there was a sore place, already breaking out into pustules; it might have been caused by harmful unguent, or a rubbing with powdered glass. Naryshkin spoke to the frightened beast gently and caressed it and had it led away, and himself mounted one of the servants' horses; but before doing so he said to me, "You're a good lad. I might have broken my neck. What is your name and where do you live in Moscow?" I told him and then blurted out, eagerly which is not my way for I have learned to be cautious, "Great lord, can I come and work for you?" For I had had enough of the old woman and her pies and knew it in that moment. Thrice in my life I have loved someone at sight and this was the first time.

Naryshkin nodded and, not wasting breath in the midst of the gaping folk, said in a low voice, "Come to the stables behind the Kremlin tomorrow and ask for the head groom there. Tell him that Ivan Kirilovich sent you." Even then I noticed that he paused before naming his patronymic, and recalled the gossip I had already heard that Naryshkin had once been Yarishkin and that the father, Kiril, was a peasant. However, that was as might be. I went to the stables next day and there were the horses, each one covered in his painted stall, with his breath steaming in clouds against the cold; and the smell of manure and warm straw I remembered from early childhood, and nearby the great enclosed palace with its reaching spires that seemed to touch the sky and blossom there. The head groom spat and said I could stay and help to clean out the horse-boxes, and have my board and keep. I was glad, because the day before all the money I had made selling pies had been stolen by someone in the crowd while I was busied with Naryshkin's horse, and when I got back to the cellar the old woman had beaten me stupid. Now I need not return to her.

So I became a stable-boy. Because I was willing to do any task or run any errand, gradually I began to be thought of, and to think of myself, as a person to be relied on. Almost daily my joy was to see Ivan Kirilovich and to dream of becoming such as he when I should be a man. He was everything I could imagine of splendour and kindness, a glimpse of another world which perhaps even yet I had never dreamed of entering. His glittering furred robes were different every day, and his purse seemed bottomless; he would toss a rouble to anyone who led out his horse or who pleased him in some small way, and he always had a word for me. In some manner I had obtained for myself the task of rubbing down and caring for the magnificent mount he had bestridden that first day. Its name was Sasha and I slept in Sasha's box and saw to it that nobody hurt him any more with powdered glass or any harmful thing.

I would comb his coat and mane lovingly and have him sleek as satin, ready for his master. There were other Naryshkin brothers and I saw them come and go, but cared nothing for them; sometimes, also, the old father Kiril would come round to the stables when he desired to ride out by coach. Neither the father nor his other sons were like Ivan.

Ivan's sister was the Tsaritsa. The palm-screened litter used by the Terem ladies stayed as a rule in its place with us, as it was seldom used when the times were so uncertain as now. Sometimes I would get the older grooms to talk to me of the days when Tsar Alexis the Gentle brought home his second bride. The beautiful Natalia Naryshkina had been used to a freer life than that of the Terem "and in the summers she and the Tsar used to go to Preobrazhenskoe where everyone was in holiday mood, and there would be mummers and players, and the Tsar and his wife—she was expecting Peter Alexievich by then—sat out of doors under the trees, and watched. Then their boy was born and after that his sister, and presently the Tsar died, and nowadays it is different."

"How is it different?" I asked. I liked to hear these old palace servants talk of what they remembered.

"Well, there has been trouble with the Miloslavsky, the first wife's kin who preferred the rights of Tsar Feodor, the elder, and Tsar Ivan Alexievich now Feodor is dead. Nowadays Tsaritsa Natalia must stay within the Kremlin and guard her son. As for Tsarevna Sofia, the daughter of the Miloslavsky, she caused much trouble by weeping aloud at the funeral of Tsar Feodor her brother, and blaming the Naryshkini who would not even stay long enough to see him entombed. Such things give offence and it is true that they rode off early. Tsaritsa Natalia had best be careful; Sofia is less of a fool than she." The groom lowered his voice; I could smell beer on his breath. "One day Sofia will make Natalia pay for having usurped the place of her mother. Also, young Peter Alexievich is strong and forward, and that does not please the Miloslavsky either. They would like Tsar Ivan, who is feeble, to rule, then they can do as they wish and destroy the Naryshkini. Mark my words, it may happen."

But I dismissed this as drunken rumour, nor had I yet seen the little Peter Alexievich, who was kept close within the palace during the troublous times. Nor were the summers yet again spent at Preobrazhenskoe.

I forget— looking back it is as though time shortened itself—how long it took for the unrest among the streltsi, the household guard, to break into flame. They were probably bribed by the agents of Sofia; their commander, Khovansky, aspired to be her lover. I can remember mutterings of unrest, the sound of men moving by night, and then a sudden great roaring of crowds assembled in Red Square beyond the palace. The horses had been restive for days; they knew. Word came soon that the colonels, who were said to have withheld the soldiers' pay, had been publicly knouted and that all was over. But this was not so. Shortly a further rumour was set about, whether or not by the agents of the Tsarevna. Tsar Ivan her brother, who had not all his wits, was said to have been poisoned, or strangled. The crowds were shouting for him to be shown to them, dead or alive.

Almost all the grooms had gone. It was not safe to be known as having any part in the life of the Kremlin. I stayed because I had nowhere else to go. I was kept busy by the head groom, who also stayed—he had been there as long as anyone could remember, and recalled Tsar Mikhail, the first of the dynasty—and I fed and watered the horses and continued especially to care for Sasha. He was growing restless as Ivan Kirilovich had not come to ride him out now for many days. It was as though everyone, of whatever rank, was out of his proper place. The press about the palace front was so thick that even I, small and lithe as I still was then, could not make a way through. The clamour went on by day and night, and was no longer formless but a repetitive dangerous chanting. Torches lit up the sea of faces which no longer seemed human. How like animals the human race can become, or perhaps it is truer to say that animals keep a dignity which men lose! A crowd such as that has no separate thought or will; if any man differed from his fellows he would be trampled underfoot. Afraid as I was—who would not have been afraid?—I despised them, I, the pie-seller. "They could have turned 'em away by a single charge of men with levelled pikes," I muttered.

"Pikes? It's the streltsi themselves have charge of this crowd, and won't let it go till they see blood," growled the groom. "Silver has changed hands, they say, but it's past all that now. Not all the gold in Muscovy will disperse that rabble. What they want——" He bit his lip, spat as was his habit, and turned and said clearly, "It is no longer safe here for you or for me. The very Kremlin itself is hardly so; they'll be into it before they've done. However we may as well go there."

He looked over his shoulder whence the sounds came, then jerked his head for me to follow. We might remain unobserved within the palace wall, I knew, or else mingle with the crowd if it should break in. Here, we had no chance.

"What's to befall Sasha?" I remember asking. I was still only a boy, though I felt like an old man.

"It isn't Sasha they're after, it's Sasha's master and his kin. Leave whatever you are at and follow me, for I won't wait." Without more words he threaded his way between the groups of men who were beginning to drift in our direction, with the aimless look of those who mean to do harm in the end. In the shadows beyond the flung brightness of the torches we found a postern door, and went in. There was no guard posted. Nothing was as it should be. I wiped my eyes with my fists and tried not to think of the beautiful spirited horses left for marauders; they were too valuable to kill.

The Kremlin is a warren of passages opening out suddenly into rooms large and small. Some of these were chapels with a lingering smell of incense, but stronger than this everywhere was the smell of fear. We joined those palace servants who had remained and hid ourselves as best we might. I remember sidling behind a curtain which was blazoned on its front with gold threads and a thousand sequins, which caught the light when a draught came or anything moved. I was sick with terror lest my breathing move the curtain and give me away. Presently, as nothing happened, I took courage and found a worn place to look through. Everything that is gold-embroidered is not new. What I saw then was a piece of history and I think that even at the time, I knew this.

The noise of the crowd outside had not stopped. Is came in great waves of animal sound, and sometimes there would be silence which was worse than the noise and then a single voice, or two or three, would rise on a high note and harangue the crowd. Within the palace they were debating together on the great staircase, their jewelled hands wagging. Busy among them was the old man I knew already to be Artemon Matviev, who had been Natalia Naryshkina's guardian and in whose house Tsar Alexis had first seen her. Matviev had lately returned from exile in Siberia where the Miloslavsky had sent him. He finished talking at last and stood with his arm about a young boy who was so tall that I thought at first he was a man, although he was beardless. His bright eyes were watchful and he took no part in the scurry and fuss; he did not seem afraid. I knew him then to be Peter Alexievich because by his side and Matviev's was a beautiful pale woman with a look of Ivan Kirilovich, wringing her white hands and wailing. There was no sign of Tsarevna Sofia or the other Kremlin women. These were all of the Miloslavsky faction and stayed out of sight.

The noise of the crowd outside had begun again. By this time it was daylight; the faces on the staircase looked grey and wan. Presently the wolfish chant grew clearer and the voices cried again for Tsar Ivan. "Show us the Tsar. Show us the Tsar." The heads on the staircase drew together and then fell apart. Through the clustered group was led, at last, a tall half-wit in a gleaming robe and cap, with his eyes closed. I learned afterwards that he had to have them propped open when he wished to see. He was shown to the people and a great shout went up, for this was Tsar Ivan.

What followed need not have done so. Now that the people knew the Tsar was not poisoned or strangled most of them would have gone home. But there was an old fool of a boyar named Dolgoruky—that clan, as God knows, always has to have its nose in everything from that day to this—and he began to scold and upbraid the streltsi and remind them of their duty. They gave him an answer. They surged in upon him and the rest in a great shouting breaking wave, and they seized the old man and threw him up and out into the square on to the points of the uplifted pikes. Then they tore Matviev from where he stood by young Peter and did the same with him; the two mangled bodies disappeared in the press. Peter Alexievich still did not move or speak. It was his mother who did so, turning white as curd and clutching her son tightly in her lawn-sleeved arms, as though that would save him. But the killers passed by Peter Matviev's death had whetted them and they began to shout for all the Naryshkin men. By this time anyone who chose was within the palace, thrusting about with drawn swords and knives and pikes and ripping apart tapestries, curtains, cushions. I had dropped on my knees and when the tearing of my curtans came, its fragments dropped heavily on me and hid me; the destroyers moved on. Later I saw them dragging out the eldest Naryshkin brother and they took him and chopped off his arms and legs and left the trunk bleeding where it lay. Last of all there began to be a chant for Ivan Naryshkin and I heard it as if all the blood in my own body had stopped still. No one seemed to know where Ivan Kirilovich had hidden himself. The crowd took up the chant and it began that steady dreadful beating, like the sound of a great drum. "Give us Ivan Naryshkin. Give us Naryshkin. Give us the young wolf who wants the crown."

They looked and found old Kiril, but did not harm him. They said that if he wished to live he must shave his head and become a monk, and this was done at once and his life saved. But still they cried for Ivan Kirilovich, like dogs for blood. The silence fell again. Presently one of the leaders approached and said that unless Ivan Kirilovich Naryshkin were given up, all of the Miloslavsky in the palace would be murdered as well. At last Tsaritsa Natalia, weeping, went to the place in the Cathedral of the Saviour, behind the golden screen that hides the altar, where she knew her brother was. She sent word to promise that he would be given to the crowd. Time passed and he did not come.

The tide of terror had lulled while everyone awaited Ivan Kirilovich. I was able to creep from my hiding place and go to where the boy Peter Alexievich still stood in his place against the wall, as though forgotten. Even his mother had left him now. She was arranging with the priests that her last remaining younger brother should be confessed and receive the Sacraments and be anointed with the holy oils before being sent out to the people. "Make haste then," I heard one old boyar grumble, "or they will murder us all."

The crowds still waited and called. When it was time and he had been made ready, Ivan Kirilovich Naryshkin came out of the chapel and down the steps to the waiting people. "I hope mine will be the last blood to be shed," he said clearly. He held an ikon of the Virgin before him and as when I saw him that first day in the street I had thought of him as having innocence, today he looked like a young saint, with his face aglow; St. Stephen, perhaps, the first martyr. There was a great yell of triumph when he appeared and then they seized him, and carried him away, to torture as I learned later. His chief fault, they said, was that he had had himself measured for the crown. He denied this, and would betray no one. When they had broken his arms and legs and could still make him say nothing they tossed him back to the waiting crowds in the square and he was torn and hacked to pieces.

I have loved no man greatly since that day.

The power was seized thereafter by Tsarevna Sofia. Khovansky the commander of the guard obeyed her because he hoped to marry her, but after a time she had him put to death. Before then I was back in the stables and I saw Sofia often. She came and went on her own business, often in the litter, or on foot to the churches among the people. Many things have been said against Regent Sofia and her enemies have described her as ugly, with hair on her face. When I saw her lying within the palm-leaf screens her face was painted, but I did not think she was uncomely; she looked more like a boy than a woman. Her face was without expression, like that of an image. They say she was a good ruler and made trade pacts with the English and other nations. But she could never be Tsar, because the people would not accept a woman. Shortly it was decided that not only drop-lidded Ivan, but also his half-brother Peter, should rule—this followed a skirmish when Peter was to rule by himself—together as one, and the deep bell of Moscow was rung at last and a proclamation made concerning it. A double silver throne was fashioned for the two rulers and when ambassadors came from foreign Courts, the boys sat and replied together although Peter always had to wait for Ivan to catch up. The words themselves were supplied by Regent Sofia, who sat in a hidden place behind the throne and whispered through a hole made for the purpose. It was not yet customary for women to show themselves on these occasions and having won her power she was discreet.

As I say, I had gone back to the stables. Sasha had been stolen. I hope he found an owner who used him well and did not spoil his mouth or ill-treat him for once having carried Ivan Kirilovich.

I have said more than once that I went back to work in the stables, but after a little while this was my task only by day. By night I had another.

Soon after the riots—it must have been within a day or two, but the floors were cleaned of blood and the great square was empty—I was told to go to the women's quarters in the Kremlin to be seen by Natalia Naryshkina. As I had no idea that she knew of my existence, I was puzzled as to what she could want of me. I brushed the straw from my clothes and smoothed my hair with my hands, and went.

The guard let me pass—the gates were manned again—and soon a house-dwarf led me through the labyrinth of dim passages and rooms I remembered. The sight of the misshapen creature scurrying ahead of me brought back my fear of the place; such things take long to leave one's mind. But I made no sign, and followed quietly.

I found Tsaritsa Natalia sitting down doing nothing, while her ladies sewed and whispered some way off. I was shocked by her appearance; her face was puffy and pale, her eyes red with weeping for her brothers and her old guardian. There was still about her, like a ghostly presence, the likeness to Ivan Kirilovich. I clenched my fists against my coat to still the sick grief and horror I myself felt. The ladies stitched on, having raised their eyes briefly as I came in. So little happens as a rule in the Terem than any new thing or person gives rise to gossip. But they had perhaps had enough to talk about lately.

"What is your name, my child?" asked Tsaritsa Natalia. Her voice was gentle and I remembered hearing that Sofia always spoke of her as the She-Bear. She was too soft and easy-going to be likened to a bear; she was more like a white heifer, well-fleshed and mild-eyed. I answered her question.

"My name is Alexander Danilovich Menshikov. They call me Alexasha."

Natalia Naryshkina smiled a little and looked down at her white hands. I was sharp enough to realise that Sofia had no doubt set spies about her in the Terem and that this was why she spoke in a low voice. I kept my own voice low. Whatever the Tsaritsa wanted of me, I did not fancy being clubbed or stabbed on my way back to the stables.

But it was soon made clear that I was only to go back there for part of the time.

Natalia began to talk to me, not as a mistress addressing a servant but in a pleading, almost humble tone. I remembered again that her people had once been peasants and that she herself had been brought up in the house of Matviev where everyone was treated as an equal. She spoke of her son.

"I want you to sleep outside his door, be his *dentschnik*," she told me. "He may need you in the night and then you must go to him. If you lack sleep, you may take it during the day." I thought the head groom would not be best pleased at that, but said nothing. The Tsaritsa was telling me now that I should receive an extra sum of money and my clothes and food in the palace. A dentschnik is a house-guard. I still did not know why I had been selected for this honour and did not like to ask. Presently Natalia clapped her lily-petal hands and summoned another dwarf to show me where Peter Alexievich slept. I remember the dwarf wore a crimson coat furred with white, not too clean, and that his coat-buttons were of gold. I wondered if I too should be given such a coat to wear, but when my new clothes came they were not so notable. They would, in fact, have attracted little attention from the Regent or anyone else.

I cannot recall my first night outside the door of Peter Alexievich and no doubt I slept like a dog. It took a few days for the tall surly boy to address me. At that time, and in certain ways all his life, he was shy. On the second or third night I heard him cry out with terror and I slipped into his room. The moon was bright over the bed and Peter was writhing in nightmare. There was a small lamp placed high on the wall and that and the moonlight showed me his curly hair plastered damp with sweat, and his brow was beaded with it. His face twitched. "Hush, little brother," I said. It was the name that came most readily and one I would have used to any child in terror. Despite all he had seen, and his rank, he was no more. I climbed into the bed and put my arms about him, and presently his shuddering and twitching stopped and he slept peacefully. I left him before daybreak, before he should wake. I did not want him to feel foolish for having slept in the arms of a stable-boy.

Soon I was to learn that Peter Alexievich had these nightmares constantly, ever since the killings he had witnessed. In the way also that one learns such things, I knew that Natalia Naryshkina was pleased with me for the way I carried out my duties. Before long I was relieved of my tasks in the stables and given instead the day-long task of watchdog and comforter to the young Tsar. I still did not know why I had been chosen.

Later, much later, when Peter Alexievich and I began to be able to say most things to one another without shyness and had in fact become rough-and-tumble friends like any boys together, Peter told me why I had been put about him. "You were the only one to stand by me after they killed old Artemon Matviev and my uncles," he said. "Mother noticed that. So did I."

So began the rise in my fortunes.

After a time Tsaritsa Natalia and her son were permitted to return to Preobrazhenskoe. I think that the Tsaritsa liked to be there because it was at that place that she had been so happy with her husband in their brief marriage, and she was still honoured there as Tsar Alexis' widow; also, she was free of the spies of Sofia. As for the Regent herself, she had decided, I believe, that young Peter Alexievich would do no harm at Preobrazhenskoe and was best kept out of the way so that soon few in Moscow would remember him. It was easier for Sofia to govern with only feeble Tsar Ivan, who had been married by now to a young woman of good family and, despite all his ailings and failings, had got her pregnant. By the end he and Praskovia Saltikova produced six daughters, though some whispered that they were the children of her doctor.

Peter at once began to grow strong in the good clear air of the summer-palace, taller than ever and full of boisterous energy. He still had his nightmares and either I myself or one of the servants had to sleep in his bed with him. But by day he had begun to re-form his toy regiments that had been started when he was a little child, grown weary of wooden soldiers and cannon-balls made of sewn leather. Each member of the regiment came from a noble family, or else a family in the nearby Nemenskaya Sloboda, where the foreigners lived. Peter drilled and marched them and made them carry carbines. At first these were toys but later he ordered the real thing from Moscow, and anything else he wanted. He would march and counter-march the armed regiments, beating on his drum. The first time I heard him do this I was amazed at the skilful way he managed the sticks against the tightly stretched hide, and as time passed he grew better; they say he became the finest drummer in all Russia. The days passed to his rat-tat-tat and the sound of marching feet. I, though of low birth, was permitted to be of the regiments and to go through their exercises with them. It was my first lesson in the art of war.

Tsaritsa Natalia encouraged her son in this play, as she still saw it; like many mothers she could not realise that he was growing up. She would sit in the shade of the trees where she had once sat with Tsar Alexis, and she was surrounded by young girls and women. One of these was Peter's sister, also named Natalia, and like him well-grown and forward for her age. If it had not been for Tsarevna Natalia I would have been much slower in getting to know the other young women, for my manners were still rough and despite the favour shown to me, I knew myself to be a low-born fellow. At first I regarded the girls like the holy images I revered in church. I went to church a great deal, despite the mockery of Peter Alexievich who said I was like an old woman. He and I had different views of God, though all his life the Tsar described God as being on his side whatever he did. Be that as it may, it was in church that I was first drawn away from my prayers by the sight of a meekly bent white neck among the Tsaritsa's women. That day there were several new girls. One was brown-skinned and squat, though later I found she had merry eyes: Barbara Arsenieva, sister of my love. For it was Daria of the white neck and white hands I loved, mistakenly for she was never any use at anything. Lovers do not think of such things till it is too late. The third sister, Aksinia, had not yet come to Court. There was a pudding-faced girl nearby named Evdokiya Lopukhina, who was always at her prayers, and who meant nothing to me either. I spent the summer dreaming of Daria and growing clumsy in my martial exercises, so that Peter would roar at me not to fall over my own feet.

Peter loved one thing more than his regiments and drumming; that was his boats. It has been often stated that he came upon the hulk of an old vessel at Yaroslavl and never rested till he was in it on the water, but this is not all. Peter Alexievich had built many small boats with his own hands, and sailed in them, before he ever saw the Ancestor. None, however, had the facility for sailing against the wind, and as Russia had only one harbour which was frozen seven months of the year, there was no one to teach him about this. What he did was to send for a Dutchman—the Dutch spend half their life on the water—whose name was Timmermann, and who could teach Peter most of what he wanted to know. Timmermann also taught Peter how to use a sextant, which none of us understood if we had ever seen one; and —though there were many mistakes owing to the difficulty of language—how to calculate mathematics in Dutch. If Peter Alexievich had been an idle boy under his old fool of a tutor Zotov, he was by now on fire to learn. He drank in new information as other men do wine.

It was at this moment—he was sixteen—that his mother decided it was time he married. Perhaps she had reason. Sofia and her lover Golitsin still hoped for the supreme power, and Tsar Ivan's fat Praskovia had not yet borne a son. Natalia Naryshkina was still suspicious of plots on her life and her son's—poor woman, one cannot blame her— and she determined that Peter must have an heir. She chose, disastrously, that pudding-faced Evdokiya Lopukhina who was so devout in her prayers. It would have been better had she chosen a girl who could laugh. But Peter respected and loved his mother and obeyed her although he was not interested in Evdokiya, or at that time in marriage. "It will make a man of you," they told him, but he was a man already.

I remember when he left to ride the forty miles to Moscow to his wedding. Afterwards when it was night, I went out alone to look at the silent boats on the lake. Nothing would move or take life again until Peter Alexievich returned; he had kept us all hard at it, hammering, riveting, sawing. In the stillness and peace I thought of Daria and of how unlikely it was that her parents would permit us to marry, though by now I was close in the company of the Tsar. Then I spared time to wonder how Peter was faring with his bride; and a thought came to me. "He will always love ships more than any woman." But I was wrong, because by the end I think he loved Ekaterina Vassilievka more than any ship. But that would not be for many years, and how could I have foretold it?

A few days after the wedding Peter journeyed back to Yaroslavl and his boat-building and sailing. He had left his mother and his young wife in tears. "Marriage?" he said, when we jested. "What is it but a matter of mechanics? I have carried it out and now here I am. It's time to work again; before next winter we must be at sea, not caught by the ice as we shall be if we linger."

Certainly he had done his duty; before the year was out Evdokiya bore him Alexis. It was somewhat like the pairing of a bull and a cow, which results in a calf of which the bull takes no more heed. Peter thereafter followed his own concerns more than he had done before, and seldom, if he could help it, went back to the Kremlin.

Once he did go back.

I had always kept the feasts, and I was aware that the Feast of Our Lady of Kazan drew near. This is an important procession in Moscow and it was expected of a Tsar that he be present. "I will go," growled Peter Alexievich. When the time came he took horse and, with myself and others following, rode to the city. We lingered somewhat on the journey and by the time we reached the outer wall the procession had already begun. The jewelled image, censed by servers in embroidered robes, so that the incense rose in clouds above the packed square, was followed by all the Court and nobility. Regent Sofia, instead of being in her litter, walked in public procession unveiled, with her younger sister Marfa and her ladies accompanying her. I saw the quick blood flush Peter's neck and cheeks. He galloped over, and brought the procession to a halt. He faced Sofia. In all of their separate doings I had never seen this half-brother and sister face to face before, and never would again. Sofia was brightly painted; she had aged since I last saw her and a fine network of wrinkles cracked the paint. They say she took too many lovers, but I believe she wore herself out working at the business of state; no matter. Peter glared at her from the saddle, his full eyes showing their whites.

"You should not be here in public," he said. "Return to the Terem."

I saw her eyes flicker briefly as if a tame dog had snapped. Then she said, coolly—Sofia was always cool—"In public, as we are, you are making a fool of yourself, little brother. It is long now since women gained the right to appear in public processions and at other times, as they choose. Perhaps if you had been oftener in Moscow you would know more of the changes which have taken place. Best ride after the procession; you cannot alter the arrangements now."

The veins swelled in his neck. "Then you refuse to obey my order, I the Tsar?"

"You are too late," said Sofia, and signalled to the procession to move again. It did so, in straggling fashion and with some murmuring from those who were not too near. Peter Alexievich dragged at his horse's bridle and jerked his head to us to follow him. All together, as we had come, we wheeled about and galloped out of Moscow.

As I say, we were together. It has often been stated that my real intimacy with Peter Alexievich began at the time when I saved him from death by poisoning. This is not so, as he and I shared many things together before that night. I cannot even certainly recall how it all happened. All I know is that when a dish was brought to the Tsar to eat it was tasted first in the kitchens, and again as it was presented to him at table. The fear of poison had been in Muscovy since the days of Ivan the Terrible and no one thought anything of the tasting ceremonies; they were taken for granted.

I cannot thank anything but my watchful eyes, which miss no detail which might be useful to me. On that particular evening the Tsar had drunk some wine—he had not yet begun the fearful potations of the All-Drunken, All-Joking Assembly which came later and would last well into the morning, with everyone under the table but the Swiss Lefort and Peter. I saw the serving-man come in with a dish, and he raised a spoon and placed it near his lips, without allowing the food to pass them. This may have been done a dozen times in so time-worn a ritual; I do not know. I leaned over to where Peter was and said, in jest, "Give the dish to your dog first; who knows?" I saw his eyes slew round and knew that he had taken heed of me. When the food came he took a portion and threw it to one of the dogs who were always nearby, to catch the rats and live off the bones and fragments swept from the tables. The beast snapped it up greedily, but within moments it was writhing on the floor, a contorted howling thing. Shortly it died.

No doubt Peter Alexievich might have put me to the torture to find out how I knew the dish had been poisoned, and to try to decide by whom. But with the wisdom he sometimes showed, he did nothing to me, or anyone. But he was warned now against the possibility of a plot on his life. Thereafter he was more suspicious, more watchful; and I grew ever closer to him.

Other things befell. Regent Sofia still wielded the power and it might have been thought that Peter had forgotten the matter of the procession and the rebuke, but I knew he had not. The Lopukhini, poor Evdokiya's kinsmen, made a little feud at Court by trying to gain places as the Naryshkini had done. They received short shrift from Sofia and, in fact, from Tsaritsa Natalia, who had grown unaccountably jealous of the daughter-in-law she had herself chosen. No doubt Peter Alexievich took time to make his plans. One night when we were asleep something wakened me, and by the light of a shaded candle I saw the face of the Tsar. He was in his nightshirt, and his face twitched as usual. He spoke to me in a low voice and bade me be silent.

"Listen, Alexasha. Tell none you cannot trust, but tell those. Say that the Regent is sending men to murder me; the streltsi have been mobilised." The twitching grimace he made might have been a wink. "I am going away from here," he said. "Quickly—there is no time to lose. I intend to ride to the Troitsa monastery."

"It is twelve leagues." I was thinking of the cold, and of his thin nightshirt. He brushed me off impatiently. "Bring my clothes to me in the wood," he said. "Say nothing till that's done. Lose no time; time's important now."

They said afterwards that he fled to the Troitsa monastery in a convulsion of terror. If so, it was well planned. Later we heard that he had been correct and that a great massing of the streltsi had indeed taken place in Moscow under Sofia. She may have meant harm to Peter or she may not. I took him his clothes and in the black and silver shadows cast by branches, the snow and the moon, Peter dressed, took horse again and was away. It was a long ride, as I had warned him. Had he gone mad, or had he come to his senses after playing at toy soldiers all his youth?

Results proved Peter Alexievich right. There came riding to the Troitsa monastery, once word had come that the Tsar was sheltering there, all those who would support him, being weary of a woman's rule behind the figurehead of half-wit Ivan. Colonel Tsikler of the streltsi sent a message. "Send for me and fifty men, and we will come," it read. Peter Alexievich sent to demand this number and the Regent was very angry, but in the end agreed to let them go. "She will regret it," said Peter grimly. There had been no explanation of Sofia's mobilisation of the guard and rightly or wrongly, it was seen as an attempt on the Tsar's life which he had escaped in timely fashion.

Peter then demanded colonels, staff, and ten men from each regiment. This time Sofia refused outright. Instead she sent the Tsar's confessor and a boyar, a Muscovite noble with his belly sagging in the saddle and his beard full of fleas. "Why are you here?" demanded Peter abruptly. "To persuade Your Majesty to humility and peace," came the reply. The Tsar gave a short laugh and turned on his heel. I followed him.

Next day an even more notable sight was seen on the road to the Troitsa: none other than Patriarch Ioakim of Moscow himself, fingers raised in prescribed blessing to the people who knelt as he approached. His pectoral cross gleamed and he wore the tall dark headgear of an Orthodox pope. In fact the Patriarch was a foolish old man greatly given to superstition and belief in magic, but his presence lent strength to the growing tide. After it became known that he himself was at the Troitsa all ranks and all persons, submissive as they thought to the will of the Church, vowed themselves to obey the rule of Peter against Sofia. The building was surrounded by men of the streltsi who had come of their own accord without waiting for orders from their officers. Peter and his mother—she had joined him by then—stood by the gate dispensing vodka to all who came. As time passed the ranks of folk grew noisy and cheerful, like a hive of bees when flowers are out.

One day a handsome young man with a French moustache rode in on a mettlesome horse. This was Lefort, who was to be the Tsar's boon companion and adviser in matters both military and amorous. At once the two young men took to one another, and would sit all night drinking in the cells so that the peace of the monastery was no more. Last to come was Patrick Gordon, a commander of such worth that for many years now he had not been permitted to return to his native Scotland lest he never come back to Muscovy, where he had long been engaged in Sofia's wars on the south border. Peter opened his arms to welcome Gordon. "There is no one left now to come here but my sister," he laughed. "How can Sofia bear to stay behind when everyone is away? The Kremlin is empty."

He was ready. When word came that the Regent had indeed started out on her journey, Peter sent the streltsi to order her back. They left grinning. "How did she take it?" he asked, when they returned.

"She was angry, very angry; in the end, she went back. She will do as she is told now. Every woman needs a man to order her," ventured the guard, knowing the way the wind was blowing. By now, everyone knew. The day after Sofia's forced return to the capital Peter Alexievich sent orders to arrest Shaklovity, the commander of the guard, who had not come over with the rest. The streltsi turned against their former leader and dragged him to the Troitsa. A few remaining supporters of the Regent were brought also.

Now there came the first sign of what Peter was to become as time went on. Later the pattern was so often repeated that it no longer shocked one. He could be violent to his friends; once when I was dancing and had forgotten to remove my sword he felled me with a blow, and my nose poured blood. He has often beaten me in public, as well as his son Alexis, and almost everyone who had dealings with him. But Shaklovity's fate was the first of its kind that I know of. He was knouted by Peter's order, tortured and then beheaded. The men watched it. The time would come when he killed them also.

Back in Moscow, Sofia meantime was flailing about like

a blunt scythe. She was no longer obeyed, nor listened to. The man who brought the order for Shaklovity's arrest was to be beheaded, she said. Such men as remained with her replied that they could not find an axe. This amused Peter Alexievich when he heard of it. "Not find an axe?" he said. "Ho! Ho! I will show them where to find many things soon." He seemed to have grown bigger and broader since the Troitsa flight, more of a man and less of a boy, even such as he had lately become. His hands could bend iron and break wood. No one dared oppose him.

There were other punishments. Some were banished to Siberia with their tongues cut out; others, suspected of wizardry against Peter and his mother and her kin, were burned over slow fires. Not all of this was by direct order of the Tsar, but by the Naryshkini, who desired revenge for the killings long ago outside the Kremlin when Peter himself was a child. They showed no mercy, even as no mercy had been shown to them. Everywhere blood flowed, but it flowed in the open. There was no secrecy about what was happening.

Sofia's punishment was mild. She was forced to take the name of Sister Susanna and withdraw to a convent. For one of her high birth and spirit, perhaps death would have been preferable. The world was never to see her again, though her part was not yet played out.

Peter Alexievich still had his nightmares. I was with him one night when he awoke. He lay still for some moments and then rose and flung back the covers and went to the small narrow window, where there was a young crescent moon to be seen, high in the sky for it was late. I watched the giant figure and told myself that this young man would be a great and terrible ruler, and that I must mind my ways and stay close to him and endure what he willed for me, but never cross him or arouse his lasting anger. I must be agile, as I had been in the Moscow streets. If it was needed, I would even cry "Hot pies! Hot pies!" again to make him laugh. Laughter can banish anger till its cause has been forgotten.

Meantime he spoke without turning round. "I am master now," he said, and laughed suddenly. "It is only the beginning, Alexasha."

Then he came back to bed.

I have spoken of Franz Lefort, the gay and hard-drinking soldier of fortune. Out of devilment, I believe, he had come that time to join the Tsar at the Troitsa. I say this because, as a Swiss, Lefort could have no interest in which side won. He had just left service with the Duke of Courland and desired fresh adventure. He loved and sought this always for its own sake, in the same way as he loved wine and good company and tobacco and women. He could talk with ease on any subject, but when one was sober enough it was to realise that Lefort preferred to talk nonsense rather than keep silence and appear ignorant. He had a quick mind, and in the same way I myself grasped at opportunities, Lefort grasped facts and never forgot them once learnt. He was his own master and gloried in it. He had come from Geneva, a sober place "where servants are whipped for singing other than psalms and nobody laughs, and a servant girl, again, will be raped in private by her master and then denounced publicly by him for fornication when she is pregnant, and he will sit in council watching while they beat her for her sins. That is Calvinism. It is a sour and hypocritical religion. One is either saved or not. I was not saved, so I left home and have never returned."

"God save us from such salvation," roared Peter Alexievich. We were seated by Lefort's fire by then—he had early acquired a house in the Sloboda, although it was very small —and all of us smoked long clay pipes so that the air was thick. The smoke rose blue to the ceiling and left brown stains there and on our linen. Tobacco had long been forbidden by the Church in Russia and Peter's grandfather, Tsar Mikhail, had called it a godless weed and had decreed harsh punishments for those found smoking it: slit nostrils, severed ears. But men went on smoking in secret, for there is comfort in a pipe. As for Peter Alexievich, he shocked all the old popes and boyars by appearing in public with a pipe in his anointed mouth, so that many said he had given his soul to the devil. Apart from that, when he went to

England he transacted a very handsome piece of business there regarding monopoly of tobacco imports into Russia. It made him rich, and he had hitherto been poor. In any case he always did as he liked whether other people agreed or not. Also we drank a great deal of wine. Lefort could drink any man down except the Tsar, who could hold more wine than any man I have ever met. Talking, carousing, exchanging gossip which more often than not had to do with new matters from the West, we passed the nights. Old Patrick Gordon, who tried to keep up with us, usually had to take to his bed the day after a carousal; but the Tsar never tired. He would be seen next morning sawing wood at a carpenter's bench or forging iron in a smithy. Now that Sofia had gone he could try his hand at everything on a much greater scale than in the days at Yaroslavl.

He also built a larger house for Lefort and we had larger carousals.

Yes, Peter had taken his freedom with both hands; he was master, as he had said. He did not sleep with his wife Evdokiya again after she had borne a second son who died in a few days. She wearied Peter and as he remarked, he had not chosen her. Instead of his wife he took Lefort's mistress Anna Mons. I think it gave the young Tsar pleasure that he should inherit the body of a Western woman from a man of the world such as Lefort. Lefort naturally gave up Anna when the Tsar took her. It was unfortunate that she proved a grasping bitch, for Peter Alexievich did not change his women readily and it was ten years before I managed to persuade him to get rid of Anna. Her letters damned her and also, the Saxon envoy was found drowned with more of them in his pocket. It was however the Prussian envoy who was her lasting passion. No one was sad when Anna went, not even Peter Alexievich for long because I found him Ekaterina.

By that time Lefort had died. He was not old, and he died of drink. Peter Alexievich missed him sorely and not even I could fill Lefort's place. But the Swiss had left many notions about the art of making war which the Tsar had not learnt in the days at Preobrazhenskoe. That was Lefort's lasting memorial. Everything else changed when Ekaterina came and soon Peter forgot his sadness.

I have said that I loved thrice in my life. The first was Ivan Kirilovich who is dead. The second was my bride, Daria Arsenieva. With the increased favour the Tsar was showing me, Daria's parents no longer looked on me as rough and of the people. What Daria felt I never knew, as naturally she took no part in the arranging of the marriage. Perhaps she has no feelings, any more than an exquisite porcelain figure. I know now what porcelain is as I have travelled to Dresden. Daria is also idle, but I have never beaten her as she has borne me my children. As regards my marriage I came in the end to prefer the second sister, Barbara, to my wife. Barbara is good company and a good bedfellow. But none of this has anything to do with my feeling for Ekaterina Vassilievka, as I still sometimes call her to myself. It was simply that I knew from the beginning that she was the right woman for the Tsar.

Knowing his shyness I had to put them together when he was drunk, and it answered very well. Ekaterina—Empress Catherine, what you will—has never failed me, either by satisfying the Tsar and keeping me in his favour, or since his death failing to rule. How much like madness it all sounds that a camp-follower, who was never beautiful and dyes her hair, should have done all this! Perhaps beauty does not matter; Anna Mons after all was beautiful and a bitch. There is generosity about Ekaterina; she is honest at heart although in the old days, when the Tsar was still alive, she had to learn to be a trifle devious; it was I who persuaded her to send money to Amsterdam and England, in case our star ever fell from the heavens. Altogether I cannot explain her quality or the reason why a low-born woman with painted eyebrows, a bosom like a goddess and a mouth full of soldiers' oaths should have been the right one, the only one, for Peter Alexievich, Autocrat of All the Russias. It is the fact of being able to gamble on such things that has placed me where I am. Otherwise I might still be selling pies in the streets of Moscow.

The water beyond Petersburg is darker now as I look out and it is growing colder, or perhaps I am growing older. Now that Peter the Great is dead I do not know what the future holds. If Catherine has a long reign I may die in peace. If not. . . .

The son of Alexis has no liking for me, I know. His likes and dislikes are as strong as his grandfather's when we were young. If that boy comes to the throne in my lifetime, I will fall more rapidly than I rose. There will not be any more pies to sell; my fate, if that boy Peter has his way, may well be to travel to the vast bitter wastes of Siberia, and die there alone. We must all, by the end, do that. And in such immensity, as I knew long ago, one can come face to face with God.

FIVE

THE EMPRESS: THE ISLAND OF HARES

The Tsar disliked questions, being so full of them himself. If I wanted to know anything I used to ask Menshikov. If he did not know the answer he would find it out, for his own benefit as well as mine. Cautiously, without troubling him in such ways, I myself found out more about Peter Alexievich.

There had been things about him which from the beginning had made me pity him with that pity which is a part of love. He was no more lustful than the next Muscovite, but that is saying a good deal. However often at nights the Tsar would not make love but would fall asleep, weary after a day's hard labour with his axes and shovels and grenades. I have said already that he must have someone to clutch hard against him while he slept, or else he would wake crying out and grimacing in the light of the dim small lamp that burned in the tent, or in our small house when it was built. I used to wonder why he had such dreams; was it the long-ago May massacre when his uncle was murdered, or the later flight from Sofia in young manhood, or the wholesale execution of the streltsi when the streets ran with blood? Often if one knows the cause of such things one is already part of the way to their cure.

Other questions the world also asked were in my mind. Why did the Tsar of Muscovy wear rough sailor's clothes when he could have had cloth of silver lined with fur and trimmed with jewels? Why did he take his pleasure on a woman like myself, when there were handsome Court ladies ready and willing to sleep with him? I will not say that he failed to oblige them, at times, during our years together; on our later journeyings through Europe the royalties were scandalised at the sight of a baby on the arm of each lady-in-waiting, and then the next and next. "The Tsar did me the honour to give me this child," they would say. I did not mind: Peter always returned to me.

His wife Evdokiya was sometimes in my thoughts: hers seemed a sad lot. The Tsar had after all taken her young son from her and shut her in a convent, then ignored the boy except to make him drunk or terrify him. It was not that Evdokiya had failed in her duty. She had borne the Tsar a second son, Alexander, who only lived a few weeks. But her husband disliked her; he had sent word from England, from the dockyard, that Evdokiya was to be made to take the veil whether she resisted or not. This in his own mind meant that they were divorced, and some time after I came to him he married me, privately. There was a second public marriage when our young daughters were old enough to attend me to the rood-screen. By then, nobody dared say anything against my becoming the wife of the Tsar. Yet Evdokiya lived on; he did not destroy her.

Some women roused Peter's fervent admiration. When he was on his first journey through Europe as a young man, anxious and eager to learn all that was new, he was persuaded to meet the clever and well-read Electress of Brandenburg, Sophia Charlotte. The Tsar was shy and unused to such company, and when the Electress and her relatives, in their Court dress, came in, he put his big hands up before his face, murmuring "I don't know what to say." But Sophia Charlotte put him at his ease soon. Her witty mother, the Electress of Hanover, was there also, with her son and his two children. Peter ruffled the bright hair of the old Electress's granddaughter Sophia, whom they called Fifi. But he did not like Fifi's father, a small slender heavy-jowled man with sullen brown eyes which stared down the huge Muscovite savage. The Hanoverians thought a great deal of themselves because of the promised English succession. George Louis of Hanover is now King of England, and his manners have not improved since that meeting. He is a good soldier and has the affairs of Hanover at heart, and that is in his favour. For himself, he is a brute. He had lately at that time shut away his young wife, Sophia Dorothea of Zell, in prison for life because she had an affair and her lover was killed. We heard of it because the lover happened to be the brother of the King of Poland's mistress, Aurora von Königsmark. However, George Louis' own affairs were not few and he could have acted less cruelly.

After that visit, curiously enough, the notion came to the Tsar to shut away Evdokiya. If one ruler could do it, why not another? And Peter's own mother, who had chosen Evdokiya as suitable, was now dead. Nobody would be the worse off in the end, and Evdokiya was taken away to the convent in a post-cart. It is interesting that later, much later, after she had supposedly been a nun for very many years, Evdokiya herself had an affair, with a soldier.

Peter's mother, the second wife of the Gentle Tsar Alexis— he had a quick temper nevertheless, but never held grudges —was the bride of a love-match. Intrigues had formerly surrounded maidens of no particular birth who had the misfortune to be loved by a Tsar. Alexis' own first choice, in his youth, had been another beautiful girl. On the day of the wedding her hair was pulled so hard that she fainted, and her rivals hastened to the Tsar to say she took fits and he must not marry her. The next choice, Maria Miloslavskaya, who had the support of noble kindred, took her place at the altar. She bore Tsar Alexis fourteen children, not all of whom lived.

Tsar Alexis was wiser on the next occasion. He met Natalia Naryshkina at dinner at the house of a charming and worldly man named Matviev, who lived in the Sloboda. It was seldom in those days that women ate at the same table as the men, but Matviev had a Scottish wife and enlightened habits. Natalia was his ward and had been taught many things, but it appears that she had more beauty than sense. To shield her from anything like the former disaster, Tsar Alexis made pretence of choosing from a line of selected maidens in the approved fashion, his first wife having died. Natalia was the choice, and they were married and Peter Alexievich was born and then, in a year, the younger Natalia. Soon Tsar Alexis himself died, and as Peter's mother had no talent for intrigue and disliked most of the Miloslavsky relations at the Kremlin, she moved out for a large part of the year to the summer-place of Preobrazhenskoe, where she and her husband had been happy and had watched theatricals. This would not have been permitted in the capital as the Church frowned on plays.

For Peter Alexievich, aged four and a half, the Village of the Transfiguration, which is what Preobrazhenskoe means, was home. Even before he left Moscow he had begun playing with cannon and drums and ignoring his rocking-horse. As he grew older—I believe it started well before he was ten—he recruited the local boys and formed a proper flesh-and-blood regiment and drilled it and drummed for it and marched it and taught it all he knew about guns. This was a good deal; he had already found out about the workings of cannon from a German and the process of making fireworks—he always loved these—from a Dutchman, both from the Sloboda. These foreigners would not have been met with inside the city walls, any more than players would be. The Sloboda was near Preobrazhenskoe. Peter learned early that there was more to be got from his new friends than from his old fool of a tutor, Nikita Zotov. "They were going to give me a man named Menzies," he once said wistfully, "but he was taken away because he was foreign." Menzies would have taught Peter much he never knew. As it was, he developed such contempt for Zotov that when he grew up he made the old man Archpriest of Mirth.

As he grew up, accordingly, Peter Alexievich was to be seen more often at the foreigners' houses than in the Kremlin or leading religious processions, as was expected of a Tsar. His half-sister Sofia was by then Regent, and it suited her well enough if Peter stayed away from Moscow.

Peter's childhood regiment stayed with him all his life and helped to man the small boats that time they defeated the four great Swedish ships. That was in my time, but before then they had been with him on the Azov campaign. When Peter Alexievich was sixteen years old he went to Yaroslavl and by chance saw the old boat lying by the water. Nothing would do but that he must float it. He learned to make and mend boats then, but knew enough to know that there was much still to be learnt. There was no one in Russia who could teach him, and so he did what no Tsar had ever done before; he left his country and went to Europe to find out what he could for himself. This was after Azov, and he had already opened a way out to the Black Sea. He had also been married to Evdokiya and had left her, despite her letters and his mother's tears.

I know little enough about that first European journey of his; it is all overlaid with memories of the second, when I went along with him. The young Tsar had met the Hanoverians as I have said, and the Emperor in Vienna, where he would not be troubled with etiquette and hurried to the meeting at a third window instead of a fifth; this will never be forgotten by the Austrians. Then in London the Tsar met William III, who was a Dutchman and they liked one another, and Peter was able to work in the dockyards at Deptford without being followed and stared at by crowds as had happened in Holland. In England they do not mind so much if anyone is different from themselves. William III sent the Tsar his yacht afterwards in a present, which delighted Peter Alexievich and he sailed it to the end of his life.

He had meant to go on to Venice, not to see the palaces or canals but to study shipbuilding there also, only the second revolt of the streltsi happened at home and instead of going to Venice the Tsar hurried back to Moscow to chop off heads. After that there were no trained soldiers left except from his Preobrazhenskoe regiments and so he had to begin training raw recruits wherever he could find them, and this took up much of his time.

Although at the beginning wolves ate the sentries, Petersburg grew. It could not help but do so, because the Tsar, as soon as danger from the Swedes was past, moved the government departments there from Moscow, and departments have to have buildings to house themselves, and courtiers also; soon my husband was to forbid all stone building elsewhere. Each boyar swallowed his pride and his unwillingness, and built himself a palace on the Neva marshes, for the same reason as he had once built boats out of his forest timber: because he was bidden. Alexasha would have the grandest palace of all, where the hares had once run wild on their island. Peter Alexievich and I were married in its chapel.

The Church authorities resented the Tsar's leaving Moscow. Although my husband had long ago put in an obedient caretaker instead of a new Patriarch, most of the popes themselves loved the old style of living which had given them power in the dark, ignorant days before beards were shorn and the Tsar travelled to Europe and came back and opened the window on the West. So they tried a trick which is amusing to remember, shortly after a church was built in Petersburg. There was much fever among the workmen by then, as the marsh was still an unhealthy place, and ordinary folk complained because nothing but turnips would grow in the salty earth. So the church, still mostly of wood in those days, had a statue of the Virgin which was weeping for those condemned to live and die in a swamp, away from Moscow. My husband said nothing and went himself and lifted down the statue and took it to pieces. Inside was a small machine which let out a few drops of oil now and then, and they spilled down the face from behind the eyes.

"Clever, eh?" said the Tsar, and laughed heartily. He bore no grudge against anyone for cleverness, not even a priest. They did not try their tricks in that way again.

By this time ours was not the only wooden house among the stone palaces: others were built till the stone should be ready. The Tsar was in no hurry to live in a palace. He had loathed the Kremlin and at Preobrazhenskoe, had hardly ever been seen indoors. He invented about this time a double ceiling, which could be put in to make any room seem lower than it was.

This was not needed in our first abode; even I found it cramped, though we were happy. We lived in the way I had always been used to do, except that we were never hungry. There was plenty of game from the marshes, and fish from the sea. I used to bake good black bread in a small woodfired oven, and brew beer. Soon the little house had become cheerful with red and green paint on the shutters and doors, as they have them done in Holland. My husband had never forgotten the little house at Zaandam, though he had only slept in it two nights before the crowds forced him out. He built an even smaller and more private retreat now in a lime tree which grew beyond our door, and would spend many hours there; he made all our furniture, tables, benches, chairs, box beds, with his own hands out of pine and lime and birch. As the children grew we needed more furniture. There were so many children, and only three lived long enough for me to know them, and of the three Natalia has since died. But there was Anne, fair-haired and placid, who has lately married the Duke of Holstein for love, and they say is happy. There was Elizabeth, who has married nobody. What will become of her, I ask myself? She was lazy and boisterous even then; her father was fond of her. He used to play with the children and then thump his fist on the dresser and roar "Thieves! Thieves! You steal my time!"

They were never afraid of him, unlike Alexis. When Peter was at home he would sit on one side of the stove, smoking his clay pipe, and I would sit at the other mending his stockings or knitting him a waistcoat for the coming campaign. There was always a campaign coming.

He loved the sight of ships, sailing now regularly with cargoes into the new-won port, spread sails furling and pilot-boat edging in ahead on its ploughed furrow. Once or twice the Tsar himself would be the pilot, when the mood took him. The first time it happened he brought the Dutch skipper home for a meal. I gave him what we had, and the man was grateful and pulled a great cheese and a roll of linen out of his pockets, and pressed them on me. I hesitated lest it displease the Tsar, but Peter roared, "Take them, Katia, and be grateful. It's a damned sight finer linen than you wore when you were young." At this point some official, I forget whom or why, came in his great peruke and braided coat, stooping and bowing at the door before the erstwhile pilot. The Dutchman's eyes goggled and he scratched his ear, as if he knew he would only regain his sober senses when he got back out to sea. "If I say the Tsar of Muscovy piloted me in, folk'll think I was drunk," he muttered. We ate the cheese afterwards and it was good.

They say of me now that I have grown to love luxury. That is perhaps true, as I shall soon be old. But I was happy enough in our wooden house, with the stone palaces rising steadily about us against the violet twilights that fall upon the Neva.

Alexis the Tsarevich was my friend, whatever they say. We did not often speak together in presence of the Tsar, because the boy feared his father and when he was present, stayed silent unless he was forced to speak. When I married Peter I was received into the Orthodox Church and Alexis was my godfather. After that I was known as Ekaterina Alexeievna, for this reason. My names have changed often, but I am still the same. I am still the same today.

They say there were once women called Amazons who took delight in war. Other women do not. Because I have described our small home at Petersburg as happy and peaceful, it does not mean that we were always there or that the children were always with us. From Archangel to Astrakhan, from the Baltic to the Caspian, there was forever war; war with Sweden, war with the Porte, war with Persia. My husband did not wage war for its own sake but for what he might gain for Russia, that huge tract of plains and mountains without any outlet except one harbour which was frozen over half the year. That was at the beginning. By now Peter had won his port in the south and another in the north, on the Baltic. That he could not rest there was due to other people and not himself. For it is kings and leaders who wage war. I should know this; last year I deliberately avoided it with the unpleasant King of England, who was ready to fight us. But he did not yet matter at the time of which I speak; the issue was between the Tsar himself and Charles XII of Sweden.

There were great kings then. Louis XIV had made Europe the mirror of Versailles and had turned his nobles at that palace into footmen. Every petty princeling, especially in the German states, tried to copy him, and as his shadow grew shorter they began to cast their own. What did it mean to anyone at that time that the history of Poland is bound up with that of Russia because we come of the same blood, from ancient times before the race divided?

Poland had made herself our enemy. Her nobles were too quarrelsome and powerful. The King of Poland himself was nobody, being elected at the whims of others, the old ruling dynasty having long died out. Countries put forth one candidate for election to the empty throne, the rest another; we ourselves supported the lecher, Augustus the Strong. Augustus was shifty, greedy and foolish. He had no talents apart from his strength. He often betrayed my husband, but the Tsar liked him and would not cast him off.

The Swedish faction, touchy about the Baltic seaboard, supported another lecher, though not of the prowess of Augustus. His name was Stanislas Leczinski. All of this did not make either a beginning or an end to what is known as the Great Northern War, ignored as it was by most of the European powers because they were waging a war of their own concerning the Spanish Succession.

Strange persons came and went. Two come to mind particularly; one was Mazeppa, Hetman of the Cossacks, and the other was a Livonian nobleman named Patkul.

Patkul was a patriot and had my blood not been sluggish, he might have fired me with his own great love of Livonia. He came once to the little house when the Tsar was absent and drank vodka and talked and talked, far into the night. He was a lean man whose fiery dark eyes inspire those who gaze on them to agree to rash deeds. Patkul wanted all the countries of Europe to combine together against Sweden to free Livonia, and he sat there draining his vodka and talked about Charles XII. I believe that if he had been able to talk to some great council as he talked to me, they would have sent him soldiers and cannon. As it was I only listened, and remembered. I can see him yet, seated by the fire with his wine-cup turning restlessly in his thin hands and talking, talking about wasted Livonia.

"A soldier to the bone! What use is that to his Swedish subjects? He cares nothing for them, this young Charles. He came into a rich inheritance; his father ruled well and wisely. What has he done but squander it and bring misery to countless poor people? Bah! He sleeps on the bare boards of the floor, they say, instead of in bed. What is that to anyone? He is not interested in women, only war."

"A strange young man," I ventured, and filled Patkul's cup. He tossed off the drink as if to be rid of it.

"He is tall and lean and narrow, in body as in mind. He has no affection for anyone except his sister's husband, the Duke of Holstein. Together they beheaded wolves and cattle and broke windows in Stockholm, and rode through the town naked, on one horse. What kind of an enemy is that? We must defeat him."

His eyes brooded at the fire, and I filled his cup again and spoke soothing words to him, as I had grown used to doing. It struck me, looking at Patkul, that men burn themselves up for a cause instead of living life as it should be lived. Here was a young man noble, handsome, and rich, and all he thought of was to band countries together against another country. Why could we not all live in peace?

Then the Tsar came in and gave a great roar of pleasure when he saw Patkul by the fire, and all through the night they drank together and I filled their wine-cups, and listened and said no more. But I recall one thing, out of all their talk, about Charles of Sweden. "If he reaches the heart of Russia, we will defeat him. He will be too far from home."

This is in fact what happened, but it did not benefit Patkul. Charles XII had got hold of him by then. And it was our own men, our Cossacks and Bashkirs, and not the Swedes, who had laid waste Livonia.

The Tsar had taken a mercury cure as he often had to, and it left him weak as a child. Alexis was with the army and also fell ill. My husband took his bed in beside his son and for ten days never left Alexis' side. That is an answer to those who say the Tsar was always harsh with Alexis. In the end they both grew better. Meantime Charles of Sweden led his army down into the heart of our country and was by now near Kharkov. My husband had himself carried south with the men and by the time the place was reached, his strength had returned to him. The last place of all would be called Poltava.

"The fellow has no mother-wit," said the Tsar of the King of Sweden. "All he needed was to wait for a few days and the supplies would have caught up with him and reinforced his numbers. As it was, we were the ones who caught up with them—and beat them soundly." He smiled, well pleased with the outcome at Lesnoi. There is nobody like a Muscovite for fighting in wooded cover, and the Swedish main force had allowed itself to be got into a position where ours sidled up to it from all directions, sniping unseen and leaving, by the end, eight thousand dead Swedes on the field. The Kalmucks had seen to it that there were no wounded.

I sat in my place in our tent and got on with my task of darning the Tsar's cobbled hose. He could not be persuaded to throw any garment away even when it was past wearing, and went about wearing patched stockings and muddy boots. Here, in any case, everywhere was mud; it was autumn, and in the tent Peter sat as always at his table which was kept nearby the open flap, so that he could see and be seen. An enemy taking a shot at a venture, if near enough, could have hit him. But the Tsar cared nothing for that. He was talking in a low voice now to Mazeppa, the Cossack leader, who had grown old in wickedness so that his whiskers by now were white as snow and jutted fiercely on either side of his face beneath the traditional cap of close-curled lamb's fleece. I saw the sideways sliding of the old man's eyes and felt, as I had often felt before, that the Hetman was not to be trusted. But my husband would listen to no word against Mazeppa from wiser mouths than mine. "Why, he has been in my company since the first Azov campaign! He brought me a sword then." The gift had been a sabre glinting with gems, and Peter Alexievich never used or wore it, but like all such things it stayed in his mind and made him continue to trust Mazeppa. I told myself that my doubt was ill-founded. The Cossack leader had stayed by the Tsar all through his days of uncertainty and defeat. Now that the tide was beginning to turn, and a great battle would soon, they said, be fought here in the central plains, would Mazeppa change sides? It seemed unlikely.

The plain truth was that one could never be sure of any Cossack leader, who had one loyalty to his chosen band of companions as they had to him. There were Zaparog Cossacks living in their famous Fastness, unmarried like the janissaries. They had built themselves that place a century ago or more, nearby the great waterfall on the Dnieper behind whose rapids they used to live, and catch fish. They paid no taxes, worked for no lord, and disliked being counted or numbered. The rest of the Cossacks were and are more various; men who, like Mazeppa, have had a grudge, or have banded together by a common dislike of being ruled by anyone. It does not matter in whose war they fight; the prize is their continued freedom. Mazeppa was one of these. They say that in his young days, after a strict Jesuit education, he had trifled with the wife of a nobleman nearby his native village of Volhynia. The outraged husband stripped the young man and tied him naked to his horse, fired pistols and sent horse and rider careering crazily through the thorny thickets. Mazeppa, covered in blood, joined a Cossack band and in course of time was elected Hetman. But that was long ago and although lately he had been in trouble again concerning the young daughter of a judge of Kiev who was madly in love with him, he sat in the tent now complaining about his gout and saying that it would prevent his taking any active part in the coming battle. "But we rely on your men," said Peter amiably. It is odd that he so often suspected persons of good faith, but continued to trust such as this old rascal, who moreover disliked Menshikov.

As I have said, the man whom the Tsar trusted not at all and yet liked was Augustus the Strong, he of the many mistresses and natural children. Augustus made no worse a King of Poland than Stanislas Leczinski. To lose the position was however undignified, and he sent the most beautiful of his mistresses, Aurora von Königsmark, to beguile Charles of Sweden in the snow, but the young man, who was still not interested in women in any case, turned his back and walked away. "Such a good fellow, August," comes my husband's voice. A good fellow, and a good host; they say he had a way of cooking roast duck that made it melt in the mouth, but he stood by Alexasha's side while our men were being killed for him and did not say, for he dared not, that he had just abdicated and left the field and the power with Charles XII and Leczinski. That was abominable, but my husband forgave him and would, I believe, have taken him back when everything was finally decided. How differently Peter behaved to his chosen friends and to the son he had not chosen!

The Tsarevich was, as I have said, brought to the battlefields and made to carry a pike and to dig like a common soldier. The Tsar beat him often in public. Alexis made a bad soldier. He was intelligent, more so than his father in certain ways, but his tastes were for the things Peter despised and would, if Alexis had become Tsar, have dragged Russia back beyond the new light from the West and made of her again a dark country with which no other would ally itself. Peter knew this, and blamed his son for what he was. But would it not have been better to leave him free of fear?

As it was, Alexis became a liar as well as a drunkard, though he never missed saying his prayers. He had changed from the pale child I had seen in the Terem and had become first a thin boy, then a tall thin young man. With his long curly hair and long thin body and thin white face he would have been like the ikons, except that he kept his jaw thrust out to copy his father. He admired Peter at the same time as being afraid of him; I think he longed to please him and that a word of praise from the Tsar would have counted for much. But Peter did not praise anything Alexis knew how to do.

Everything about the life we led, the Tsar and I, frightened or disgusted Alexis. No doubt he remembered his mother—later we learned that he sometimes visited her—and thought, each time he set eyes on me, how different I was from Evdokiya, with her tears and prayers. I have never wasted either, but I would have liked to please Peter's son. But the smells of sweat and the men's latrines, the dirt of the gunpowder, the habit the Tsar had of letting off fireworks when there was nothing better to do; my constant mending and brewing and baking, which should have been beneath his father's wife (but we had to eat) disgusted

Alexis. I cannot recall that he ever sat down to a meal with us in the little house, although others did. Alexis' place was back in the old Kremlin of the Tsars, sheltered and full of tradition, which last his father was doing his best to smash and let in light and air and everything new. Perhaps if Alexis had had both parents with him for longer in his youth he would have been different and less afraid. I do not know.

All of the army knew of his fears. He had been made to live among the men too soon. When he was drunk he talked a great deal, being a Muscovite, and the things he said made the men have a contempt for him. As for the officers, I believe they thought they were pleasing the Tsar by degrading his son. I have seen Alexasha Menshikov seize the Tsarevich by his long hair and drag him to the ground. That should not have been permitted to happen. But I could do nothing for Alexis then or at any other time. When I ventured to speak to the Tsar, he rounded on me.

"So you're coddling him as well, eh? Time to stop; he'll be a grown man soon, or what passes for a man, and what use is one that can't use a pike or carbine and doesn't know north from south or land from water?" For the Tsarevich was also a wretched sailor and feared going to sea. After that I saw less of Alexis and I think the Tsar had given orders that he was to be kept from me. So the fact that I was now Ekaterina Alexeievna meant very little, though I was never, as they said afterwards, my young godfather's enemy.

What can I say about that heroic time? We lived through the bitter cold of the worst winter in memory. It was worse for the Swedes than for us. They had lost their supply-wagons; a little later they lost most of their horses. Later still, after the winter was over, the Tsar himself helped the men dig, in one great night's work, the trenches which were to help win us victory at Poltava. But I, being a woman, remember little things; frozen birds lying on the ground, the sight of gaping wounds; boys dying in my lap at last as though it was their mother's. I tried to mother them, all those men. They are all, and always, children at heart. To me it did not matter then about the coalition of rival states and rival Polish kings; it did not even matter that Patkul the Livonian, having made the rounds of all the countries he might to plead his cause, finished by paying court to a rich widow in Switzerland and settling down, then was kidnapped by Swedish agents and brought back across the frontier. Patkul was the Tsar's envoy, but Charles XII tried him and broke him on the wheel after torture, then beheaded him; after four strokes of the axe Patkul was still not dead. It matters less to me now than the memory of soldiers dying in the bloodstained snow.

I tried to cheer the men on campaign. Before they went into action at Lesnoi and Rashevko and Poltava, I would ride up and down the lines saying, "Cheer up, lads, it's vodka does it; here's a tot for you, Ivan, and one for you, Vaslav, and one for you, Ilya, and you, and you." I was pregnant with Elizabeth but, God knows, that did not matter by then. The vodka made them cheerful and they went in with courage, and some of them came back. That is war. Our last disaster had been at Grodno where they had had to leave some of the cannon in the river, but after that the luck seemed to turn. It turned and we won, in skirmishes and in evasion, all the way down into central Russia, where Charles of Sweden had been fool enough to lead his men, thinking he could not be conquered. But my husband was not enough of a fool in his turn to risk a full-scale engagement before he had to.

At Poltava, it came. Before then word had been received of the flight of Mazeppa the Cossack. He had deserted to Charles and to the fortunes of Stanislas Leczinski, who had been wooing him with letters and with bribes for years. "The Judas!" said my husband, and was much hurt. I did not say that I had known for a long time, perhaps from the beginning, that Mazeppa would fail him. Others had tried to say so and had had no success.

The Tsar sent Menshikov to ensure the quiet of the Cossack country, and Alexasha subdued it within a year. There is nothing now where there was once the town of Baturin, nor was a living soul left in the countryside. Sometimes when I look at Alexasha I marvel that he can be so many men at once; soldier, courtier, adviser, buffoon, the rest. Without him we might still be at war. It would have been foolish to show mercy in the circumstances.

The Tsar felt his strength returning; after the mercury treatment he had gone to build ships at Voronezh. "While I busy myself with the Swedish army, the Turks try to betray me in the south," he grumbled. It was prudent to overhaul his navy. When he came back, Alexasha was able to tell him about the night attacks, false alarms, deceits and artificial famines with which he had tamed the Swedes. Loss of food and sleep, uncertainty and cold, in the midst of enemy country plays havoc with the bravest of armies. As a result, the Swedish numbers had fallen greatly. Alexasha and the cruel winter combined to prepare for our victory. But we could not have won it without the Tsar. He came back at last, for the kill.

Charles XII by then was besieging the town of Poltava itself. It had no more ammunition and the Swedes pounded the walls without reply. My husband at such times was more than human. He stood and watched, then, at the very last moment, gave orders to move. I saw the unending lines of our men go forward in the twilight that is neither of night nor morning. The trenches on our side were still silent. There began the sound of drumming. It was summer by now and there was much dust, and the men's feet shuffled in it and made no sound above the drums. This drumming continued and did not stop as the regiments prepared to cross the river. Surely the Swede will not let them, I thought; surely now he will turn and fight. But there was no resistance as they waded through the water. The sun rose at last on the sight of our banners, bright on the other side. I had helped to sew them. Now my part was done till the wounded should come back, if they came.

It is incredible that the advance was not prevented. No doubt the fierce young King, who himself fought in every skirmish, thought that now we were to come to grips he and his hardened troops—only the hardest had survived the winter—would fight and win. At last his great enemy was before him and his dream was coming true. But fate has a habit of snatching at dreams. So it was that day. Charles of Sweden rode out in the summer morning to survey the positions, and went through a wood. He was alone. Some Cossacks who were still loyal to us were hidden there. The King shot one and then, as if he had been flushing game-birds, slid down from the saddle intending to finish off the rest. A bullet was fired. It hit the King in a curious way, from the toe of one foot to the heel. We saw no more of him till he lay bandaged in a litter on the field of Poltava, and our men soon shot that from under him and he was carried then on two crossed lances. He had had to give the command to one of his generals. They say he was much enraged at the loss of his glory.

My husband was exultant, not only by reason of Charles's wound but because he said ours was the better position and the Swedes had no ammunition left. "We are firing their own guns back at them," he said, remembering the capture of the supply-train. Peter Alexievich, not in love with war like Charles, stayed cool. He took time always to decide which course of action was best. "There are four of ours to one of theirs," he said, and his voice was calm. The drumming had continued all this time and the guns remained silent. They were keeping the ammunition till the right moment to fire. Soon it came.

The sun rose higher. Word had already come in that by dawn, some of the Swedish infantry had made a fierce attack on our cavalry, a thing almost unheard of in war. They had inflicted much damage and captured some officers. The Tsar told the cavalry to retire to the woods, into cover. The Swedish infantry plunged after them and suddenly the cross-fire rang out from our trenches and they were mown down almost to a man. That part of Charles's army was not to return for the main battle. Menshikov rounded up the stragglers and captured two generals in the forest places, and some foot.

I have tried to describe the unceasing drums. They sounded on through the growing day, with the glitter of carbines at last as the men stood in their places. When they were drawn up in full array the sun was above them, and behind them in the woods the roaring of flames came, and soon smoke hid that. The Tsar was everywhere at once, seeing to the men, encouraging them, noting positions, deciding what should be done. He was like a giant chess player, as unhurried and cool. Further off, Charles of Sweden, cursing and pleading at once, had had himself carried on his crossed lances into the heart of the fight. It continued back and forth for two hours, and there were the clashing sounds of conflict and the thunder of guns, and the screams of wounded men and horses. Then suddenly it was like seeing a wall crumble and subside, and our men began yelling for victory and the Swedes cried out to save their King.

He was not worth saving. He was only a great child with toys. But somehow they got him away and he escaped across the river in an open boat. With him was Mazeppa.

A strange thing had happened regarding my husband, whose life had from the beginning been in constant danger, for he took no heed to it. Perhaps God protected Peter Alexievich and would not let him suffer so much as a wound. He was shot once through the hat, again in the saddle, and a third time a bullet glanced off the cross he wore on his breast. Afterwards he ordered that thanks be given for the victory. The Tsar and his generals and all our men knelt as they were on the field of Poltava, and gave thanks among nine thousand Swedish dead.

"We can live in peace in our little house at Petersburg now, Katinka," he said to me afterwards. "August will be King of Poland again. We can have whatever we ask, after this fight. Do you know that that old villain Mazeppa got away with two barrels of gold?"

He feasted that night with the captured generals. In Moscow they rang the bells of all the churches for eight days and the Tsarevich arranged a banquet for the European envoys at Preobrazhenskoe. There was free beer in the streets. Everyone rejoiced, and then the Tsar fell ill again. It was as though he had kept his worst illness till after the battle was won, as though his will could fight it till then. We went back to the little house in Petersburg and I nursed him there till he was better.

If in my youth I had heeded Pastor Glück enough to learn to read and write, it might have been of some use to me in the time that followed. As it was, all I could do, when Peter brought me the first newspaper printed in Russia, was to stare at it and then lay my hand upon it, in a kind of reverence. He was full of pride. It was a part of all he wished to do, the beginning of a new age; everyone was to be educated, to know what was happening, what the army was doing, how many cannon we had, what Europe was saying and thinking. Dimly I knew all this and was able to say to him, "You have done well," and look again at the spread white sheet with its black unreadable betters like the spells of a magician. But at any rate it was the right thing to have said. The Tsar had indeed done well; now I know, and perhaps even then began to feel, that this was of more importance than anything in his life, more so than Poltava. But there was my big peasant's hand spread flat on the paper. I wondered if the thousands in the country who could not read either would feel resentment, bewilderment, even anger, as they did as a rule towards anything new the Tsar thought of. They would have preferred to be left alone in their darkness. But Peter Alexievich would not leave them alone.

Now he talked of opening schools, and of employing not only Muscovites but Swedish prisoners who could teach any subject. He became involved also with that strange alien people, the Finns, in what we called our little war; I think he wanted some territory to bargain with, but the strange land, once won, caused more trouble than the victory was worth and I best remember how it ended in the marriage of the Duke of Courland to one of the fat blonde daughters of Tsar Ivan, who still lived on in the Kremlin and were not even permitted to go and see the new theatre Peter had caused to be opened in the Red Square. Otherwise, he neglected Moscow at this time. All activity, building in stone, making plans for book-printing and the history of Alexander the Great and the government offices and the road-laying and the drunken parties at which Peter's former tutor Zotov, the Archpriest of Mirth, presided, took place in St. Petersburg, and before there was anywhere to put them Peter ordered the royal family to move there also. All of his new stone houses and palaces had chimneys; fires of pitch blazed in the streets to warm the workmen in the snow. Many of these were criminals, who were no longer sent to Siberia but brought here to work, at the new capital. For such it was now to be, and the Tsar had sent for the bones of St. Alexander Nevsky, who long ago had saved Russia from the Swedes and Tartars, and had them placed in the new Cathedral of St. Samson; the city was now St. Petersburg in truth.

I myself was useless among all this culture, so I held my peace. But nobody can say I was not of use to the Tsar in the campaign which followed. He had forgotten one person; his enemy Charles XII, who had by now become the guest of the Sultan in Constantinople, where guests are sacred, and was pestering that ruler again to pursue his old war with Muscovy in aid of Sweden.

"I shall send Sheremetev and the rest to deal with them. You and I will follow at our leisure."

It was two in the morning. He stood at the window of our little house beyond which a storm was blowing, with all the painted wood shutters straining and creaking in the gale. It would be swinging the corpses on their gibbets at the four corners of the market square, where there had been a fire lately and they had been caught stealing goods from the ruined shops. "No more wooden buildings," said the Tsar. "They must all be of stone." But he did not destroy our little house, or speak of doing so. He stood now with the storm-blown moon outside showing up his huge figure in its night-shirt. I knew that he was looking out at the water, white-capped now by the moonlight and the storm. He loved water, and Petersburg, and our house. I was glad he spoke of taking me with him again on campaign. I watched him from where I lay on our bed and then spoke very carefully.

"Is Alexis' marriage to take place?"

"Later, later," he said impatiently. Alexis had consented to be betrothed to a young princess he had met once some years before and had not disliked. It seemed as good a reason for marriage as any other. Her name was Charlotte of Brunswick-Wolfenbüttel. She was sixteen. If she bore Alexis sons, they would inherit. This did not trouble me. It would be better for the Tsarevich to be married to a loving companion who would listen to him and comfort him. Father and son are alike in that, I thought. Another thought flashed across my mind then; I remembered the rejoicings after Poltava and the way Alexis had arranged the triumphal arches and the decorations and the feasting in Moscow, and how when men drank healths in the free beer they said it had not been "God save the Tsar" but "God save the Tsar and his noble heir, Alexis." And Alexis' likeness had appeared on the painted banners beside his father's. I knew Peter remembered all this, and judged, and would not forget.

He turned to me now. "I will sign the marriage-treaty before we leave, or perhaps on the way," he said. Then he lay down at my side. "I do not want to leave here," he said, "to leave Petersburg."

"You are growing old, little father." I could say this kind of thing to him and he did not mind.

"Old? Am I, Katia? I will show you I am not old," and he did so. Afterwards he said, "This place to me is Paradise." And then he slept.

In a few days we made our way south-east across the plains where we had travelled on the journey to Poltava. I knew the coming campaign was in Peter's mind above all else. What I prayed was that he might not take it for granted that because he had won one victory, he would win two. I thought I knew his caution and his prudence in such ways, and as usual I kept silent.

It was hard to imagine Charles XII of Sweden as a guest in the land of seraglios and veiled women. Mazeppa meantime had died in bed, which no one would have expected either. As we made our way south, strange rumours reached us. One had already been spread in the Cossack country that all their women were to be forcibly married to Germans— many of his subjects suspected Peter's attachment to German dress and habits—and so they married a hundred each day for a week and rang all the bells and feasted. It was the last feasting for some time. A man named Goly the Naked then summoned all the poor to rise, but there was little they could do once they had risen. There were no tilled fields and much famine, and a plague of locusts settled on what crops they had. That, at any rate, was one excuse made by Cantemir, whom my husband had made Hospodar of Moldavia, for sending no supplies. By then, we ourselves were very far from home.

I myself, despite everything, do not believe that Cantemir betrayed us. He knew too well where his good fortune lay and in addition, the Turks had executed the former Hospodar. After the locusts his province was laid waste by fire and sword, so it was better for Cantemir to attach himself to us in St. Petersburg and to live there. He fancied himself as a scholar and had written a history of the world in Latin and was about to write another history, this time of Turkish music. He also had a pretty, pert little daughter named Maria. I will say no more yet.

It has become fashionable to state that I saved the Tsar's life on the Pruth, where we were at last surrounded by the enemy and where the Bessarabian foothills bristled with Turkish cannon amid their scrub, and the same sun that had shone on Poltava now showed us the many glittering curved swords and banners of the spahis and janissary troops. Charles of Sweden himself would have favoured the janissaries. They had been reared to live for nothing but war and did not sleep with women, and were marvellously fierce in battle. They outnumbered us by five to one.

I tried to act sensibly, as no one else had done so. Sheremetev had been laggard, and we ourselves late in arriving as the Tsar had been ill. We were by now in the exact position the Swedes had reached the previous summer at Poltava, though without enduring such blazing heat as here in the south. In short, we were in a trap and could not find a way out, and our gunners were roasting.

To fight was useless; there had already been enough blood shed in the rearguard action. Before us now lay marshes, the river, and the great broad sweep of the Sutan's army: behind us were the victorious Turkish rearguard and a single narrow escape route into Moldavia. When matters first became desperate the Tsar had wanted to take this way and escape with me, leaving the army. It was not cowardice, but common sense; a country needs its leader more than its fighting men. But there was one better plan, and I thought of it. I say this because it is the truth. There comes a time when with all their bravery and their boasting and their swords men can do nothing, and this was such a time. The Tsar paced up and down his tent, and the heat was fearsome; beyond was the pitiless sunlight and the dry summer marshes and the Turks. Peter grimaced and twitched in his old way and was not to be approached. He was like a beast in a trap, and I sat there watching him and remembering how ill he had been, again, on our journey through Poland. His convulsions then had been frightening, and he had passed blood with his water in great pain.

Presently I said, "Peter Alexievich, let me speak with the generals. It may not do any good but it can do no harm." He stopped in his pacing and scowled and said, "Be silent. There is nothing to be done. All of last night I went over the ground in my mind and still, today, there is nothing. They will take us prisoner. They may even treat us as they treated Tolstoy"—Tolstoy was the envoy, who had been made to ride half naked through Constantinople and had been spat on by the populace and thrown into prison—"or they may hold us to ransom. Yes, they may do that. They would not dare kill me. But you, Katia, that you should have to endure, for my sake, what I——"

"Listen to me," I said. "If there is to be a ransom it had best be paid now and not later. Money answers all questions. They say Charles bribed their Vizier with some of Mazeppa's gold from his barrels, and with loans from an English banker. If we——"

"How much you know," he said at last, stopping in his pacing and looking at me, for the first time in many hours, as if he knew me for who I was. "You are wise, Katia. You——"

"Then let me use my wisdom to persuade our friends, if you will. It is worth trying, is it not, to bribe the Vizier? Charles of Sweden did as much."

After it was all over we learned, too late, that we might have threatened to fight them after all, as their intelligence was poor and they had not been informed of the disaster with the rearguard. We learned also that Charles of Sweden had not been permitted to ride with the host but awaited events some way off, at Bender. If he had been present, I doubt if words would have carried the day. Afterwards, when he learned that we had been successful in parley, I believe he rode furiously and with speed to the Vizier, who had been bribed by both himself and by us, and flung himself down on the couch with his spurs on, talking fast and discourteously. Possibly we ourselves had a better understanding of the Oriental mind. However that may be, it was with great relief that I heard the bugle sound for truce and a silence fall over both armies.

They did not accept our suggestions at once. It became as they say conditions are in Turkish markets, perhaps any market, when one haggles over the price of something greatly desired without letting the seller know how much one covets it. So it was with us, but at the second attempt we were permitted to withdraw; there had been comings and goings between the two camps with money and promises, conveyed by a fat red-haired Jew named Shafirev who was as proud of his great belly as any boyar. Then there were more promises and more money, vast sums of money, some promised and some at hand. There were other demands also. Peter had to swear to part with his beloved fort of Azov that he had won in his earliest victory. It was very bitter for him. The other Black Sea fortresses were to be destroyed. All this had to be agreed before they would let us go. The bargain was a hard one.

But at least we were free, with whole skins, though much the poorer, and could go back to St. Petersburg with the assurance, devoutly given—and a Moslem does not break his promise—from the Porte that they would not oblige the King of Sweden in such warlike ways again and would rid themselves of him as soon as was courteous.

Charles became thereafter an even more ungracious guest. By the end of his visit the Turks were besieging him in his lodging and he lost four fingers in the shooting. By this time no European power regarded him highly and although he was returned, in the end, to Sweden it was not for long that that country had to endure the king who never troubled to rule. He was killed by a bullet while warmongering against Norway in 1718. After that his sister, peaceably married to a peaceable husband, ascended the throne. By that time the Tsar and I had other matters on our minds than the Great Northern War, though relations with Sweden and Denmark would never be easy again.

But for the time, at any rate, there was relief and laughter. The Tsar was no longer like a trapped wild beast, and even his health seemed better. When word came that the Sultan had accepted our terms at the Pruth he came to me and took my face between his huge hands and said, "Ekaterina Alexievna, you have saved Russia and its Tsar. I will put a crown on your head: I will make you equal with myself." I told him to get along and said he owed me something, because if the Grand Vizier had taken us both prisoners I might have become the Sultan's chief wife. "Think what he's missed," I said.

But he would not laugh and his great eyes looked at me gravely. "I had come to an end, and you saved me," he said again. "Do not mock at it, even when we are alone." Then he suddenly started to think and plan again and said, "Do you know, Katia, I believe that I shall tell them to leave the foundations intact at Taganrog? Perhaps some day——"

He did not part with Azov in a hurry either; he left a garrison there, but it had to be marched out in the end. It was like drawing blood again to get him to part with his first successes. The Porte was understanding; the whole business was spun out in a leisurely manner, except that they wanted the money at once. Nobody but soldiers will wait for their money. Be that as it may, the Turks respected us by now as a nation which understood bargaining and would not spoil the rich fabric of the Vizier's sofa with sharp and muddy spurs.

After Poltava we had become a great Power, and everyone knew it. A year earlier, no one would have bargained with Muscovy.

We went on to make merry in Warsaw. My husband had always been able to put the past behind him, and he never again spoke of the black hours in the tent by the Pruth. Two things seemed to fill his mind; the first was his meeting with Augustus the Strong at Dresden, where the two powerful men vied with one another at bending and crumpling the silver dishes served at table. The other was Alexis' marriage to the Princess of Brunswick-Wolfenbüttel.

Poor Charlotte; I can well remember her. She was a retiring and gentle creature and her long face had nothing about it that was remarkeable except the pock-marks; she had had smallpox as a child. She had been a dutiful daughter and would make a dutiful wife. There was no reason why Alexis should not have been happy enough in his marriage. Perhaps, while it lasted, he was so. At the beginning, however, he was placed at a disadvantage. The sixty thousand roubles now in the Vizier's grasp in Constantinople had made my husband close-fisted with regard to the marriage. Alexis was sent off to Wolfenbüttel to try to arrange for a smaller price for Charlotte. It was a humiliating mission for a bridegroom, but the bride's parents took to him despite it. There was less trouble from them than from the Tsarevich's confessor, Ignatiev. He did not like the marriage; the bride was a Lutheran. "Perhaps when she comes to live among us she will change of her own accord," said Alexis hopefully.

The marriage was to be at Carlsbad. Meantime the Tsar took ill again. I was not with him, and no doubt the feasting with Augustus the Strong had undone the good of the latest mercury cure. He was carried in a litter for part of the way, then before the town was reached sat up and demanded a coach. He was always very particular as to what kind of carriage he used, but no doubt on this occasion there was little choice.

I was at Thorn, living in a monastery. All of the other buildings had been destroyed by the war.

Peter reached his lodging and took to his bed and to a gradual water cure which finally reached forty mugs a day. After that he went to the baths. Meantime Alexis and his betrothed were growing better acquainted at Torgau. Suddenly the Tsar burst in upon them, his health recovered.

All of the polite customs went by the board. The couple must be married at once, he said; and married they were. On the fourth day, Peter removed his heir from the festivities and his bride, and sent Alexis to me at Thorn. But he did not arrive. The Tsar came, and was angry.

"The Danes are besieging Stralsund," he said flatly, without comment on my surroundings. "I sent Alexis Petrovich here to organise supplies for the campaign."

"And made him leave his wife of four days?"

"The marriage has been consummated," said Peter, as if it were part of a military programme. But the Tsarevich himself had not yet left Torgau. Some days later he appeared, shamefaced.

"What the devil," roared the Tsar.

Alexis stammered that he had been trying to arrange to bring his wife. She had ordered a travelling bed and it had not been delivered by the time Alexis left. "I hope you will excuse the delay," he said miserably.

It was in fact two months before Charlotte did arrive. After that the couple had almost eight weeks of one another's company before the Baltic war separated them again. I was troubled. Such upsets did not seem to me good for a marriage, but after all my own had not been peaceful and here I was. I could only smile at Alexis' plain bride as I did not speak High German. She returned my smile, but looked unhappy. She did not seem haughty and her forlorn state touched me, torn as she had been from her mother and family and set down suddenly in the midst of war at sixteen years old, with a strange husband who was sometimes there and sometimes not.

"Now we will go to Petersburg," said the Tsar with satisfaction. He had two things on his mind at this time, other than the campaign and the question of whether Charlotte might, or might not, be pregnant. One was my palace of the Ekaterinhofsky, which he had ordered to be built for me partly as an honour because of the Pruth, and partly since as I have said the market-place had been destroyed by fire and there were to be no more wooden buildings. He had, as it were, done his duty by his heir; now he would please himself.

We reached Petersburg. The Tsar married me again in public with none other than the well-born Praskovia, Tsar Ivan's widow, in attendance. She did not look too pleased. After that there were the customary revels with the elected Princess-Abbess. old Rzhevskaya, presiding to have her breasts kissed. I wondered what Charlotte thought of this lady of misrule, who was the female equivalent of Zotov, Archpriest of Mirth. Alexis' wife was not a young woman who said much, even in High German. At no time, despite the opportunities at what generally ended as a drunken riot, was she ever seen to misbehave. I think that the Tsar, to his own surprise, conceived a respect for his son's wife. But he had already left them at Thorn without any money to buy food, and Charlotte had had to borrow it and later, when she was left alone, fled back to her parents. Men seldom trouble about such things, and the Tsar was no exception, though Charlotte's flight made him angry and he fetched her back again.

Hatred is alien to me. It is one of the things about which I could not help my husband, though I used to try in the early years. If somebody does one an injury, it hurts at the time. Then it is over and done with, and to brood on it makes it worse, like picking scabs. In such ways I could now meet Sheremetev, who in his time had flogged me and turned me into a public whore, without embarrassment, even without dislike. I said to myself that he was a brave commander and the servant of the Tsar, and the General Field Marshal in his turn thought of me now, when he did so, as his master's. But to Peter Alexievich to hate was for life. One carried on hatred, like God's punishment, to the third and fourth generation. That is what happened with Alexis and Charlotte and their children. The Tsar had ended by loathing Alexis' mother Evdokiya, who paid homage to ikons and no matter what he did to her, said nothing in complaint; if she had browbeaten him in return and boxed his ears, he might not have sent her to a convent. But to Peter, Evdokiya came to mean the ancient dark he was trying to banish from Russia, the dark of the Terem and the bearded popes and gleaming idols of Tsars who were seldom seen in public and seldom spoken of abroad except as savages. Then Alexis grew to be such another. It showed in the famous affair of the geometry and fortifications.

I know nothing of either. I had seen the Tsar making marks with a compass over maps of the Black Sea ports when we were in the south. But according to the reports he received of his son, Alexis was following a course of study prescribed by his tutors. No doubt in the boy's younger days Peter had been too busy to notice what he was taught. But now he suddenly demanded proof of Alexis' ability to conduct a siege and other such things, and although the Tsarevich had ably organised the celebrations after Poltava, that was not quite the same thing.

His fear of his father showed now. Instead of going straight to Peter and telling the truth, which was that he had spent his time in drinking, not studying geometry, he took a pistol and tried to wound his hand so that he might say he could not use it to draw. It was like Alexis to misfire, and all he did was to burn his hand with the blast of the powder. He came to the Tsar bandaged and laggard, with wine on his breath. "Get out of my sight," said Peter, instead of examining Alexis' knowledge as he had planned.

In such ways, his son was a disappointment. Perhaps Peter still hoped for an heir to the marriage who would turn out as he wished. But Charlotte arranged things badly; she produced a girl. "I am going to Carlsbad," said Alexis, looking round the door as she was in labour. Perhaps he had already begun to ill-treat Charlotte after her return from her flight home, following the lean time at Thorn.

The baby was named Natalia.

There was talk of our visiting Europe. When the Tsar was a young man he had gone abroad to learn. Now, he wanted, I believe, to show himself as a powerful ruler who had conquered the unconquerable Charles XII, had won himself ports in which to exchange trade, and had a navy and a capital no longer in the strange heart of Russia, but by the open sea. I was to go with him, and already, though it was still some time before we were to leave, I began to get ready my dresses. There was one I was particularly proud of, with a double-headed eagle, the Tsar's emblem, sewn on it in feathers studded with diamonds. All my ladies who were to come made ready. Now that it was to be left again, I sniffed the salt air of St. Petersburg lovingly. Whatever happened this place had been home to me, the only home of my own I had known. Some while back it had only been marshes, islands and sea and wild animals; now it was becoming a great city, like Paris or London or Amsterdam, yet different from all these. My husband had not thought of beauty while he built it; suddenly, it was beautiful, as though the half-finished stone palaces and the part-laid roads and the mended shops in the market-place had become one perfect whole with the river running through like a great shining thread, binding everything together. Whatever else Peter Alexievich did badly or well, there are his two achievements; the newspaper in the Russian tongue, and Petersburg. He will be remembered for that.

Charlotte was pregnant again. I knew she was not happy, though I did not like to pry or tell tales. She had mastered a very little Russian, enough for us to have some stiff uneasy talk, and she used pleasant, pretty manners to me and to the Tsar. She never complained of Alexis. I do not know how it was that I found out he now kept a mistress, a peasant like me, a fat carrot-headed Finn named Efrosinia Fedorova, who had already been the kept woman of his tutor Vazhyonsky.

If the second child had been begotten of reconciliation, this did not last. Shortly before she was due to take to her bed Charlotte was said to have fallen upstairs, and to have bruised her side. But I heard from my woman Anisa, who always heard everything, that the truth was Alexis had kicked his wife in the stomach. It may not be true. Weak persons who are afraid can, however, be cruel.

The child was born and this time it was a boy, to be named Peter Alexievich. Perhaps Charlotte got up too soon after the birth: at any rate she caught a fever. The physicians tried to get her to take medicine, but she shook her head. "Do not try to save me," she said. "I do not want to live." She was twenty years old.

She died, and after her death Alexis wept for three days.

Love is as strange as hate. When I see lovers walking hand in hand by the Neva of an evening I think of their thoughts of love and what it must say to them. Then I remember my own life and the man who filled it. He was a man like no other and yet, for this same reason, more of a man than any other. Had I been a young girl in love, made foolish by it like the romances, I should have grown very doleful, for Peter Alexievich regarded other women like tobacco, there for the sampling and to give pleasure for the time. But just as he could not have done without his food and drink and live wholly by smoking his clay pipe, so I believe he told the truth when he said he could not do without me. Bodily, I satisfied him as well as the rest; he used to speak of me as a fine vigorous wife and boast of me to men less fortunate. But that did not prevent him from sleeping with every pretty woman, and some ugly ones, he met or from debauching himself with the Princess-Abbess or the Archpriest of Mirth. It was as though pleasure itself were part of a military programme; now we will drink, smoke, dance in a ragged circle, sleep with each other, kiss the Abbess, change partners again, and so on. I know there were such occasions; Zotov as a senile bridegroom and his young bride put to bed and everyone sat on chamber-pots and watched what went on, and there were other goings-on where Peter mocked the Church and the Patriarch (he had never since the beginning of his reign permitted a Patriarch, and the man who was called Exarch, Stefan Yavorsky, always did exactly as he was bid) by electing so-called prelates on holed chairs so that their sex could be tested, after a story the Tsar heard about Pope Joan. He would make more than anyone ever had done of such things, and it was all of it a part of the great lust for living that was in him that would not be satisfied with restraint or authority other than his own. Yet he was religious, as I have said, at times like Poltava.

If one is to live with such a man at all, it must be on his terms. These did not always mean hard work. We used to send presents to one another when we were separated. Mine would be such things as a knitted waistcoat for the cold winter, lemons and cucumbers which the Tsar liked to eat, anything I could find that he fancied to keep him warm and fed. The gifts he sent me were all of them different. Once it was a pair of fluttering doves from Finland, and a tame fox. Another time—this was from Dresden—it was a pretty watch, which must have cost Peter a great deal of money. He never gave handsome presents to his casual mistresses (my own, after all, had once been a ducat). He sent me ruffles of Mechlin lace, which I had sewn on to my sleeves and wore when I had my portrait painted by Benner and the rest. I did not let them paint my hands. But we wrote letters through our secretaries, and we sent these presents to one another, and often when he was away from me the Tsar would write and say he felt very lonely.

By now all of our wars looked as if they were over, and with the arrival of a son to Alexis the succession seemed certain. Perhaps for this very reason we were more contented together than usual, without thought or care for the future. All I know of it is that wondrously, so late in my life and marriage, after so many stillbirths and miscarriages and girl-children, after the damned pox marred my fertility, at last, at last I gave birth to a son who would live. I can still savour our joy.

SIX

I, ALEXIS

I have known, I think, from the beginning that my father would kill me.

When I speak of the beginning, I must have been about eight years old. Until then I was in the Kremlin with my beloved mother, the true Tsaritsa, Evdokiya Luphokina, and the Tsar never visited us. My mother was all my world and she loved me and was gentle with me. When I think of her, which I still do sometimes, it is to remember her as she was then; the years and sorrow have changed her and they say that by now she looks like an old woman. But in those days she was a tall plump girl, full-faced and with a brilliant red-and-white complexion that never needed paint. She always wore the seemly dark furred robes and headdress of the Terem, and being devout she spent a great part of her day in prayer and taught me to do likewise. I was glad to obey her in everything; her voice was quiet and she never shouted orders.

The other women were different. There was my aunt Maria, who seldom spoke and kept her eyes downcast thinking herself lucky not to have been made to take the veil like her sisters Sofia and Marfa. Then there was my young aunt Natalia who shouted and played pranks. I did not like her or my grandmother, Tsaritsa Natalia, who was not always kind to my mother and acted as though mother had failed her in some way. Probably the reason was the Tsar's indifference so that he never came to the Terem. I can recall a time when mother used to write letters to him and weep, but no answers came and she stopped writing and prayed for my father instead. Otherwise I was her world as she was mine. Together we read the holy books long before my tutor Vyazhemsky came. I loved to read and it was as well, because later, in my loneliness as I grew up, I read the Bible five times through. Also, I secretly visited my mother who was by then in her convent. What son could have done less? Yet it is one of the many things for which my father lately blames me and out of which he fashions evidence to try to prove that I was plotting to overthrow him and take the throne. Even so I do not hate him, although I greatly fear him; he has never given me a moment's love in all my life, and has beaten me often.

I know that Menshikov and Tolstoy and the rest will soon come for me and that then I shall be taken and tortured ready for questioning, and thereafter I shall not be able to write. I want to set down matters as they happened to me, not the lies I have been forced to put down by my father's agents, flattering him and making myself out a drunkard, a hypocrite and liar. I may be the first—they made me so—but to myself, now, I can tell the truth as God will see it when I am dead. For I do not think I shall live through this questioning: the Tsar has intended that I shall not. Which will give him the greater pleasure, the cat-and-mouse game of recent months, or the sight of my dead body?

No one, not even Menshikov and his spies, shall ever see this testimonial because I shall hide it too well. Perhaps one day my son will find it. I am alone in my room in the upper part of the house on the Neva, where I lived for three years with my wife Charlotte. The two children are abed and the servants have gone about their duties for tomorrow. Tomorrow! When I think of what it may bring strength fails me, and my hand shakes as I hold the quill. My father has devised such desperate cruelties for others that I shall not be spared them. He delights in inflicting pain, and especially on me.

It began early. My mother was taken away before my eighth birthday. They came to the Terem and forced her to go with them and she was bundled into an ordinary postcart and taken out of Moscow. No one would tell me where she was or what had become of her; I was told that I must not mention her name or pray for her. Those who know nothing of such things, like my aunt Natalia, think that because a little child does not weep it feels nothing. But children in great fear and bewilderment can grow pale and silent and changed, and so did I. I began to be furtive and would hide in corners and behind hangings, to shut the others out that I did not love. These were the tutor Vyazhemsky—later the Tsar found me a German tutor as well—and the aunts and my grandmother who now, in her turn, was constantly writing letters. From her I learned that she wrote to the Tsar who was still in England. I did not yet know geography, only that it was from that place that the order had come to remove my mother and hide her away as a nun. I soon learnt this from my aunt Natalia in whose charge I was put. She would tell me most things I asked, but I distrusted her. She was a tall strapping young woman who liked such rough exercises as were available in the Terem, such as flinging snowballs and sliding on the ice in winter and throwing a leather ball in summer. She would force me to go with her, grabbing my hand and calling out, "Come on, slow-feet! Boys like slides," or catching leather balls or whatever it might be. I often missed the ball and then she would mock me. I liked reading best and made progress at that and Latin.

The Tsar still had not come home.

When he came unexpectedly, it was by reason of a further revolt of the streltsi. They had once revolted in his boyhood, but that was a more widespread affair; this one could have been put down quite easily and without bloodshed. It had happened in fact because the Tsar had been away too long; this I learned later. Muscovites do not expect their Tsar to be absent from them. But my father thought differently.

I can remember him now, a giant, striding suddenly through the Terem apartments towards my grandmother's. Presently I heard him shouting at her and wondered if they were quarrelling. He had not noticed me, and this may have been because I had grown since he last saw me; presently I was sent for. The Tsar was still roaring and shouting and did not stop it as I went in and made my prostration to him. He said, "I will dig up old Miloslavsky out of his grave——"

"It is not a Miloslavsky matter," said my grandmother.

"—and let them see the maggots on him and that he has died like other men. Then they will die also. I will cut off their heads myself and let the blood pour down into the coffin from the scaffold as if they were goats for the sacrifice. Not a Miloslavsky matter? Be bound it is, and that Sofia has her finger in it, the same as last time. I won't leave a man alive, I tell you; I'll string up a row of corpses outside her cell window and leave 'em there to stink. Then she can say her prayers for them, Sister Susanna." Then he saw me and my white face and that I was going to be sick, and growled something, and went out. But I was very frightened and my aunt Natalia, who enjoyed such things, told me that the Tsar had indeed dug up old Miloslavsky, kinsman of the first wife of Tsar Alexis, and indeed he was all covered in worms, and my father had executed two hundred streltsi over the coffin with his own hands in one day, and Menshikov and the rest hundreds more, and now there were no streltsi left. I said timidly, "What will he do for a guard?"

"You mustn't ask questions of that sort. The Tsar will find men."

But indeed my father soon complained bitterly because there were not enough trained troops for his wars, and he had to comb the countryside for peasants who ought to have been tilling the fields, and teach them how to use the weapons he had learned about in Holland and England.

I was made to learn to use these also.

It was almost as bad as when they took my mother away. I had never before left the Terem, and suddenly word came that I was to be taken from my books and tutors and sent off to the Swedish campaign. It was bitterly cold on the journey and my guards saw that I was shivering, and laughed. "They will make you dig to keep you warm," they said; they were not respectful as the servants in the Terem had been.

I remember when camp was reached at last and at once, as it now seems, I was taken to where my father was standing knee-deep in snow, handling a pick by the side of the men. He looked at me and muttered something and I was given a spade which was too heavy for me, and made to dig with it. Soon I was crying with the cold and the weight of the spade, but the tears froze on my face and no one heeded me. If I had known for what purpose I was digging it might have been better.

At the end of the day I was taken back to the Tsar's

tent. Someone—I believe it was Menshikov whom I have hated ever since—laughed and said, "The Tsarevich is cold. Give him wine to warm his guts." They brought the wine and I disliked it, and tried to thrust away the cup after the first taste, coughing at the same time because the air in the tent was foul with the smoke from the commanders' pipes. I heard my father saying, "What, a son of mine can't hold his drink?" and then there was some jest I couldn't hear, but everyone laughed loudly and I felt a fool. Then Menshikov came over and took hold of me and held my nose between his fingers so that I had to open my mouth to breathe, and so he forced me to gulp down all of the wine. Afterwards I was sick.

They made me drink wine every day after that, and work at digging and regimental drill. I loathed all of it, but soon grew used to the wine and by the end there was no need to force me to take it. Wine is a comfort because it dulls the senses. It did not matter so much, for instance, if the Tsar beat me while I was drunk. My father beat everybody, especially Menshikov when the fit took him. He carried a heavy stick which would swing to and fro with his arm as he walked, and he did that so fast that everyone else had to run to keep up with him. He made me very much afraid. It was impossible to tell what he would want, or do, from one minute to the next. He had brought back ideas from Holland and England and Germany and was determined that they should all be used in Russia by the Russians.

One thing in particular sickened me; my father had taken lessons from a barber-surgeon in Amsterdam and fancied himself at the pulling out of teeth. He would bear down on some courtier with a rotten tooth and heave it out with strong pliers, and if he had drunk enough he would pull out sound teeth as well. The victims dared not complain. I used to live in terror that he would pull mine.

So passed my boyhood.

Sometimes I was returned briefly to my tutors to learn further. Vyazhemsky had been with me longest; he remembered my mother, but I had always thought of him as a Tsar's man. So was the German, Huyssen, whom my father found. I read theology and the classics with Vyazhemsky and French and German with Huyssen. I liked history also, and Greek plays, although my father said these were useless to me. In the midst of my learning he sent Huyssen abroad for four years on state business. If he had been present the following events might not have taken place so readily.

I was still reading Latin with Vyazhemsky although the Tsar disapproved. Everything I liked or had a natural aptitude for my father condemned out of hand, and so it has been throughout our lives. No doubt it is my fault for being my mother's son. One day during the lesson my tutor whispered that I had a visitor; the Tsar was then absent at the wars. Presently a big man with a kindly face and the erect bearing of a soldier entered. He was made known to me as Captain Glebov and I was told to do exactly as he bade me, but to say nothing to anyone. His manner did not alarm me, and I let him and Vyazhemsky put me into a peasant's cap and tunic. Then I was led out to where the horses waited; they were sturdy short-legged steppe ponies and not the spirited, nervous beasts from the palace stables. Glebov saw me up into the saddle and then mounted his own pony, and we set off at a steady pace, our heads down against the cold. I had tried to ask where we were going, but the captain shook his head and had so merry a look in his eyes that I could not distrust him. Free of my father I am not a coward, and I was beginning to relish the adventure. We rode some little distance out of Moscow. It was late autumn and the trees had shed their leaves.

Presently we drew rein at a place I had never seen before. The captain helped me to dismount and tied our horses' reins to a post in the yard. All this time there had been a kind of stirring of movement about the place, and I heard stifled laughter; presently two women whom I recognised as lay-sisters came out, smiling broadly, and bobbed to me. Behind the windows other nuns were watching. "It cannot be a very strict convent," I remember thinking. I had some idea by now of why we were here and my heart had begun to beat rapidly in my breast.

Glebov and I were greeted by more smiling, curtsying

women, and they led us into a cool whitewashed interior, very plain, with no ikons or crucifixes. Then a door opened and my mother was standing there, and held out her arms. She was not dressed as a nun and wore her familiar fur hood and dark cloak. I felt shy as I kissed her. She said, "My son, how tall you have grown!" Then we could not seem to think of anything else to say for some minutes. Glebov had remained by the door. I saw a kindly, loving glance pass between him and my mother. I am glad she had such a lover to console her. She had grown stouter because at that convent they fed well.

Mother asked about my studies and if I said my prayers. I told her I did, which was the truth, and added, "And I remember always to pray for you silently," and then she looked as if instead of smiling she would weep. "And I for you, Alexis," she said. "Come." She led me into the chapel which lay beyond. It was like other chapels with painted walls and a carved and gilded screen before the altar. Mother led me towards this screen and I looked through, while we both knelt. Beyond, on the altar itself, was a stone tablet with carved letters.

"Read it," she said, "but do not tell anyone."

I read aloud as I was accustomed. The stone said, "Long life and health to Tsar Peter Alexievich and Tsaritsa Evdokiya." I understood.

"A holy bishop says that all will come about as it should in the end," said my mother comfortably. She crossed herself and added, "I live in the hope of that."

I learned later that the bishop had told her she should bear my father two more sons: also, that many people in fact came here on pilgrimage to the Novodevichi convent and knelt before my mother as if she had been a saint. But the prophecy itself has not come true. When my father learned of it all, which was not for some years, he tortured the bishop and Glebov to death and forced my mother to shave her head and put on a nun's habit and live as a nun, in a convent many miles from Novodevichi so that no one could visit her. As for myself, my visits are made a part of my father's accusation against me now. He found out about that quite soon.

Yes, I visited her often, and in the end my father sent for me to rebuke me. He was at a place named Zholkva. I was very much afraid, and he beat me cruelly and told me that I would be watched in future so that the visits must cease. He did not at that time suspect Vyazhemsky or know about Glebov; that came later. "I am sending you now to Smolensk," he said, "and there you will direct supplies and mobilisation. It is time you learned the whole business of war."

Is it a crime that I am not by nature a soldier or commander? I travelled to cold, bleak Smolensk, where the real work was done by others put over me, and then I was brought back to Moscow to be shown how to fortify the city in case of attack. Nobody has attacked Moscow in old men's memories, and they are unlikely to want to as it is too far inland. If they did try, it would fall at once.

My father was disappointed in me for my lack of interest in the Moscow defences and wrote to complain that I was living an idle and useless life. By this time Ekaterina Vassilievka was with him and although she cannot read I wrote to her to try to stave off his anger. Whatever they may say, and whatever I myself may have said when I was drunk, my relations with Ekaterina have always been friendly. I do not seriously suspect her of trying to poison me. I think that at the time I mention she must have placated my father in the way she can generally do, because I suffered no more from his anger at this time and was allowed to return to my studies with Huyssen when he came back from abroad, and Vyazhemsky, who as I say had escaped suspicion.

I still prayed for my mother. No one could stop me from doing that. I still do.

One thing I tried to do well to please the Tsar may well have helped in my downfall. I had been ill at the time of Poltava and had not been present at the battle. Afterwards he wrote to say that there were to be public rejoicings and that I was to direct the celebrations in Moscow. I put all my renewed energies into this task, which was one that appealed to me. I forget how many classical myths—they had to have explanations attached to them, as few in the old city knew what they were about—wreaths, lanterns, fireworks and hogsheads of wine and beer there were, but one thing I remember even though I was fully occupied with the banquet for visiting heads of state at Preobrazhenskoe. I should have dreaded this memory of mine. It shows that I was innocent of fault in that I did not understand, at the time, how much harm it could do me. At the end, in the streets, the joyous and dutifully drunken people called for our healths. They did not call for my father's health alone. My toast was drunk as well, as the heir. After all, I was so. Why should he have grudged me this recognition? The Muscovites know me better than my father, who was never much among them. Moreover he had just won a victory over a foe they knew little about, in a place they had never before heard of. They meant no harm by drinking to me. They meant no harm.

I think my father has ended by thinking of himself as God, with power over life and death and change. He certainly believes that because he says or does a thing, so must it be, whether or not it breaks every law God made. And how could Ekaterina Vassilievka be my father's wife, despite the marriages in public and in private, when my mother was still alive and forced to the pretence of being a nun, which she never wished to be? Yet I have never dared to address Ekaterina as what she is, my father's concubine. Like everyone else, I bow to her as Tsaritsa.

Had I become Tsar in the natural order—how it has become twisted and defaced! I shall never now rule—I would have put everything back as it was in the good familiar days before my father forced on everyone his violent changes. The old, secret, dignified Russia with its mystic Tsar would have lived again, and have been self-sufficient as for centuries; we do not need armies and navies if there are no wars, except with our internal enemies. Pope and peasant could have grown beards again without fear of being disfigured (it is because my father cannot grow a beard himself that he hates them so?); the Church would have upheld its laws as of old; there would be no more trafficking with foreigners, no German ways, no filthy tobacco. I love what I remember of the old things, the old churches, true houses of God. As Tsar I would have made Moscow the capital again, the great heart of Russia steadfastly beating, not a new hastily-erected site above shifting marshland on a spur of foreign country near the sea. Our ancestors grew great by using the rivers. They were great in the days of Novgorod, the days of Kiev. It is moreover useless to try to turn a Muscovite into a German as my father thinks he has done. The peasants whose beards he cut off keep them inside their shirts to render to St. Nicholas at the gate of heaven when they die.

O God, how near I myself am to death!

Charlotte my wife was a German. I met her first the year my father sent me to Dresden to complete my education. My betrothal with Charlotte had already been arranged before I saw her; it was still a triumph for a Tsar to achieve a foreign alliance. I myself would have preferred to marry some young noblewoman from a Terem such as they still have in country-houses in Russia, where my father's barbarous habit of forced assemblies for mixed sexes has not been imitated. Such a one would have understood Muscovite ways, but I was not consulted. Charlotte was a Lutheran and had no notion of religion as we understand it in the Orthodox Church. I used to hope that she would change, but she never did so. However in herself she was harmless enough and did not displease me. She was a tall thin girl of sixteen then—I myself am tall and thin—and although her features were good enough there was no doubt the smallpox had marred them very badly. This does not show in her portraits. When one considers it, a portrait seldom tells the whole truth about anyone. I myself have been painted in armour with an expression like my father's, so that anyone seeing it would no doubt think of me as a born commander. It is also true that when we first met, I bragged to Charlotte of my military accomplishments. I did not want her to know that I was shy and had no talents of the kind women admire. So I told her—and in its way it was true—that I had commanded mobilisation and supplies at Smolensk and had been present at the capture of Nyenskanz, and other places. I saw her blue eyes open wide. "How clever Your Highness must be, to have done so much at the age of eighteen years!" she said. There was no mockery in the words; she had believed everything I had told her, and afterwards she informed her mother that I was clever and had pleasing manners. I hoped for as long as I could to keep this picture of myself in Charlotte's mind, but the Tsar spoilt everything; my father ruined my marriage as he has ruined my life. If it can be believed, four days after the wedding he ordered me to prepare to go to the front with detachments; I was sent to Thorn, where the Tsaritsa was, and after a few weeks Charlotte joined me. Not only had our honeymoon been interrupted—I remember there was a scene with the Tsar because I had delayed to try to find a travelling-carriage for Charlotte—but we were short of money. Nothing could have been more humiliating for me. My wife had been gently bred in her Brunswick home. Now, day after day after we were left alone she must sit down with me to poor fare at a wooden table, within walls which dripped with damp, and the guard outside spitting and swearing he had not been paid, which was true. Sometimes we did not know how to buy food. I knew, although Charlotte never complained, that she was beginning to wonder if her life with me would always be one of discomfort, poverty and danger.

My own sojourn at Thorn came to an abrupt end. This time, the Tsar had ordered me to Pomerania. I suppose that, with his usual habit of considering persons as chattels, he had decided that Charlotte had had time to become pregnant; as it happened, she was not. At about that time she was forced—she did not tell me of it—to borrow money from Menshikov, who visited us; he lent it to her out of the army funds. I was furious and it caused our first quarrel, if one may call it so with only one partner saying anything at all. Charlotte said nothing, and only looked at me with mournful eyes; this made me still angrier. I expect I bullied her; it was the first time I had met a person who would obey me. We did not part on loving terms and I left her looking as miserable as I felt. At the same time the Tsar was writing to ask for news of a pregnancy and I was obliged to ask my wife to let me know post-haste concerning the matter if it should arise.

There followed the only time Charlotte was disobedient. It was partly due to the fear in which Russians are held abroad. She was afraid of being murdered if, as the Tsar demanded, she travel to St. Petersburg alone. The next I heard was that she had fled back home to her parents in Brunswick, and that the Tsar was very angry.

I do not know what happened next. I was not present, nor was I informed. The Tsar journeyed to visit Charlotte and by some means other than terrorising her, persuaded her to return to me. Thereafter she was never afraid of him, was friendly with him and Ekaterina, and even after our daughter was at last born, wrote him a joking letter saying that next time it must be a son.

I was very often drunk by then. What did they expect of me? I knew, I could not fail to know, that the Tsar had by his own methods taken away Charlotte's good opinion of me, so that she blamed me for our situation at Thorn and elsewhere. By now she would watch me with suffering eyes like a dumb animal ill-treated by its owner. If she had only answered back sometimes! Her humility made me unkind to her. It made me feel of more importance to myself.

The worst thing of all happened before our second child, our son, was born. Charlotte was already big with him, and I came in the worse for wine and taunted her. She did not reply and I do not remember what happened next. I swear I do not remember. When I came to myself it was to find Charlotte bent double with pain and her hands to her belly, and the servants in the room fussing all about her. Her eyes met mine and I heard her say in a clear voice, "It is nothing. I fell and bruised myself on the way upstairs. Perhaps if you will unlace me and put me to bed, it will be better." She always spoke to the servants in this way, as if they were her equals. She had no pride.

I stumbled out of the room and downstairs, to Efrosinia. Yes, there was Efrosinia by then. Soon afterwards when Charlotte gave birth to the boy and died I remembered my many unkindnesses and how good and dutiful she had been and how, at the end when they were trying to save her, she had told the physicians to leave her in peace. "I do not want to live any longer," she said. I wept for her, too late because she was dead. I would have liked her to know that I was fond of her.

My love for Efrosinia was like a flame, which devours me still. There is no reason for such a love and indeed it feeds on unreason. My mistress is a Finnish serf, red-headed and without beauty, and had been Vyazhemsky's mistress before she became mine. She had an odour, which made her different from my wife—Charlotte was always fastidious—and as Efrosinia went upstairs or about the house I could smell her acrid female sweat, which had a quality about it to inflame a man's lust. Everything about her had this effect; her thick white flesh, her lewd quick jests and loud laughter when her mouth would open to show square wide-spaced teeth. She never pretended to be other than she was and so I need not pretend either. We made love like pigs in a sewer, wherever we might meet; across Efrosinia's pallet, on the floor of the Neva house, in closets, on Charlotte's very bed when she had left it and gone out to wait on my father and Ekaterina (they used her like a servant, to fetch and carry). Once Charlotte returned early and found us together. She said nothing, did not complain to the Tsar or anyone, and she did not, as most wives would have done, beat Efrosinia and have her dismissed. No doubt she knew I would have found another house for Efrosinia. But her eyes grew sadder and as I have said, she lost the will to live and in the end had her way. Meantime Efrosinia was to me like a drug, like more and fiercer wine. In our love-play she used to jerk and bite me like a mare with a stallion. It was as if she drained the strength from me and left me empty. I can feel the urge for her rise in me even now, when she has betrayed me. If she were to enter the room at this moment I would fall at her feet and kiss her gown's hem. I do not know what will become of her or whether or not our child was born alive. I am not told such things any more and dare not ask. But the Tsar knows all.

I am reminded of one time, before all this, when he sent for me to question me on my knowledge of geometry and fortifications. I understood very little of either as they did not interest me. I was terrified, and in order not to have to attempt drawings and measurements before him I resolved to maim my hand. I took a firearm and drank plenty of wine and when I was drunk enough, pulled the firing-lock against my right palm. The blast did not go off properly and I was badly burned, that is all. I went to see the Tsar with my hand bandaged, and again I had drunk a great deal to give me courage.

"Get out, you idle wastrel," he said, his jaw grinning like a wolf's.

It may have been then that he began to think of giving the inheritance to another. He could not forgive the fact that were it mine, I would rule like my ancestors.

Some were on my side. Kikin, whom my father had raised to the Admiralty, was secretly with me. "Wait till the day comes," he would whisper, "endure all now, and wait. His excesses will not promise him a long life."

I have waited, after my fashion. But my father will outlive me. He arrested Kikin as well, and the man has been executed.

It was the Tsar who drove me to flight. No one can understand my reasons who has not spent the best part of three years in fear from day to day. First of all he sent a letter saying I was an unsatisfactory heir and that I must mend my ways, then, when Ekaterina had borne him a son who might live, he wrote to say that I was to be deprived of the succession. At first I did not greatly care provided he let me be. But gradually it became a choice between turning into what he wanted me to be, with geometry and fortifications and drilling and campaigns, or—this idea was mine—taking the tonsure and becoming a monk. I had made the last suggestion because I was desperate, but I knew it would not suit me. If it had not been for Efrosinia, I would have troubled less; monasteries are peaceful places. "The cowl is not nailed to one's head," murmured Kikin. "Your own grandsire Tsar Mikhail's father Philaret was forced into a monastery, and later disavowed it and reigned alongside his son for the rest of his days." But Philaret had not loved Efrosinia. Every man who has ever been in love will know my feelings. Moreover she would have laughed at the idea of me in a celibate's gown, and perhaps have gone off with some soldier.

"I won't ever get my backside into a boy's breeches. They'll know us at once for what we are, before we go any distance. 'S'not as though you were nobody, or looked like anyone else. Mad, I call it. But just as you say."

"You must do it, Efrosinia," I said desperately. "Look, I've cut my hair."

"That's something, for you."

It was true, and she knew it: I had been proud of my long curling locks, and felt as a woman might when the shears clipped them and they fell to the floor. I threw them on the fire and they burned. Efrosinia was struggling into the page's livery I had procured for her disguise. The room was full of the smell of burning hair.

I was to be one Khokhansky, a traveller on my own business. I would wear a wig of a dark colour, and unremarkable clothes with a hat pulled down over my eyes. Only my height could not be done away with; to stoop was only to draw attention to it. Efrosinia had by now finished her transformation and made me a leg and a bow. She could never take most things seriously. She was a squat, comic little creature in her boy's garb and a German wig with powder. I wanted to pinch her bottom in the breeches. Nobody would look twice at us once we were beyond the frontier.

"Make haste," I said, fretting because I had drunk no wine to leave my head the clearer. At the last moment, would one of my father's spies, or Menshikov's, prevent us from leaving? If that happened, I could not think beyond it.

"I'm ready, aren't I? Make haste yourself." Her eyes looked at me obliquely with their accustomed mixture of affection and contempt. I did not know whether she despised me for myself, or only because all men are to be despised by such as Efrosinia. But at least she had said she would come away with me. I knew in my heart that she probably feared arrest and questioning if she were left behind when I had gone; but I tried to pretend to myself that I was valuable to her. In any case, whatever she thought of me, I could not do without her.

"There's the carriage," she said, lifting aside the window-curtain. My heart stopped; she had no discretion, and might betray us. "For God's sake," I said, "don't let yourself be seen."

"It's dark."

It was so, only the carriage-lamps showing, and the further glow from the pleasure-boats my father had decreed should cruise up and down the Neva of an evening. We went downstairs and out to the coach and entered. I heard it rumble off with a great leaping of my heart. I crossed myself and said a prayer. There was nothing else to do now till the frontier was reached, and if we were stopped . . . if it happened. . . . "Efrosinia must be let go free," I told myself. I tried to occupy my mind with this and other things till we had trundled out of the city. At least we had not been stopped yet. Then to Riga; there should be horses waiting. After that we were to take a common post-coach for Libau, where Kikin would meet me secretly with funds. Thereafter it should be possible to lose ourselves in so large a place as Danzig, in case we were followed. The final goal was Vienna. I had resolved to go to my brother-in-law, the Austrian Emperor, who had married Charlotte's sister, and tell him my life was in danger from my father and ask for his protection. The fact that I had a page-boy with me would not arouse his anger or his wife's. Later, I could let it be known that my mistress had accompanied me.

"It's your step-mother you have to blame for it all." The country we passed through was flat and dull, and Efrosinia would chatter. "Wouldn't surprise me if she'd have you poisoned to put you out of the way, now she's got her own son." I hadn't the heart to quell her. In any case, would it not be politic to say in Vienna that the Tsaritsa was my enemy and had been unkind to Charlotte? Otherwise they might have no sympathy for me in my plight. And Ekaterina could persuade my father to anything she chose....

I would speak of it somehow. The Tsar was away in Copenhagen. He expected me to join him, and no surprise would be expressed for a time in St. Petersburg at my absence. It was a good time to go; some weeks must elapse before he could know for certain that I was no longer in Russia. In all the wide continent of Europe surely, surely there would be a place to shelter us, a roof to hide our heads?

"It's a pity you don't have a trade, like your father," Efrosinia was saying. "*He'd* have made a living wherever he went, as a blacksmith or carpenter or shipbuilder. But all you ever do except in bed is read, read, read."

I knew she despised me.

It was night when we reached Vienna. I asked to be shown the Vice-Chancellor's house and, alone and almost unannounced, I waited on him. Presently he came in his bedgown, a fussed pretentious man with formal manners. Unwittingly I thought of my father's visit to Vienna long ago and how he had shocked them there by hastening to meet the Emperor Leopold at the third window instead of the fifth.

I began to talk to the man, whose name was Schönbrun. I had drunk a great deal to give me courage for this interview, but it did not have the effect of steadying me and I heard my voice rising high like a woman's. I was suddenly full of fear that they would send me back to my father. I began to give Schönbrun all the information I had in my mind about myself, my life, my father, my fear of him, the way he and Menshikov had forced me to drink to undermine my health. I said I feared for my life under the Tsar. I said my stepmother and Menshikov were working against me and would do away with me, and had maltreated my wife. I do not know what else I said. I believed it all at the time. The shocked little Vice-Chancellor pressed more wine on me and the more I had the more I talked, and wept, and walked rapidly up and down the room. I could see that my arrival was something that had never happened before in diplomatic circles and that it had taken them at a loss.

At first they had not believed I was myself. Now they believed it. The Emperor should be informed of my visit, the Vice-Chancellor said soothingly. "Without delay?" I said, knowing something of the time such things can take and the hands that have to be bribed before anything at all is done about it, at least in Russia.

"Without delay." He bowed low, and I went out into the night. He sent his officials to follow me and see that I was reasonably housed.

I never saw Emperor Charles VI. We were lodged at first in Weierburg near Vienna and then taken in great secrecy to the castle of Ehrenberg in the Tyrol. It was a solitary place of gorges and pine trees and high mountains. I felt closed in, nameless—the very servants in the castle had not been informed who I was—and passed my days with books, my nights with Efrosinia. Lying with her in the close-drawn, intimate warmth of the bed-curtains, it was possible to imagine that I was back in my mother's womb. I nuzzled my face in Efrosinia's armpit and smelled her odour and let her talk baby-talk to me, or bite me, as she would. She had remained placid through all our changes of residence. "I'm pregnant," she told me once, as if she were talking about the weather. "Know anything about it? I swear you do."

Her child I knew would be incredibly dear to me, dearer by far than Charlotte's two children whom I had barely seen or come to know, and who were the property of the nation. Perhaps we could live on here out of the reach of the world, I thought; perhaps my father would never find us. I knew that, by this time, he must be searching.

I asked to be sent an Orthodox confessor, but this was refused. In Vienna they think of us as heretics.

They found where I was hidden. In the end, they found me.

There is a devil whom my father employs and his name is Peter Tolstoy. He has endured many things for the Tsar and my father trusts him. Tolstoy has no mercy and no sensitiveness; there is nothing too cruel, too brutal for him. It was only after his arrival in Vienna that the pursuit of me quickened. They told the Emperor—it was not true, I knew nothing, I swear—that the Mecklenburg guard was ready to kill my father and place the Tsaritsa in a convent, and then the government was to be given to me. It is true, and I know it, that the people have long wanted me, and have hated my father.

The Tsar sent a letter to the Emperor concerning me. Later it was shown to me by a secretary. In it my father requested my brother-in-law to send me back to him under escort of officers. When I heard this I broke down. I walked from room to room of the castle sobbing like a woman. I remember meeting Efrosinia in a doorway. Her eyes looked at me in the way I knew and there was contempt in them. She said nothing. The Finns have a belief in fate.

Presently the Emperor's secretary caught up with me. He began to talk to me in a low voice. "All will be well," he kept saying, "all will yet be well." I was to be sent, it appeared, in further great secrecy to Naples, a place ruled also by the Austrian Emperor. Surely this, I thought, would be far enough away; surely there was somewhere in the world beyond the reach of my father, his spies, Tolstoy, the rest. I had to drink a great deal on the journey. Efrosinia was dressed as a page again. The child hadn't started to show yet. She felt the heat as we journeyed south. I felt nothing. I did not care where I went, to frozen wastes or burning deserts, so long as my father's arm could not reach out and drag me home.

It was all useless. They followed us all the way to Naples, hiding themselves.

This was the time when Tolstoy threatened the Emperor with war if I were not delivered up to my father.

They were cunning. They embroiled not only the Emperor with threats of war, but my mother-in-law, the Duchess of Wolfenbüttel, who was at the Viennese Court. The Tsar would punish her grandchildren, it was implied, if I were not returned to Russia. The Duchess wrote to me begging me to go home. By now the Emperor was persuaded to let Tolstoy and the other Tsar's man, Rumiantsev, see me; he had prevented their doing so at Ehrenberg, but he did not desire war. They came upon me suddenly, Tolstoy with his winning ways of diplomacy and Rumiantsev with his great height and strength; physically he is like my father. "You have come to kill me," I cried. They should have done so then. They tried to persuade me to return with them but I would not be persuaded.

Soon I became aware of a change in the manners of the Emperor's representative in Naples, who had at first been welcoming. His courtesy did not alter, but it acquired an oily quality, as though he wrung his hands to protest his own innocence. It was made clear in indirect fashion that the Emperor was alarmed at my father's threat of war if I were not returned; he would not force me to an issue but would, in fact, be relieved if on my own accord I should go home. How can one stay on with an unwilling host? Efrosinia was right and I should have been able to earn my living in some obscure way and never more be found or recognised. But I could not, and now it was too late.

Worse came. I blame Tolstoy for it: he was old in such games. They came several times; they must have bribed the Viceroy's men to let them in. First of all they said my father was coming with an army to Italy, to dig me out. After they had gone I said to Efrosinia that we were no longer safe here and must appeal to the Pope. She looked at me with her unfathomable eyes and said, "Don't be a fool. The Pope thinks you're a heretic. Didn't you say so yourself, at Ehrenberg? He won't protect you; why should he?"

I wept. Presently Tolstoy and the others came back. This time they were triumphant as they had found the right solution. "We have orders to take away the woman," Tolstoy said, looking me between the eyes. I knew then that their bribes must have been large ones. Nothing would prevent them from taking Efrosinia; an appeal to Vienna would be too late.

She was all I had. Looking back I still do not find it strange that I gave way then. Efrosinia herself was sullen and said little; she was still feeling the heat and the child grew in her. Perhaps for enough money she would have left me of her own accord. I was certain of nothing and nobody; I drank, whored with her and wept. "I'd be glad to see the north again," said Efrosinia. "Can't make a page out of me now, can you, eh? The front's as big as the back."

She strolled to the narrow stone window of that place, which was called St. Elmo, and looked out at the arid land and sky. There may be some who flourish best in the south but they are not our people, who were reared in mist and snow.

If they took Efrosinia, I thought, I might as well die. If I agreed to return to Russia, perhaps my father would permit my marriage with her. After all he himself had married a woman who was low-born. I would do anything, sign anything to be allowed to keep Efrosinia. I would travel anywhere.

I said I would go back to Russia with them. They looked at one another, bowed low, and left. Later they returned, and did not leave me even when I made it clear I was weary of their company.

There is a shrine to St. Nicholas at Bari and I went there and prayed beside the blue heedless Adriatic. I tried to seek guidance, but Tolstoy and Rumiantsev stayed with me all the time now and never left me. I felt cut off from God.

Later on our journey I saw Rome, which I had longed to do. I was between the same gaolers, however; it would have been impossible to see the Pope. The ancient grandeur of the city, where I should have liked to linger, passed me by as in a drunken dream. It hardly seems true now that I was indeed there and was able to say to myself, "This is Rome; this was once the heart of the world, as Moscow is the heart of Russia." They would not let me stop to look at a single arch, a single broken column. I shall never see Rome again, or any other place.

It was the same, or rather worse, in Vienna. I could see the familiar shape of St. Stephen's, the Hofburg, the places I knew already from our earlier halt at Weierburg. I said to Tolstoy, "Let us pay the Emperor a visit." I felt, however foolishly, that if I and my brother-in-law came face to face many things would be better understood. Besides, I wanted

to thank him for his kindness. He had done his best to shelter me and had only been deterred by the threat of war. My father's name was dreaded after Poltava.
Tolstoy's face lacked expression. He said carefully, "There could be no purpose in such a visit."
"I want to see him—to thank him——"
"Our orders are to proceed direct to Moscow."
"It would not delay us long——"
"Our orders are to proceed."
Did the Emperor indeed still think of me as a free agent? I was hustled through Vienna like a State prisoner, Rumiantsev my gaoler and Tolstoy my judge. No doubt by now my father had written to Charles VI in honeyed terms, which he knows very well how to use in letters. He had written also to me, promising me a full pardon. But my heart was sick when we crossed the Russian frontier. Now I know my misgivings had reason. Perhaps the news that will soon reach the Emperor will convince him that I was not raving, in the beginning, when I said to Schönbrun that the Tsar desired my life. Peter Alexievich is not such a loving father, despite his letters, despite his promises.

I was brought before him at last in Moscow. He deliberately chose the old capital for this humiliation of me.
He sat on his throne. On this occasion he did not seek to resemble a carpenter, a shipbuilder, a bombardier, or give the glory to his buffoon he calls the King of Pressburg. He was himself. He wore the gleaming robe of the Tsars of Muscovy and surrounding him were all the nobility of Church and State.
I was brought in without my sword.
I had prepared a speech. Nothing of it remained in my mind now. I fell on my knees. I heard the voice above me, cold and remote as a heathen god's. God sat on His own throne, mocking me.
"What do you want of us?"
I felt the saliva drool from my mouth; I was a drunkard, an animal. I quavered a reply and felt the contempt in which I was held; it weighed me down.
"My life, and mercy."

The travesty proceeded. I do not remember what else was said. They had taken Efrosinia away and I did not know where she was; my plea to be allowed to marry her if I returned to Russia had come to nothing, although my father had promised it, in writing, but I dared not remind him. How many things he had promised! But seeing him as he was that day, robed and surrounded by supporters who feared and would obey him, I myself was filled with more fear than ever before in my life. I knew, now, without any further doubt, that he would soon kill me.

Can there still be more to say? The rest was degradation. He kept me by him and presently Efrosinia was brought back so that she could see to what I had been brought. My father's intentions were as clear as if I could see them in a mirror. The weeks passed, the months passed, and he asked questions, questions all the time. Often he used to beat me in front of Efrosinia. She was wearing a new satin dress. I could see that she had given birth to the child, but dared not ask where it was or what had become of it. I remember most clearly the antics of the seal in the fountain at the summer-palace of Petrodvorets, where we all three drove or walked up and down, up and down. The Tsar let me assume that he tolerated Efrosinia's presence. No doubt he thought that there were matters he still did not know of, and would learn in this way. But Efrosinia said nothing on our drives and walks. I think the Tsar had already questioned her and she had told him everything he wanted to know, or that she knew. Perhaps he had threatened to flog her. She would have become like a howling animal at the threat of pain. Women are physical cowards.

In the end we returned to Petersburg. The Tsar could do whatever he chose there, free of the support I was said to have in Moscow. We still supped together. How often have I eaten and drunk beside my father, my murderer!

They had already questioned my mother about my visits, which I had never altogether ceased, and sent her to the further convent at Ladoga and killed her lover. They tortured and killed all those whom I had been tricked into naming as my accomplices or as those who had aided me. The only one to escape was Vyazhemsky the tutor, whom the Tsar pardoned. Why do I think of him now? I do not know what I said when I was drunk. I am sober now. It has been said of me that I made no effort to save my mother, my friends, my servants from the Tsar's anger. How could I save them when I could not save myself? From the hour of my birth this has been coming upon me.

I do not know at what hour they will arrive, Menshikov and the rest. They will take me away to prison and to torture. Soon there will be nothing but the pain, the pain. . . . I pray for death. Perhaps I will die soon.

SEVEN

THE EMPRESS: ABSALOM

The birth of Peter Petrovich, our Shishenka, happened at a bad time for his half-brother. In fact my husband altered the date of a letter he had already written to the Tsarevich just before the birth. He had in any case been thinking of finding a more satisfactory heir, and though he did not fully commit himself to this in the letter, he described Alexis as the idle servant who hid his talent in the earth. "I will wholly cut thee off from the succession, like a gangrenous limb," he wrote, adding triumphantly, "Do not say to thyself that thou art the only son I have and that this is only written to frighten."

Alexis however was already so frightened that nowadays he was hardly ever sober. Efrosinia, drink, and peace seemed to be all he wanted. He took no interest in his two little children. As for other things, the Tsar had already been made very angry by the discovery that Alexis had been visiting Evdokiya in her convent. This to me was natural enough and would cheer the poor woman, but Peter also knew—and by now it was one of the chief causes of his rage against Alexis—that no matter how many sons I bore they would still, in the people's eyes, be bastards, children of a concubine. The glittering public wedding had meant nothing to them. Evdokiya was the Tsaritsa, Evdokiya's son would in time be Tsar, and all would be as it had been before the coming of Antichrist. They said nothing and showed no anger, only waited, and prayed for Evdokiya.

"I will disinherit Alexis," Peter said again and again, glancing sometimes at the cradle in which Shishenka lay asleep, his round cheek having put on flesh, his mouth milky. When he was awake he would laugh if we shook his rattle, and try to grasp it. His father adored him. Perhaps Peter Petrovich would grow into a fine man who understood geometry and fortifications. All this was in the Tsar's mind, as I knew. Peter himself strode up and down the nursery, and presently announced that he would give Alexis the chance to become a monk. "It is what they used to do in the old days with those of whom they wanted to be rid," he said. "It is an old-fashioned cure; that should please him."

Alexis accepted this prospect so meekly that I was not surprised when Anisa told me that his friends had advised him that a cowl need not after all be nailed to one's head. Meantime the Tsarevich sent cringing letters to his father. "Though I had no brother, now, thank God, I have a brother who is in good health," he wrote. He commended his own motherless children to the Tsar's care. "Your most humble son and slave, Alexis," seemed to have no more spirit left in him. On receiving this particular letter his father took ill. This time the fits were very bad, and Peter took the last sacraments. Then he grew better. "It was all a pretence," said Alexis' advisers. I think, myself, rage saved Peter.

"It is the long-beards who advise my son," he said repeatedly. There were still such persons left in Russia, wearing their tax-token pinned to their adornment. Presently a priest came with Alexis' written submission and the agreement that he would enter a monastery. They are uncomfortable places, as I knew from Thorn. At the same time the young man himself was desperately trying to scrape together enough money for Efrosinia to live in comfort in his absence. Meanwhile, I spoke very cautiously to the Tsar. "If they are able to say afterwards that you forced him to take vows, those will be worth nothing," I said, "like Philaret's." Philaret Romanov had been the father of Tsar Mikhail and his enemies had forced him to take the cowl, which he quitted on his son's becoming Tsar and for many years ruled with him. Peter grunted in reply, but did no more about the matter; war threatened again and he set off for Denmark. I was left with my son. I was beginning to be troubled about Shishenka. He was slow in learning to walk, and the sounds he made could not as yet be called words or anything like them. I was full of fears that he might turn out to be slow of wit and tongue-tied, like

Peter's half-brother Ivan. What a curse lay on that family! But perhaps my strong peasant blood would save Shishenka; perhaps he would learn to walk and talk in time, and gain strength, and grow to be a man like his father. In the meantime, there was still another hope. I was pregnant again. I hoped that it would not prevent my forthcoming visit to Europe with the Tsar. Everything was prepared for that, and both I myself and my women would suffer great disappointment if we might not go. It would be less strenuous than riding on campaign; I would be in a coach, with soft beds to sleep in on the way. There should be no danger.

I was smiling, and the smile had grown stiff on my face; inside myself I was very unhappy. Stiff, also, was the giant household guard drawn up in formation before the palace of the King of Prussia. They were all of them giants, like Peter Alexievich. He had promised King Frederick William a hundred such men, and had brought a hundred and fifty. Frederick William was delighted. Like the Tsar, he was a huge man, and the two enormous creatures roared greetings and slapped one another on the back and lit their pipes and smoked and drank to the confusion of King George I of England. One had to be careful, however, because that insolent and newly-crowned monarch was the father of Frederick William's Queen, whom he still called Fifi. She had been the little girl whose hair the Tsar had ruffled long ago on his first visit to Europe, and now she was a full-blown young woman with children of her own. Two of these, a cowed boy called Frederick, and a sharp little girl of nine years old named Wilhelmina, caused a part of my discomfort. It was evident in the glance of the Princess of Prussia that I was low-born and a dowd. She may have been only nine, but she had the eyes of an old woman. The Tsar kissed her all over her face and she boxed his ears. I did not like Wilhelmina and she did not like me, but we preserved courtly manners to one another and I even caressed the little bitch in my turn. She went on staring at my dress. I had been proud of it; it was the one which had the double-headed eagle of Romanov sewn on with feathers and diamonds. Now I felt the dress was a bundle, the feathers ridiculous and the diamonds too small to be worth mentioning, and my hands and feet seemed like boats. "You are not even a consort," said the Princess's glance. "You are a concubine, and a laundress, and getting fat, and you do not know how to conduct yourself at a civilised court; one does not stand about and say nothing." I still thought it was the best thing to do, and smiled on; but I have not often been made to feel low-born or unsuitable since I first took up with Peter Alexievich, and when it happens it hurts me. But one can always smile.

Something had happened lately which was worse than that. It was because George I of England was also Elector of Hanover, and at the moment unfriendly to Russia. I had gone alone through Hanover in my coach, on my way to join the Tsar, and the coach was stopped by the crowds and they burst open the door and stuck their hostile faces inside, and thrust and jostled me. As a result I lost my baby. He was a boy and would have been christened Paul. The Tsar was furious with the Hanoverians and it did not improve his relations with King George. I made myself stop thinking of Paul and started worrying again about Shishenka. I had hated leaving him behind. This made me feel worse than before, so instead I tried to understand what was happening about foreign relations and why we were now in Prussia.

The beginning of it all had been that Peter had made marriages in Europe for two of his nieces, which was a triumph. The first had been Anna who was already married to the Duke of Courland. She was a daughter of Tsar Ivan V and Praskovia of the pancakes, and she was a greedy, mean young woman I had never liked, but I was sorry to hear that her marriage was unhappy and that the Duke of Courland was given to unnatural vice. The second bride, her sister Catherine, was to marry the Duke of Mecklenburg. Catherine was a harmless creature and I wished her well. Unfortunately, as a despatch from England put it, the first wife of the Duke of Mecklenburg had not yet been properly divorced. Instead of the marriage the English had offered us an alliance, but by the time word reached my husband it was too late and the wedding was over.

The King of England continued to display bad manners. He ordered his admiral, Norris, to seize all Russian ships and also, if possible, the person of the Tsar. This was because Peter had promised the town of Wismar as part of the Mecklenburg dowry, and England kept a wary eye on happenings in the Baltic. However, Admiral Norris, a big red-faced man with a snowy peruke, whom my husband already knew, had refused to carry out the order: it had been sent in the name of the Elector of Hanover, not the King of England. George always thought of himself first as a Hanoverian, which was a source of great chagrin to the English, not all of whom had wanted him in the first place. "Tell them," growled Peter, "that we have enough Jacobites living in the Nemenskaya Sloboda outside Moscow to man a squadron of warships, if it should come to that." It was however doubtful if the Jacobites would want to go back home; as I have said they had made themselves very comfortable in the Sloboda now for some generations, and had grown richer than they would have done in Scotland.

The English also feared that we would join with Charles of Sweden to oust King George and bring back his rival, the son of the Catholic James II. Perhaps the English do not understand the workings of other minds in such matters. Nothing would have induced my husband to ally himself with Charles, after Poltava and the Pruth and Golotchkina, where the Swedes had defeated the Russians early in that war. They were still our natural enemies.

However nothing seemed to solve the problem of who should have Wismar. The port was desired by England, Saxony, Denmark, Mecklenburg and Sweden. A contingent of our own had already been sent there and forced to turn back. My husband kept his temper.

"I will go to meet the King of Denmark," he said. As he grew older the truth was borne in on Peter Alexievich that it is better to meet, to talk, to drink together, than to fight. He went to Denmark, therefore, but it was a disappointment. In return for the doubtful friendship of the Danes, Peter was asked to make another attack on the Swedish mainland. As it happened, he fell ill again at this point and went to take the waters at Pyrmont.

Afterwards, he went down to Warnemunde where he supervised the arrival of stores. But the Danes did nothing, even though the Tsar sailed to meet them at the head of his fleet. The fuss and delay of the Danish Court, where everyone stands on dignity, made him impatient and in the end he sent for me. This made me happy again. I was sorry when Peter was miserable, but it was a joyful thing that it was still myself he wanted, stout and growing old as I was. I could still pillow his head on my breast, still stroke his hair; it had not grown thin with the years. "The Tsar has given every one of the Tsarina's waiting-women a baby," wrote Princess Wilhelmina in her diary. It did not matter, though the diary was read and widely talked of. I expect she wrote it with the help of her governess.

Copenhagen was flat, dull, greedy, and afraid. Neither of us liked it and I was made to feel out of place as I had been in Prussia. In the end the Tsar, twitching with rage, set sail for the north to see what had become of the supplies, and on the way back he surprised much Swedish shipping concealed in the bays and inlets. They were making ready for war, he wrote to me. "There are at least twenty thousand men."

They opened fire on him and almost sank his ship. As before, like the time when three bullets failed to pierce him at Poltava, there was a miracle. Peter escaped, but perhaps this second deliverance made him face the fact that he could not live forever. As soon as he had time he wrote again to the Tsarevich Alexis, asking him to come to Copenhagen.

But Alexis did not come.

The Tsar left me at Amsterdam while he went on to Paris. I was happy enough among the cheerful, friendly, hardworking Dutch. I had not wanted to risk sneers at Versailles, the most polished court in the world. The Tsar travelled on there and met the Regent, who everyone said had sold his soul to the devil, and also the little King, Louis XV, who was only seven years old. Peter tossed him up in his arms and later carried him up the grand staircase, I think the notion had already come to him that this little boy would make a husband for our Elizabeth. The stiff and formal courtiers were much abashed at his informal way of handling the King.

He went to see the aged widow of Louis XIV, Madame de Maintenon. This lady had been the governess fo the late King's bastard children by his beautiful mistress, Athénaïs de Montespan. After she was accused of witchcraft Louis dismissed her, and shortly set this surprising woman in her place and married her on the death of his first wife. Madame de Maintenon was not beautiful, and very devout and strait-laced. I asked Peter afterwards what she looked like. "Oh, she was in bed," he said, "and had drawn the curtains so that her face was in darkness. But I pulled them back and had a good look at her. She may have been handsome once."

He was never anyone but himself. Back in Prussia, the night of my reception by Wilhelmina, we had had a banquet. In course of it Peter Alexievich began his convulsions, which often happened. I was used to them, but the Queen of Prussia was much alarmed; there was a knife in Peter's shaking hand and she was afraid it would harm her. He said, "Do not be troubled," and tried to grasp her wrist to reassure her, but the grip of Peter Alexievich is not soft. Fifi squealed, and the Tsar laughed loudly and told the company my bones were not so flimsy.

Perhaps, in the end, I scored over Wilhelmina.

Denmark and England continued to cause the Tsar annoyance. But the worst news was of Alexis, and when I could I sent for Alexasha Menshikov who would know what had happened while we had been away. Alexasha said the Tsarevich had visited him in his palace in Petersburg, pretending that he was going to join the Tsar in Denmark and borrowing money for the journey. Then he fled abroad. We found out fairly soon what his first movements were. He had gone as far as Libau with Efrosinia, then disguised himself while she put on a page's clothes and wig. After that there was no further trace of them, though the Tsar sent out enquiries to all the foreign Courts.

He himself was still occupied with the Danes, who by now had barricaded Copenhagen in the mistaken idea that the Tsar meant to make war on themselves. Whether or not he was still ready to attack Sweden once more no longer mattered. "A waste of time," said the Tsar. He made himself, I think, speak rather of war than of Alexis. At least Frederick William of Prussia remained his friend. Before we had all parted that time, Peter received an amber cabinet and a yacht, in exchange for the hundred and fifty giants. As Frederick William was known to be close-fisted, this was handsome.

So ended our tour of Europe.

I can remember the first blessing of the Neva, and many later. There had always been an annual ceremony at Moscow, which was one of the few where the Tsar behaved like his ancestors and submitted to being blessed in a golden robe and, on his head, when the ice melted, the Cap of Monomakh. I think this was because all his life he had felt the call of the rivers and the sea. He did not resent the waters; he respected them. Now that St. Petersburg was our new capital there had, naturally, to be a similar rejoicing there. However it was not at the melting, but at the freezing of the ice. This meant that the roads were hard and passable by sledge, and many of the boyars and their wives came to live in the town-houses they had built, although these still rocked on their swampy foundations in the warmer weather.

A hundred fools were kept by the Tsar, and there were his monsters and his dwarfs and two negroes who had lately been sent to him. At the freezing of the ice there was a parade of fools. When the ice would bear it was first tested by iron rods, then a clown stepped out upon it and beat a drum. How often and in how many places have I heard drums beating! But this was not for war; it was not even to remind us of the homeless families from Taganrog and the Black Sea ports, or the massacred people of Moldavia. A great flag was unfurled, and everybody was in a spirit of carnival or, if they were not, must seem so. The fools danced and made play with their axes and shovels and hooks. At Zotov's wedding to the young girl, which I have spoken of already, they wore costumes made of cat's tails. The Tsar and I wore Frisian peasant costume, and I kept mine to wear again at the celebrations for the Peace of Nystadt.

Follies, whims, dance in front of me. There were bears let loose; there was a blind man of a hundred years old, with coloured lanterns hanging from his dark spectacles. Rodomanovsky, whom the Tsar called King of Pressburg and before whom he pretended to lay all his victories, wound a barrel-organ on the ice. Bands played, fireworks exploded, and everyone who could do so beat on drums. The sound of the drums will go with me, I think, when death comes. They remind me of the Tsar himself, the best drummer in Russia, beating, always beating a tattoo to which the rest of us must march and dance, or if we would not we were hurled beyond the fitful light cast by the pitch-fires and coloured lanterns and fireworks. Even an elephant came and knelt; it had been a present to Peter from the Shah of Persia. Everyone obeyed, and made merry; everyone except the Tsarevich Alexis. In the days when he was still among us he showed no pleasure at such scenes, and afterwards, after he was gone, the feasting and the merriment rose to such a height as to seem the screaming of madmen, the crying out of fools.

It is a pity that Alexis did not come to his father and face him. Peter would have respected honesty, but he has never understood fear. The flight of the Tsarevich hurt him deeply, and as time went on he became angry, like a bear. It took many months to pick up the trail of the missing Tsarevich and his mistress: in fact, we might not have done so if a clerk in Alexis' employment, at the Austrian Emperor's castle of Ehrenberg in the Tyrol, had not betrayed his master for money. Alexis had been so carefully hidden away that most of the servants and peasants in the villages nearby did not know the name of the tall thin man who was living in the castle. He had been calling himself Khokansky. Efrosinia was with him and had they not been discovered, it is possible that they would have stayed there till Alexis died in bed.

He had fled to the Emperor. Dead Charlotte's sister was Empress of Austria and her mother was living at the Viennese Court. Alexis arrived at the Vice-Chancellor's residence without warning, at night; at first he had difficulty in convincing the servants that he was indeed the Tsarevich, and on being admitted at last, flung himself into a chair and talked wildly and long. Among other things he said that I wished to poison him, but chiefly he blamed his father. "If I return it will mean my death," he said over and over again. "The Tsar means to kill me. He has given me no peace since my wife bore children," and so on. The embarrassed Vice-Chancellor consulted an equally embarrassed Emperor. They were sorry for Alexis, but did not wish to upset relations with St. Petersburg. In the end Alexis, with his mistress, was sent to Ehrenberg, which was remote enough to make his discovery unlikely. But the Tsar's men found him.

After he was found he was sent under the Emperor's guard to the castle of St. Elmo, in Naples, for greater safety. Efrosinia was still with him; Alexis would not be parted from her. He was already frozen with terror, and the letters the Tsar wrote promising forgiveness meant nothing to him; he knew that his life depended on his staying out of Russia. If he had not been a coward I think he would have taken poison himself instead of blaming it on me. "My stepmother and Menshikov will see me tortured, poisoned," he wrote and said again and again. I had tried to be his friend. Why did he blame me so harshly? Later he was to write to me, abjectly, to intercede for him with the Tsar. He wrote three times and I did what I could. But by then it was too late. Peter would not forgive him.

The Tsar's men, Tolstoy and Rumiantsev, had not been permitted to see Alexis at Ehrenberg; it was made difficult for them to do so even at St. Elmo, but they contrived it. The Emperor was disposed to pity the Tsarevich and to be rid of such pity, Peter's envoy, Tolstoy—he had been ridiculed and imprisoned for us in Constantinople—brought his intelligence to bear to think of a plan. In the end he succeeded by deluding Alexis. It was whispered that Efrosinia would be taken away from him; that if he did not submit to his father the Russian armies would march into Austria and make war. Peter's reputation since Poltava was a fierce and alarming one. There is no doubt that the Emperor was wavering.

Last of all, they went to Charlotte's mother. The Duchess of Wolfenbüttel wrote to Alexis begging him to return to Russia lest vengeance fall on his two children, Peter and Natalia. He had cared so little for them that it is strange that this argument was the one which by the end won him over. Secure, as the Emperor thought, in the promise of the Tsar's pardon for Alexis, the Tsarevich left Naples in the company of Tolstoy, Rumiantsev, captain of the guard, who had been ordered to kidnap Alexis if he would not come, and lastly Efrosinia.

They hurried him through Vienna. He was not permitted to visit the Emperor, his brother-in-law. Offence was taken at this, but by then the journey was more than half over and the party was within sight of the Russian frontier. Efrosinia was about to give birth to Alexis' child and they left her at Riga, on the Gulf of Finland. I do not know what happened to the child. It was not a part of the Tsar's plan. Afterwards, he himself was to question Efrosinia and her statements helped to condemn her lover.

What was the truth of it? It may indeed have been that those who hated Peter's reforms saw hope in his heir. This is why Alexis was doomed; but it was wrong to promise him forgiveness and then withdraw the promise. A great many things about Alexis' story are wrong. Perhaps there is some way in which I am to blame, but I did what I could, which was the same as doing nothing. In the events which followed I had no voice at all.

Shishenka staggered a few steps on his thin little legs. We were in the new palace the Tsar had had built for me, which still smelt of damp plaster. It had shutters with flower-bunches painted on, like the small old house only grander. Down in the city there were now rows of wooden houses like that we had lived in, and government officials worked there.

"Come, then," said the Tsar to Peter Petrovich, his new heir. "Faster, faster." He spoke gently. He was never anything but tender with the delicate little boy. Shishenka tried to run to him and tripped and fell, and began to cry. His giant of a father picked him up and comforted him.

"Perhaps he will grow stronger," he said to me afterwards, when the child was back with his nurse. "When I was his age I was very quiet and shy. Picture it now!"

I laughed, to cheer him and myself. We both knew by now that Shishenka would never be strong, but we did not say so to one another.

Alexis had gone before that to pray at the shrine of St. Nicholas. Tolstoy and Rumiantsev stood by him, like a bodyguard. The wretched man knew no peace through prayer. He went on to Rome. There a letter from his father was brought to him. "Thou askest forgiveness," Peter wrote. "I now confirm it. Of that you may be certain." He added that other wishes expressed by Alexis would be granted, but did not put in words the plea of marriage to Efrosinia. Tolstoy had already seized on this as likely to offend the Emperor by casting a slur on Charlotte's memory. The net was tightening.

At Petersburg, the Tsar received bad news and came to me with it. "Zotov is dead," he said briefly. Doubtless the famous marriage had sped the elderly bridegroom's departing. Somewhere in my mind I recalled hearing that Zotov had tutored a small boy named Peter Alexievich in the Kremlin in the old days, and that every lesson was started with the swinging of censers and blessing of the books. "He taught me nothing of use," Peter used to say briefly. It had been in scorn for the old man's lack of learning that he had afterwards made him Archpriest of Mirth. Now there must be a new one. I sat in my carriage and watched the procession of voters, headed by the Tsar in a scarlet cloak which flared bravely in the light of pitch-fires. Drums beat again; there was the sound of fifes and singing. One of the dwarfs dressed all in black came bearing the list of candidates' names in a book. Behind him, lying on a door carried shoulder-high by peasants, were two drunken men, as Bacchus and Silenus. They brandished chamber-pots and were very drunk. Last of all came Caesar, laurel wreath and all. The procession and the noise and fifing and laughter passed on into Zotov's house where the voting was to take place. After they had all gone the tar-fires spluttered and the night seemed dark, and I went home to Shishenka.

It was after that—they had in the end elected a man named Buturlin as the new Archpriest of Mirth—that Alexis was brought back to Moscow. My husband set out at once. I did not go with him.

It was Alexasha who brought me the news of the conspiracy. He came to me where I sat with my son in the Ekaterinhofsky, on a winter's day when the sconces were lit early. By the light of candles old men look young, and women too; and a delicate little boy less waxen. Alexasha took up one of Shishenka's toys and made droll play with it, so that the little fellow reached out for it and laughed. He was affectionate and fond of playthings and kisses. I had been happy with him, for lacking the Tsar St. Petersburg was a peaceful place, with the sledges gliding noiselessly past under my windows and the gardens sleeping under a drift of snow. Perhaps next year my son will be playing with snowballs, I thought; but not yet, not quite yet.

I looked at Alexasha, who had bowed low before me on entering; his manners were always polished and courteous, as though I had been of royal blood. For moments I wanted to laugh at our solemn ways with one another. This was the pieman, my one-time lover whom I had often seen beaten with the Tsar's stick. But he was also the brave commander who had helped win the Tsar's wars, and who had rescued me from Sheremetev in a time so long ago it was forgotten except when I chose to remember it. I chose to do so now. I looked at Menshikov's face, seeing despite the gentle light the lines and pouches of debauchery, the sideways glance of the eyes that reminded me of Mazeppa, the traitorous Cossack Hetman long ago. Court life and intrigue makes one appear thus. Menshikov had to be constantly watchful to keep his place, I thought. And I? But I was assured of the affection of Peter Alexievich. I was the mother of his son.

Suddenly I thought of Evdokiya, locked in her convent these many years. She too had borne a son to Peter Alexievich. I listened to Menshikov idly. He was talking now about a man named Alexander Kikin whom I remembered slightly; he was the kind of harmless, goodnatured creature one meets in palace corridors, but never in a position of influence. He was known to dislike Menshikov.

"—and we put him to the torture, Serene Majesty, and he admitted everything. I have sent him on to Moscow. The Tsarevich is to be questioned further to find out who are his other accomplices."

My mind rushed back to the present, this room, what Menshikov had been saying. "Torture?" I heard myself asking, and remembered Kikin's harmless, fleshy face. I put Shishenka from me into his little chair. He would repeat nothing; he could not speak yet. "Tell me all of it," I said to Menshikov.

They had made the Tsarevich kneel before his father to promise submission. In the Cathedral of the Assumption they had made him swear by God in the Trinity to renounce the succession for ever for himself and his descendants. They had forced him to acknowledge Peter Petrovich, my little son, as the rightful heir. Then they had gone on to destroy Alexis. He was not to be permitted to retire to the country and marry Efrosinia. He was not even to be given a monk's cowl. He was to be destroyed as surely as God destroyed the cities of wickedness. But Alexis was not wicked, only weak.

The questioning had spread not only to poor Kikin, but to hundreds of those who perhaps knew and blessed the name of the Tsarevich, no more. They may have been those who drank his health alongside his father's at the time of the Poltava celebrations. Even Evdokiya in her convent was not spared. She was found to be living not the life of a nun, but of a woman; she had a lover. His name was Stefan Glebov and he was a soldier, and a brave one. He was put to death after long torture, first by being stretched on nailed boards for three days, then by gradual impaling on a wooden spike. The Tsar came to watch him in his death agony.

Glebov spat in his face.

Evdokiya was made to shave her head and live as a nun in a stricter convent nearer Petersburg, so that she might be watched. Many of the nuns in her former convent at Suzdal were knouted. Evdokiya's crime was not the affair with Glebov, but that her son had been to visit her. There were smaller affairs; a noble lady who had spread gossip from convent to convent was birched in full view of the drawn-up guard, then made to become a Princess-Abbess of debauchery in exchange for forgiveness. The trouble was that the Bishop of Rostov had had a vision. He had prophesied that Evdokiya and Peter should reign again together on a joint throne, that Evdokiya would bear two more sons to Peter, and that their names should be said together in the nation's prayers. I was not to be prayed for. The Bishop was degraded, tortured, questioned, broken on the wheel, then had his guts torn out and his severed head set on a pole.

As for Kikin, his torture by Menshikov was only the beginning, though all he had done was to advise Alexis to flee. In Moscow he was given twenty-five strokes of the knout, then made to write a statement which meant nothing and helped no one. Finally he was executed, not swiftly. Other friends of Alexis were brought to Moscow in chains, questioned, tortured, beheaded or sent to Siberia. A clerk who had refused to swear fealty to my son, and who admitted to faith in Alexis, was tortured three times, then broken. One could go on repeating such tales.

In all this time no bodily hurt had been done to the Tsarevich. I give Alexis that name purposely; I meant him no harm. He had been kept in his father's company after swearing the oath of renunciation in the Cathedral; he was too much afraid to say a word for his friends, a word for his mother. But when he was taken with the Tsar to meet Efrosinia, who had borne her child and was afterwards brought to Petersburg, he broke down. I believe Efrosinia was the one person Alexis truly loved in the whole of his life. And she betrayed him.

Spring came to St. Petersburg. Down at Petrodvorets, the palace which my husband had begun for himself which was to rival Versailles, there was smooth grass and smooth water, and young buds bursting their coats. The Tsar walked there with two puppets, jerked on strings; Alexis Petrovich and Efrosinia. They were made to praise the grass, the rising stone palace, the fountains, the water. They must walk and eat with the Tsar day after day, and be questioned by him. Sometimes for whole days he would ask nothing. Yet again, on others, he would fall upon Alexis and beat him with his *doubina*. This unmanning of a man before his woman was not needed. Efrosinia had already told the Tsar all he needed to know.

"She did not put up any fight," he had said contemptuously; he had come to me after first questioning the Finnish woman in the fortress. "When I threatened to have her flogged she came out with everything; how he'd babbled to her this and that, including his happiness when he heard there was a mutiny in the army here. A mutiny, indeed! They know I'd have their heads for any such thing. That was a lie."

If it was a lie, I was thinking, there was no harm done in the matter. But I did not say so to Peter Alexievich. He was striding up and down with the look on his face of a wild animal, the look I knew. There was a time—had it been in Prussia—when he'd noticed a marble statue of a man with an erected phallus, and said to me, "Kiss it, Katinka." I wasn't going to make a fool of myself in front of our hosts, and I refused, and he grew ugly and shouted, "Kiss it or I will have your head off." He was like that now. There was nothing to be done but obey, and listen. He was in a mood to crush whatever opposed him.

He went on talking about what Alexis had told his mistress. "She says he read in a gazette that Shishenka was ill. When he read it he laughed and said, 'Father wants things his way, but God will win.' You say nothing; do you not care for your son?"

"You know I do," I said, and let him rave on. More had been said, or claimed to have been said, to Efrosinia. The woman was like a slow heavy animal, without attraction that I could see. Others seldom know why love is inspired between this woman, that man. Alexis loved Efrosinia as he had never loved Charlotte. Yet Charlotte, had she been alive, would have tried to shield him. Efrosinia had given way at the first threat. The shame of it was that the Finnish serf was still with Alexis; by his side, night and day, known to be informing against him while he could not do without her. The devil reigned in St. Petersburg that spring, as he had done in Moscow, and at Suzdal.

"He wrote to the bishops to say that on my death—ay, that—he would leave Petersburg to rot. He said he would make Moscow the capital again, fail to keep up an army and navy, make everything as it was before, as though I had never existed. Is such a one to succeed me? Now, though, I have enough to finish him." Yet he still did not finish; the wretched business dragged on. Perhaps Peter was saying to himself that the Emperor, in Vienna, would never forgive him if he withheld the promised forgiveness from Alexis.

I spoke of that, carefully. I hoped that this would be what would save Alexis; his value abroad. He could marry another princess; he was eligible, liked well enough except for his drinking. As a Tsar, he would have been no worse than some. But my husband's life's work meant more in the end than a cut from Vienna.

Spring had turned to summer. On the fourteenth of June the Tsar sent guards to Alexis' house in Petersburg to place him under arrest.

I heard the rest from Alexasha, who was one of the hundred to sign their names below the death-warrant of the Tsarevich. If they had not signed, they would have been tortured and killed. I could not blame them.

This is what he told me. In the first place the Tsar tried to gain support from the Church. But even the Exarch, Yavorsky, who obeyed him in all things, quoted the parable of the Prodigal Son. This was of no value to Peter Alexievich. So he turned to the Senate. If anything was said abroad, he knew, he could say. "But I left it to my advisers it was they who insisted he must die." He could say that if he wished.

The Tsarevich was brought under guard from the Peter

and Paul fortress to face the senators. The president was Tolstoy, who had been one of those sent to bring Alexis back from abroad under promise of forgiveness. Tolstoy is a hard man. If he had not been, he would scarcely have endured his own harsh imprisonment in Constantinople and the public ridicule before it. He knew what suffering meant. It should not have been so easy to inflict it on another. Without Tolstoy's demand for evidence, it is possible the rest might have come to another decision, perhaps of life imprisonment; perhaps not.

A demand for evidence means knouting. Alexis was taken out and given twenty-five strokes of the knout to make him speak. The knout is not like any other whip. It is a stout leather thong with metal ends, borne on a handle. The victim is first stripped and then hung up by the wrists, and to ensure that his arms are put out of joint his feet are weighted with a great log of wood. In this position he receives the blows. Eight or nine are said to kill a man. Alexis was not strong physically. I can only pray that after the first he was senseless and felt nothing. But it is likely the questioners would not permit this. He would be revived, and the knouting would continue.

They did not bring back any useful evidence afterwards. The prisoner was left in the fortress for three days. I did not see anything of my husband; he was closeted with Tolstoy and Golovin, who had also signed as part of the hundred.

Tolstoy was given a letter from the Tsar and with it, he went to the fortress and again questioned the prisoner. I have seen some of the answers and I do not think they came from Alexis, but from Tolstoy. One said that in his youth, Menshikov alone did him good and prevented him from wasting his time with priests and monks. I know Alexis loathed and feared Menshikov as he feared many others. His times with his confessor and with priests, when he saw them, were the few lighted places in his life. He would not think of them as a waste of time.

Next day he received fifteen more blows from the knout.

The Senate then pronounced him worthy of death. Having done this excuses were made for the Tsar, and his promised pardon. Reasons were put forward why the pardon no longer held good. This no doubt was for foreign Courts to listen to. It was stated that the Tsarevich had placed his reliance on foreign aid to obtain the throne by the death of his father.

Any lies will do if they serve well.

Next day again, my husband, Alexasha himself, Tolstoy, and some others went to the fortress at eight o'clock in the morning. They carried instruments of torture, and stayed three hours. That evening word was brought that the Tsarevich was dead.

In Moscow, the deep bell of Ivan the Great tolled its mourning note over the city. Moscow was the place where Alexis was best loved, and where there had been hope that with his coming to rule, the old days would return. Now there was no hope. The people knew nothing either there or in St. Petersburg. Absurd stories began to go about; they said the Tsarevich had been executed after torture, in the fortress, by his father's own hand; they said that next day a Livonian girl named Krammer had been ferried across to sew the head on the body again for the lying in state. That came, and the body itself, with the face and right hand exposed, was viewed by hundreds of people who filed past in the Church of the Trinity before Alexis' burial. I saw it myself. It was pale as parchment and the face had no expression; it might have been that of a man who had died in his sleep. The Tsar was by me and we said no word to one another, then or later, concerning it.

There would have been no need of any execution. I remembered Patkul, the magnificently hardy Livonian nobleman whom Charles XII broke on the wheel. After nine strokes of the knout Patkul had screamed a prayer to them to cut off his head, for he could endure no more. But Alexis lived after forty strokes.

One of the stories arose in this way. At the last minute, hearing of what was being done, I sickened of all of it, and sent for a physician I trusted. "For the love of God, if he isn't dead yet, cut the poor devil's veins," I said to him. Afterwards they said, "Tsaritsa Catherine killed him. She had his veins cut and he bled to death." There was nothing of the kind needed, any more than execution was needed.

The bells tolled in Petersburg also, their Dutch jangle sounding too frivolous for death. Peter had had them made in Rotterdam. I remembered that and all the other things he had had done, and tried to think of him as a good ruler freed from the threat of a successor who would undo all his work. I sat stroking Shishenka's curls which were like his father's. Some of all this had been for him. He, not Alexis, was now his father's heir. I tried to feel joy.

Alexis had died on the seventh of July. Next day was the anniversary of our victory at Poltava. As always there were festivities, a banquet, and a ball. There was no Court mourning because the Tsarevich had died a criminal. Two days later was another occasion for feasting; the birthday of the Tsar. He had designed a boat and it was launched and named *Liesna*. Everyone made merry.

Next day again was Alexis' funeral. No foreign envoys had been invited. The preacher announced his text and it was, "O Absalom, my son, my son." I stared straight ahead of me and did not look at the Tsar. Others who had been watching told me afterwards that the tears poured down his face.

They buried Alexis and Charlotte together. Charlotte's coffin had been exposed since her death to the wind and rain below a leaking roof which was unfinished in that corner of the cathedral. Now they are together. Efrosinia was dismissed with a large gift from Alexis' goods. I do not know exactly what happened to her; I believe she married a soldier in the guard, but I have never seen her again.

They say God is just. During all that year I had been noticing small things, trifles of no account, missing from my rooms at the Ekaterinhofsky. I thought I knew who was at fault, and because of it and the disturbances about Alexis, I held my peace for long.

Mary Hamilton had come from the Sloboda. She was a kinswoman of Matviev, whose Scots wife bore the same name. The earlier Mary Hamilton had helped bring up Peter's mother. Natalia Naryshkina thought of Matviev as her guardian; he died on the pikes of the streltsi in the Red Square. Peter and his mother saw him thrown to them. Perhaps for that reason the Tsar had always been kind to the younger Mary. Later she became his mistress. She had the clear bright colouring of her country-women, and a pretty smile with dimples. I am not beyond seeing the good points in women Peter admired. I knew also that Mary was vain, arrogant and selfish. Now it appeared she was dishonest. When something I particularly valued went at last, I complained to the Tsar.

I should not have done it. I should have made myself ignore the losing of small things that did not matter. My husband after Alexis' death was not as he had been. For a man to kill his son is against nature, and now it seemed that Peter Alexievich sought all ways of showing his cruelty. That he had such a streak I had known from the beginning. Now it seemed to drown his other qualities, his affection, his faith in God, his sudden kindnesses. There were few in that year.

Mary Hamilton had other lovers. The favourite at that time was a man called Orlov, to whom it was later found that Mary passed the stolen goods for resale. After my complaint the Tsar sent for this man and set about him with his stick, his *doubina*. Orlov was a coward and began to whimper information. Yes, he had received such a thing, and such another and another, from Mary Hamilton; yes, he had been her lover; there had been a pregnancy, whether his fault or not, and she had destroyed it; no, it was not the first time.

Most young women who take lovers have the same problem, and solve it as Mary did. I myself had had to do the same in the days of Sheremetev. If it is not convenient for a child to be born, it can be got rid of early, with herbs or hooks. Anisa and I had helped one another in this way in the old days. It had never been called a crime in Russia. Now, my husband, for his own reasons, decided to call it murder, and he had Mary Hamilton arrested and flogged. He was present. I regret to say that at that time he often stripped young women and flogged them. He never did it to me. Under the lash of the whip Mary told everything:

there had been three pregnancies and a still-birth. On that occasion she had strangled the child to make sure.

"She is to die," said the Tsar. I tried to do what I could for Mary as for Alexis. Nothing would move the Tsar. On the morning of the execution he rose early as usual and got through much paper-work before going out to the scaffold. One or two early townsfolk saw the giant figure and drew together into a crowd to watch. Presently Mary Hamilton came out, her dimpled cheeks rosy in the cold March day. She was wearing a white dress with black ribbons, as the Tsar had ordered. He took trouble over such things. Perhaps Mary hoped at the last moment, if she looked attractive, to win a pardon from him. She did not seem to expect death. She knelt before the Tsar and he turned away, and whispered something to the executioner.

"She is pardoned," breathed the crowd. At the same moment the axe swept bright through the air. Mary Hamilton's head flew from her shoulders and the headless corpse knelt on, with its white dress slowly soaking in blood. Peter picked up the girl's head, still warm, and kissed the mouth. Then he turned it about and gave a lecture to those listening; he knew the names of the different veins and arteries, the form and making of a skull. Afterwards he kissed the head again and dropped it in the dust, crossed himself, and walked away. Later he sent orders that the head was to be preserved in spirits of wine in a bottle for the Academy of Sciences, which is still being built.

This execution happened on March the nineteenth. A month later to the day, our little Shishenka died. I do not forget the date. It was spring again and the grass was green and the water blue and the sun shining.

I still cannot speak of Shishenka without tears. I had loved him better than my daughters, perhaps better than the Tsar. To his father also he had meant much. Now, it was unlikely I should bear another child. Could it be said that Alexis had died in vain? That was a bad time. I cannot yet think of it. I will go on thinking of Mary Hamilton.

A strange thing happened about her. Some of the Scots in the Sloboda, hearing of it, must have written home. However it happened, Mary's death was made into a ballad. From the beginning it was said to have happened in the reign of Mary, Queen of Scots, who had four waiting-women called Maries. But there was no Mary Hamilton among them. She died in Petersburg in 1719, and was soon forgotten by most.

It is common enough to hear Europe described as a chessboard. But there are too many kings and queens for one game of chess. I often wonder if the fate of countries would have turned out differently had Peter Alexievich not made one European journey in his youth and another in middle age; had he never disliked the sight of a slender insolent Hanoverian whose brown glance despised him for a savage; had he never made gigantic friendships with Frederick William of Prussia of the huge guards, or Augustus the Strong of Poland with whom he crumpled silver dishes at dinner. There was also the strange regard he and Charles of Sweden had for one another, although they passed the years making war.

I, being a woman, cannot see countries except through their rulers. The brown-eyed German was now King George of England, not too secure on his throne; he himself regarded England hardly at all, Hanover much. He had accepted the English crown to strengthen Hanover. Like ourselves before the coming of the Tsar, Hanover itself had no ports; George was anxious for Bremen and Verden, and he wished his son-in-law, the friendly giant of Prussia, to sever relations with the Tsar. He used all possible means to bring that about, and ended only by causing Frederick William to swear friendship to one side openly and to ourselves in secret. That was as far as anyone got.

Augustus of Poland had tired himself out with women. He could not, if he would, stop the Tsar from marching troops through his country. Again, the liking between the two men stood the Tsar in good stead. But he was never to recover the friendship of the Emperor in Vienna after Alexis' death. He did not go abroad again.

Charles XII was dead. His sister—they did not elect the elder, who was married to Holstein, and our daughter Anne was in love with the young Duke by now although, poor dear, it was long enough before we could let them be formally betrothed—his younger sister Ulrica had become Queen, and was less warlike than her brother. George of England twice sent ships to protect Sweden against Russia, and Russia's answer was to land and invade the Swedish coastland and set fire to towns and villages. That made the ships withdraw and George's Parliament laugh at him and his orders. He understood no English so this would hardly affect him. But Admiral Norris, our old friend, felt foolish. The Kalmucks had made good work of destroying Swedish farmsteads.

Peter, his generals, all the people, were weary of the Baltic war. To end it seemed impossible in anyone's lifetime. There had been attempts at peace, between the hurried building of ships for war and the landings to burn villages on Swedish soil. But the Tsar refused to part with Petersburg although having conquered Finland itself as ground to bargain with, he would give way as to that when the time came. He juggled with power, like a clown, keeping his mind cool. He tried to be friendly with France by speaking of an alliance for Elizabeth still; this time to the Duc de Chartres, the Regent's son, whom he proposed making King of Poland when Augustus should die. Once the bridegroom was to have been Louis XV, but reports had reached the Court of Versailles that although attractive the Tsarevna Elizabeth was uneducated. This was Elizabeth's own fault; she was lazy and her sister Anne learned more than she did from their tutors. But my husband had hopes of a French alliance if only to trouble England. The English have always been enemies of the French, not only because they still lay claim to the French throne; there is some difference in their minds. They were cautious now both with ourselves and Sweden; they suspected Charles XII in his day, and then Russia, of being about to invade them on behalf of the Pretender. But Peter Alexievich was never interested in that affair.

It was all very hard to deal with, especially as Queen Ulrica withdrew from an agreement at Aland which should have suited everyone. Shortly afterwards she gave the crown to her husband, who became Frederick I. Despite the fact that we had attacked a squadron of Swedish vessels at the beginning of his new reign, he was friendly. This held out great hope of peace.

The Tsar was now without a male heir except for the young son of Alexis, whom he refused to see. It would have hurt him to set eyes on the tall well-grown child, remembering Shishenka. I know how greatly he had set store on a son of his own for heir: at Shishenka's death they told me the Tsar had put a pistol to his temple, but did not use it. I was too sad almost to care. I had borne Peter Alexievich many children, and few had lived to grow. Some said it was the curse of the Romanovs, whose sons are always weaker than their daughters. But I knew it was the curse of the pox. Otherwise I had been strong and well enough; even the pains of labour hardly troubled me. Now he could have no hope of sons from me. He never reproached me, nor was he anything but loving towards me; but by now I had seen something of the world, and I began to watch the pretty young women about Court. Had I been a man in Peter's place, I would have chosen one of them to bear me a child and get rid of the old laundress-wife. Perhaps he would do so. Maria Cantemir had grown into a handsome young woman and the Tsar spent much time with her and with her father, the book-loving Hospodar of Moldavia. I knew that Menshikov, Tolstoy and the others were watching all this, as well as myself. All of us watched and said nothing.

Looking back, I cannot feel that in the end I committed any crime about Maria, I who on the European journey had gone surrounded by women with children in their arms that they said were the Tsar's. I had cared nothing because despite all these affairs of his, he had always come back to me. But now? I did not know.

Meantime the Tsar had news of peace, and boarded his yacht the King of Prussia had given him and sailed towards Sweden. He bade us pray for success and we did so. No word reached us for some days, and then all was changed to rejoicing except in my heart. But I let no one guess it;

it was right for us to celebrate the Peace of Nystadt, and to cheer the Tsar when he sailed back in triumph and leapt on shore brandishing the peace-treaty and then almost ran to the Cathedral to give thanks, and afterwards drank before everyone to the Russia he had made in a bumper of wine, and everyone cheered him.

The celebrations were in Moscow and were like nothing ever seen. Now in the quiet I can remember them, though I could not see everything because I myself was a part of the procession. I sat in a red-hung gondola with a brazier to keep me warm. It was needed, because I had to change my costume frequently, appearing sometimes as a Frisian, in the dress I had worn with Peter at Zotov's wedding, then again in a red gown or another in blue. I smiled as was proper, and fingered my diamond sword, but I still had a thick head. The banquet had been for a thousand guests, and Peter Alexievich locked everyone in while he himself went to let off fireworks, as the men already told to do so were drunk. So were we. Alexasha fell under the table, and his head is strong. Now behind the Prince-Pope, the Marshal-Jester, and Bacchus, led by cardinals, the Emperor's fool sat in a carriage drawn by pigs. Neptune followed, with a beard as white as the snow that threatened. Everyone was made to attach golden ducats to this false beard and at the end, Peter went and cut them off himself and kept them. He always had a great respect for money.

The Princess-Abbess with her breasts bare—she must have been frozen—was led by monks, and sat in another gondola on wheels. Alexasha followed with his servants, dressed as abbés, and Daria, who was in the procession, and either Marfa or Anna, I forget which, were in Spanish costume in a barque. There followed the King of Pressburg in a skiff on wheels and full of white bears, but these were stuffed. Praskovia had been made to come but she wore as might have been expected, a costume of old Muscovy, with one of her fat daughters dressed as a shepherdess. There was a galley with spread sails manned by an admiral; there was a three-masted ship mounted with guns, and dragged by fifteen horses. The Muscovites stared and cheered; many had never seen a real ship. The Tsar was on board, and a drum beat and Peter Alexievich climbed up on the rigging. I could see what he was doing as I rode just behind, with my eight horses for the gondola. He was as active as a boy.

There were harlequins and dragons and masked ladies and bears. There were sledge-dogs and foreign envoys and the Duke of Holstein, whom Anne loved. There was a Turkish ship with cannon firing in answer to the salutes from the Tsar's ship. In it sat the Hospodar of Moldavia, Cantemir. He was comfortable enough on a pile of cushions. No one followed him except the servants, dressed for the show, and their sledge was disguised as a sausage. The whole procession passed through every street in Moscow for five days. It was much harder work than the banquet.

Peter did a strange thing then; he decided to burn down his little house at Preobrazhensky, in which he had thought of starting the Swedish war twenty years earlier. While it blazed he marched round and round it, beating on his drum as he had done while he formerly lived there, a boy raising regiments.

After everything was over he came to me. I received him gladly; he no longer looked troubled, ageing or ill, and I thought he would be able now to live in peace and dig his Petersburg garden and prune his lime trees and roses and barberry bushes and watch the cypress grow. He sat and drank wine with me and then said, "Katinka! The way is clear now for war on Persia. I have wanted the caravan routes to India all my life; it will set the seal on our achievement."

I said nothing, except that I would go with him.

It was summer when we reached the Persian frontier, and the heat was fierce. The Tsar had had his curly hair cropped before he left. "Keep it for my return and we will make a peruke," he told the barber, and I hoped that if this were done, it would stop Peter Alexievich from snatching the wigs off other people's heads when he felt cold in church. But there was no cold here: we would have been glad of it. I myself had copied my husband and felt relief from the heavy burden of my hair. We wore helmets on campaign; I, Peter, Tolstoy and Apraxin the Admiral, and Cantemir the Hospodar and his daughter Maria.

Behind us rode thirty thousand men, who had been increasing on the way, joined by strange hordes in stranger clothing that recalled to me the first barbarian I had ever seen in the Livonian camp outside Marienburg. The Cossacks joined us, which meant that we were expected to win the war, for they do not trouble to join a losing side. Their karakul caps stank in the hot weather. The Tartars and the Kalmucks came, yellow of skin and at home on the backs of ponies. There were the mountain chiefs and, last of all, to the Tsar's pleasure, the most royal Ayuta Khan, the Kalmuck of Kalmucks. He brought his wife and daughter who were sent to my tent. We smiled and talked through an interpreter while I tried not to stare at their costumes of Persian brocade, fur-trimmed with matching bonnets, below which their black hair stuck out in many tight pigtails. We were by then nearing Astrakhan.

I must make myself think of Maria Cantemir. Of all Peter's mistresses she was the only one who scorned me and did not try to hide it. She was as confident of her place as Anna Mons had been long ago; I tried to remember Anna's fall and hope that the same thing would happen to Maria. But Maria had a weapon that Anna had not used. She was pregnant by the Tsar. The long riding over rough roads had not brought on a miscarriage.

We left her at Astrakhan, where she said she felt unwell. We ourselves were embarking by sea. The sight of the sparkling water cheered Peter Alexievich and made him forget the sad sight that had greeted him lately at Yaroslavl, where his earliest ship of all was found rotting. "Tar her! Save her! Next year we will return and have a great feast for the ancestor of the Russian navy, and sail her down the Neva." He was very angry about the neglect of the boat.

But here was the dark glitter of the Caspian and a seaworthy ship. Peter cast off his gloomy mood as soon as we were afloat with the supply-vessels following, and so far as I know never gave a thought to whether or not Maria was in premature labour.

I stayed by him listening, as usual. I avoided particularly the company of Tolstoy. He had found me a Greek physician who would treat Maria Cantemir with herbs. They would not kill her. It was not so discourteous. I had, after all, learned some fine manners on my European journey. But why should I lose all I had gained over the years of waiting, hoping, fruitless bearing, watching my husband with other women? Why?

There was another thing. Looking down at the water as we went, I remembered how, over the past few years, on the advice of Alexasha Menshikov and others, I had sent money to be invested in my name in London and Amsterdam. It would be enough to provide for my old age if the Tsar tired of me now I was growing older and had given him no living son.

But on the voyage, and later after we had reached Derbent, he showed no sign either of being weary of me, or of longing for Maria. He sniffed the tarry smells of the bitumen which lay everywhere, past which Peter walked with his customary hurry so that the rest must always run to keep up with his stride.

Word came then of Maria's miscarriage in Astrakhan.

He did not seem to grieve much, or to guess anything. He remained in good humour. After his triumphal entry into the Persian city he said cheerfully, "Alexander built it; now Peter has captured it." Perhaps he reflected also that Alexander the Great, like himself, left no son.

Some time later he was talking to me. He said, "I don't want to add any more land to the empire, God knows. What I need is water, water, water."

I should have recalled earlier that after the Peace of Nystadt the Senate had begged him to accept the title of Father of the Fatherland, Peter the Great, Emperor of All the Russias.

Later a storm sank our ships and we ran short of food. I ate horseflesh with the men as I had often done before, but that left us short of horses. It would in fact take a year for Peter to wring a favourable treaty from the Shah. I had to comfort him when we rode out of Derbent, where he had left a garrison behind. "Do as you formerly have and harry the enemy, with small forces here and there," I said. "They'll never know how many more are waiting to follow." But there would be few to wait. However the Persians had a bad spy-system and the uneven country lent itself to deception about numbers. After he believed that he had thought of the idea himself, my husband took it up. In the end, he won the whole Caspian seaboard and the Turks, still ill-informed as to the real nature of things, agreed that he should be left in possession of what he already had.

"Take comfort, Bombardier Mikhailov," I said to him, remembering the name he had chosen for himself in old days. "Now you have your ports and your trade will come from east and west and you will be Emperor indeed, and richer than anyone." But Peter moved restlessly and said his inside was hurting him. "I may have water, but I can't pass any," he said wryly.

I looked at his face; it was thin and drawn, and I knew he was in much pain. "You shall see a physician when we get back to Moscow," I told him. He agreed with me absently. "Moscow, yes: when we return to Moscow." Both of us knew St. Petersburg was too far away.

EIGHT

THE CAP OF MONOMAKH

The Moscow doctors patched my husband up, and as soon as we might do so we travelled to St. Petersburg; I knew this was better than any cure. He was homesick for the sight of the sea and the islands; oppressed in the heavy inland air. Again within sight of his beloved city he was like a new man who wanted to live. As I had hoped, he spent much time now with the gardener, seeing his newly planted spiraea and lilacs bloom; he could even sit, talking ceaselessly in his old way, beneath the limes which now, with constant care, were growing tall and thick with tender green leaves to give pleasure.

In the evenings he slept in a boat on the Neva. He said it made him feel better. I know he did not spend all of the night in sleep; he roamed the streets with drunken parties. Perhaps it was a sign that he was better. I slept alone and listened in vain for the sound of the sweeping Saturday brooms on the Nevsky Prospekt, that long street paved with stone, which the Tsar had insisted must be kept clean once a week by Swedish prisoners. They had all been sent home now after the Peace of Nystadt which had demanded their return. "You'll have to go with them," Peter had joked to me. "I wonder what they'll do with you now in Livonia?"

About this time, left alone so much, I grew foolish. I would be the last to deny my folly, or that ageing women often fall in love unsuitably, making themselves laughed at, no doubt. I thought that no one knew except a few, but the news always leaks out. My lover was the brother of Anna Mons of long ago. He reminded me strongly of that time I had seen his beautiful golden-haired sister in her coach, driving through the Sloboda. William Mons had Anna's features and her colouring. He was too pretty, they said, to be a man. But he was not a woman in bed. He handled me delicately as if I were made of Dresden porcelain. His sister Matrena, who was married to a man named Balk, helped us.

Perhaps I was too much occupied with William Mons to know at this time what the Tsar was thinking. Who would have credited that strange mind with a plan to crown me, at that time, in Moscow as a reward for the long years, the hardships, the days when I had perhaps saved him on the Pruth?

He had many other plans for everything, as usual. There was the supposed execution of Shafirev the Jew, that same one who had gone to Constantinople to make terms regarding money at the very time the Tsar remembered now. I told him that he was cutting off his own head with Shafirev's. "He saved us once," I said. "He may be of use again. Jews always know everyone, even in a foreign city." So Shafirev was saved, just in time as it turned out; they had had difficulty in fitting his huge belly in below the block, and in the delay this caused, the Tsar's word arrived to save him. This happened also to Osterman, who had helped draw up the Nystadt treaty. Their sentences were altered to exile for life, which can mean that they will in the end return to St. Petersburg.

Other plans concerned the punishment of dishonesty, or taking bribes in the law courts, bribes everywhere; in this the Tsar was not successful. He had established countless governors of the provinces, and the more governors there were the worse the bribery became; no one was free of it. Yet the land was so vast after Peter's conquests that no one man could govern it alone. There were more decrees to alter customs tariffs; there was a ukase to state that the Tsar might name his own heir. This last roused much unrest, as everyone rightly saw it as an attempt to rule out Alexis' young son from the succession. The right of naming has fallen to me now and I will name young Peter Alexievich when the time comes for me to go. Everyone agrees on this, even Alexasha.

Peter himself was never still nowadays. He paid visits to his needle factory he had founded, his schools of mathematics that were still short of teachers (the Swedes had been useful), his planned tapestry works (but nobody could spin cotton) and the growing Academy of Sciences which he would not live to see completed. He jotted down ideas for digging a canal between the Caspian and the Baltic; one had already been started between the Volga and the Don. He gave street lights to St. Petersburg. He arranged for fortresses to be built in the Crimea and for more boats to be built at Yaroslavl to retake Azov for Russia. He wanted an expedition to set out to find if America is joined to Tartary. He wrote letters to the King of Madagascar to explain how much better off that island would be under Russian rule, but the King did not agree, that I know of. Above all, Peter created a new nobility. It no longer consisted of the boyars of ancient blood, but of men who had served him and shown their talent and loyalty, like Menshikov the pieman who was made a prince. There was much ill-feeling over this last creation, but nobody could stop it.

On the anniversary of our marriage the Tsar set off fireworks beneath my windows. They were very ambitious, designed to show Peter's initials and mine twined together within a great heart surrounded by symbols of love. William Mons watched them with me and behind us were the ladies and Maria Cantemir, now no longer of importance to the Tsar.

The coronation was to be within a fortnight. My crown was made by a famous goldsmith, and it weighed four pounds and had a great ruby on top. I was glad my hair had grown again and would support the weight. My coronation robe had come from Paris and was heavy with gold thread, showing the double eagle on the mantle. The Tsar's costume was to be of gold also. We went to Moscow. Shortly before the ceremony, when I was to drive to the Cathedral of the Assumption in a great gilded coach sent from France, Peter strode into my rooms. He was carrying his golden robe and shook it. Gold sequins fell off and strewed the floor and lay there shining.

"Look at that!" he roared. "Enough to pay a grenadier! Why don't they teach their women to sew?" And I remembered one of his other ideas, which had been very successful; this was to take our own women away from the fate of sewing which had befallen them in Terem days, and place them in assemblies held in private houses, where they might meet well-mannered men and dance with them and make polite talk and drink water or tea. Peter was most particular that these assemblies should not become drunken. At first everyone had been ill at ease but now they were accepted, and brought about many marriages.

He had mentioned the grenadiers. They had not been paid.

My coronation took place in the towered city where the ancient Tsars had been crowned. I think Peter was trying to say that I was fit for this. There were no unusual happenings; the crowds in the streets cheered as they had been bidden, though they did not know me; we had hardly ever come to Moscow. After the anointing with the holy oils I was so much moved that I knelt and clasped by the knees the tall golden figure beside me, as though he were God. The Tsar raised me up with great tenderness. He laid in my hands the golden globe, the symbol of power. I saw in their place our young daughters in their rich robes and behind them all the nobility of Muscovy, both old and new. It was a great moment for Sheremetev's laundress. I do not remember clearly, but I think tears coursed down my face and I was thinking how Shishenka should have been here today and was not, and there was nobody to take his place. Apart from this it should have been the happiest day of my whole life. I do not know what more I wanted. I went to pray at the shrines and then we returned to the Kremlin in the gilded coach and there was feasting and everyone kissed my hands.

So many things come to mind; the Tsar sailing the mended Ancestor from Yaroslavl down the Neva to the flutter of flags and the booming of guns in salute from all the Russian fleet: our own evening cruises on the water, for the Tsar had decreed that every citizen of Petersburg must have a boat, and he appointed an official to see to them if they leaked, at the owner's expense. The city of an evening was like a great drifting water-party, with friends calling out to one another above the splash of oars and swing of sails, and coloured lights making reflections in the water. Or again, it might be a gala occasion at my palace or Peter's, where I would wait for him with my ladies by the fountains, which played. My dresses were very grand by now; I do not think Wilhelmina of Prussia would have scorned them. Nobody at Court was allowed to copy them. So glittering a figure had I become that, when the Tsar found my Skavronsky brothers for me after Nystadt, they came to the Ekaterinhofsky and gaped and twisted their hats in their hands and did not know what to say. But the Tsar had been like that himself long ago, when he visited the Electress of Brandenburg. I did not know what to say to my brothers either. After a little while of attempted talk I handed them over to Anisa and she entertained them. They stayed on at Court and by now we get on more easily, especially Karl who still loves horses.

Court life is tiring, and when the Tsar arranged to visit the fleet at Voronezh that summer I took myself and William Mons into the country to rest. William was my chamberlain and this could have been the reason for taking him. I felt tired and languid, too much so even for making love. We had a few days together. The house where we stayed was by the water; one cannot get away from water anywhere near Petersburg. One morning I saw a ship come in close. It was the Tsar's yacht, not the Prussian one but the one he liked best that the King of England, William III, had sent him long ago after his time of shipbuilding there. The messenger came ashore and there was a letter for me. I had Mons read it out. His fair cheeks flushed and the gold-tipped lashes were lowered over his eyes; I could not stop looking at him, he was so beautiful.

This was the letter. *When I go into a room and you are not there, I want to run out of the house. Everything is empty lacking you.*

The Tsar must have come home early from Voronezh. I told the women to pack my gear at once. We would go back to Petersburg.

Yes, I think Peter always loved me. He was over fifty when

he wrote that letter. He had become ill again with a recurrence of the old fever, the old enemy, and also passed a stone which gave him intense pain. I sat by him day and night and would not leave him. He was like my child at such times. Before he was better, as always happened, he insisted on getting up and going to see one of his new ships launched. "I am very well, very well indeed now," he would say impatiently. He began to celebrate with the ship's crew afterwards and when I knew they had all drunk as much as they could hold I went to fetch him.

"Come away, little father. It is time you were home."

I took part of his weight and the huge body sagged against my shoulder. It was all bone and muscle with Peter Alexievich; he was never fat, like the boyars. I knew he was not as well as he pretended. Yet he would not stay in bed and now instead, to cure himself in his own way, rode off across the freezing marshes to inspect the canal-digging. He used to keep a constant eye on this because the forced labour, thousands of serfs driven each year out of their homes, would not stay if they could escape, and Peter was like a foreman with a work-force. He would get down himself and show them how to dig, and see that they did it, then come home with wet shoes. This time, he did not even come straight home; he went on into the heat of the smith's forge he had founded at Clonets and worked it himself and sweated a great deal. Then on the journey home he saw a boat in difficulties near the water's edge and got a dinghy and told the crew what to do, how to haul on the ropes, and they did not do it properly and he jumped out of the boat so that the icy sea was waist-high about him, and tied the ropes himself and helped to haul. He saved the crew that night, but made himself ill again. Yet he was only in bed for two days after he reached Petersburg.

That was the moment they chose to tell him about my affair with William Mons.

The horror was his silence. He had never before been silent. Many times I have seen him hotly angry, or cold as with Alexis. But now he contained his anger, and this was more dangerous than anything.

I tried to deceive myself. Perhaps after all he did not know. There were many other things which might be keeping him from me. But nothing happened for two weeks, two whole weeks. At the end of that time we all of us sat together at the supper-table. The Tsar asked for the time. I looked at my little Dresden watch he had bought me long ago and said, "It is nine o'clock." I was proud of having learned to read the figures.

He seized the watch from me, twisting the hands violently as though to break them. "No! No! It is midnight!" he shouted. "Everybody must go to bed."

I went to my room. There was nothing to do but obey him in these moods. Next morning Mons did not come for his day's orders as usual. I heard later that they had arrested him within minutes of my leaving. Matrena Balk was arrested also. "They have been dealing in bribes, the brother and sister," the rumour was put about. "They have taken presents for obtaining favours from the Empress."

My name was not otherwise mentioned. I said not a word and waited. How often I had done this! Now, there was nothing else I could do. I did not know what was to happen to me. I did not try to think.

Mons was condemned to death and Matrena to exile. Later I heard that the Tsar went to see Mons in prison. William was wearing a gold ring I had given him. Peter fingered it, and said, "This was for love, wasn't it?" and went out.

Mons was beheaded on the twenty-eighth of November. The same day the Tsar sent for me to drive out with him. I put on furs and a heavy pelisse of lined velvet against the cold, and I rouged my cheeks. When I reached the sledge and found my husband waiting for me, I smiled as usual and made my curtsy, and went to take my place.

"Where are we going today?" I asked, as he remained silent.

"I will show you." He lashed out at the sledge-dogs, who quickened pace. Then he made them slow down; we were approaching the public scaffold. There were still a few watchers scattered about in the cold. I saw, as though it were a scene in a theatre, Mons' headless body at the block, wearing the pale-blue coat I had known. That was how I knew the corpse. As we went past, my velvet skirts brushed against the blood-stained satin. I could feel the stiffness of the dead, like wood, touch me. I smiled on. Presently I began to chat about something. I do not know to this day what it was. We finished our drive and went back to the palace. I parted from Peter, still amiably. Everyone must see that the Empress is smiling; there can have been no truth in the rumours that went about earlier.

When I reached my rooms, Mons' head, bled white and preserved in spirit, sat in a jar on my mantel. I took no heed and went and took off my furs and the velvet and gave it all to the women so that they could brush off the snow. Then I had them lace me into another gown.

That night he came to me. I do not know if he expected to find me weeping, guilty, horrified, swooning, begging for mercy. I was none of these things. I greeted him as usual and asked if he would take wine.

"No," he replied gruffly, not looking at me. "Drink if you will. You drink too much."

Presently he turned and said, "You killed Cantemir's baby, didn't you?"

"Yes."

I poured myself a wine-cup and sat down again. The pallid thing on the mantel was between us. I continued sipping my wine and making polite talk, such as he liked at the assemblies. "It seems a long time since your Imperial Majesty visited me. If as they say you may marry your younger daughter to the King of France, they must surely approve of her mother. Elizabeth is a good dancer; she will keep in step. I would have done so myself had I learned young. She would make a worthy Queen, do you not think? Perhaps it will all come true one day. A pity your Imperial Majesty will not drink with me; it is not comradely, but do as you will."

Suddenly he rose with a roar and smashed the Venetian mirror with his fist. The fragments showered about the floor and Peter Alexievich stood there with the blood running from his cut hand and from a place on his chin, glaring at me.

"So I will do to you, to—to you, to all of yours, you——"

I saw that he was about to take one of his fits. I rose to my feet and said calmly, "You have ruined a piece of furniture that wasn't cheap. Is your home more pleasing now?"

I had laid down the wine-cup. He stood there quivering and twitching, and more than I had done in the whole of my life I felt pity for him, and a lifetime's love. But that must come from him now, never myself. In this moment I had either lost him and my life, or else gained him forever.

Suddenly he gave an oath and a sob and held out his arms to me. "Ah! Katioushka! What does any of it matter save for our two selves?"

We had ended in bed. The brazier had died down and the flames no longer sparkled reflected in the smashed mirror's fragments as though rubies strewed the floor. The candles were low, and had ceased to cast their steady light on Mons' head, in pickle on the mantel. It didn't matter. I had seen worse, after all, on the battlefields. What mattered was the man who lay in my arms, a man the like of whom had never before been seen and will never, I know, be again; Peter the Great, the giant, genius, madman, murderer, my lover; the only lover fit for me. I remembered the first night we had lain together in Alexasha's house and even now, wondered if this would be the last. He had not, I knew well, long to live. While he lived, and whatever he did to others and to me, I would stay by him.

For some years, perhaps since the murder of Alexis, I had been troubled with a dream which was always the same. It took the form of a beast on whose head were three lighted candles, and it spoke in a tongue I could not understand. I told the Tsar of it and he said to me, "I too have a dream, and it is of blood, always blood. It spills and runs over the high walls like washing-water." But to dream one must sleep, and nowadays Peter Alexievich hardly slept at all. He was again in a fever of energy, like a light that burns the brighter in the last moment before it goes out. Partly he was occupied by the election of a new Prince-Pope of buffoons, as the last had died: there was the business of the chairs and the conclave and each voter swallowing spoonfuls of brandy, and all the rest, lasting two nights and a day. Later the new Archpriest was married to Zotov's widow, with celebrations. Then, at Epiphany, there was the blessing of the Neva, and the Tsar behaved with dignity here, as at each blessing of waters since he had been young.

Following this we had a grand reception at the Winter Palace, and a banquet afterwards. The Tsar seemed well then. But by early morning he was crying out with pain and I sent for his physician.

"We must perform an operation," said Lazarotti. Italians make good doctors; they have gentle fingers and know their business.

"What will you do to him?" Whatever it was to be, I would stay in the room. Alexasha Menshikov and a man named Repnin—they disliked each other and were rivals for the favour of the Tsar—held Peter's hands, while a cut was made in his abdomen to release trapped urine. It all gushed forth mixed with blood, and he made no sound. Afterwards the two men showed me their bruised wrists. "Man's a poor animal," the Tsar was muttering.

At last, after many years of mockery at the Church, he agreed to have a chapel consecrated in the next room, so that by having the door open he might see it. The bishop came and Peter made his confession. He took the sacrament, but it did not stop his pain. Soon he could no longer keep himself from crying aloud. His groin and thighs were a mass of sores and the blocked urine coursed like poison through his blood. Yet his mind was clear. He thought of a charity to perform to save his soul. If any convict was not guilty of a capital offence, he said, the man was to be set free.

That same day he received extreme unction. Anointed with the oil, he continued in charity. He freed by then all military prisoners except murderers, likewise pardoning those nobles who had fled from Court. There were not a few of them. His brain still dealt with detail. The day wore on and I sat by him listening to his cries. I tried to pray for him and to ask that he be freed from pain. When the bleak winter sun had reached its height and the shadows were shorter, he asked for writing-paper and a quill.

He tried to write. The words he set down were *Give all back to* . . . but there was no name. He called then for Anne, our elder girl, whose wedding he had promised to attend soon. She came in, weeping. I think that he had wanted to dictate the rest to her to write, but when she came he had already grown faint, and did not know her. We were glad to see him out of pain. Perhaps God had answered my prayer.

He was dying. Presently the silence was broken by the clanking spurs of the guard. One after another the men came in, saluted, and left. The Senate followed. Its members looked at the death-bed awkwardly, saying nothing. Perhaps they did not yet believe that this time the Tsar would not recover. But I knew. "They'll believe it when he is dead," I told myself. "They'll have plenty to say then." A part of my mind was clear, knowing their thoughts.

Alexasha had gone away. Through my weariness I wondered where he had gone. It was almost certain that he and Tolstoy or Repnin would be giving orders to the guard and quarrelling with each other about who was to do it. They could get on with it, I thought, and decide what they might. I had no time now for anything except my husband.

No more words came. "I believe, I hope," he had murmured at the last, kissing the crucifix. I kept saying the phrases to myself, losing sight of their meaning while I watched Peter's face. Outside it had begun to grow dark early and the lights below the ikons made little glowing places on the walls. The Tsar's eyes stared and his breath grew rasping. But still he struggled for life. He had taken life with his two hands, wrought at it, twisted and used it like metal: he would not part with it easily. It was many hours after that that the struggle ceased.

When it happened, I closed the poor staring eyes. It was the last thing I could do for him.

They say he was hated. But after he lay in his coffin a strange thing happened. I have spoken of the man Yaguzhinsky, who had once been a bootblack. By now he was one of the new nobility and had roystered with Peter and served him well and badly and been beaten by his *doubina* like the others. Yet through the night he went weeping into the church and tore the pall off the coffin and sat astride it and beat on its two sides, like beating a drum. And he called aloud, "Peter Alexievich, come back, come back!" He called again and again, and there was no answer and they came in the end and led him, still weeping, away.

He was drunk, of course. But perhaps everyone did not hate my husband.

That happened afterwards. Before then, when I went out to leave the priests to pray by the newly-dead corpse, my women were already waiting to array me in the formal mourning of a Tsaritsa: the straight black robe, the muffling veil. I let them do as they would. It was merciful to be no one, only a woman behind a veil like the women of the Terem. Nobody could watch my face and eyes, or guess my thoughts when I should think again. For the present, I could not. I could do nothing of my own will. Next day perhaps would be different. But now, even for an hour, I wanted to be left alone behind my veil. So it was with anger that I heard Menshikov desired to see me. I wanted no one.

"What now?" I said to him when he came. I did not care what he wanted; when part of one's life has died there is this blankness, this breathing-space before the full knowledge of loss sets in, before one knows that an empty chair will never again be filled.

Alexasha was bowing before me, kissing my hands.

"Leave that," I said. I wished he would go away. In my mind something had begun to stir again, because of Alexasha and his bowing and kissing. I began to wonder who was to be Tsar. It ought to be Peter's grandson, young Peter Alexievich, who was kept hidden in the suburbs with his sister and never seen at Court. Peter—the name hurt—must be about ten years old now; so much time had gone by. That would mean a regency. I remember one of the Scots commanders named Roman Bruce telling me that they always had child kings in Scotland as they had mostly murdered the fathers, and there is a Bible saying there, "Woe to the land whose king is a child." It would be the same in Russia. Nobody could take the place of the dead Tsar. The dead Tsar; my husband was dead.

Alexasha was talking. He said he had bribed the guard. Why? I started to listen idly. It was nothing to me what the answer might be. I had been a man's wife for twenty years and now I was his widow. The word had a lonely sound. I wished there was some wine to drink. Perhaps I should ask the women to bring me and Prince Menshikov wine. Would that cause scandal? I didn't care; I wanted a drink.

"Repnin was angry," Alexasha was saying. "He asked who had dared give orders to the guard and he was told they were under orders from the Empress. You are to rule, Ekaterina Alexievna. Do not trouble your head about anything but saluting the guard. Once that is done, you may leave it all to me."

"The guard," I said stupidly; I was still thinking of wine. I believe I ordered it and Alexasha said, "No, no, no, there is no time for that now. You must see the guard first. Then we can proclaim it to the people later: there is no hurry for that. But now, you must come with me. Put your veil back. Let them see you as they know you. That is all they will want; to see you and hear that you agree to rule us."

"As Regent?" I said doubtfully. I knew enough to know that there had to be an election, a council of regency, and that everyone might not agree on it. But with a Tsar of ten years old—"Katia," said Alexasha, "for the love of me, for the sake of my head—I'll lose it for the day's work if you do not do as I say—for the love of God"—he was a religious man—"come with me to the guard. Only to the guard, my Katia. Then you shall be left in peace. Poor woman, you are very weary. You shall sleep soon, Imperial Majesty, when you've drunk your wine. No, no, my Katia; no wine till you've been to the guard and taken the salute. Do you want them to say to everyone that you came to take it with wine on your breath?"

"Damn you, I've drunk more vodka with the men on campaign than you ever paid for in the whole of your life," I said, and heard myself saying it; I was coming back from somewhere. "You want me for Empress? How the devil can I be? They won't accept a woman of the people, a——"

"You knew the late Tsar's wishes well. You were his closest counsel. There is nobody better fitted to take his place after all your years with him. He anointed and crowned you. Come with me now. Damn you, Katia, if you don't come they will murder both of us, Repnin and the rest. We sink or swim together, as we have from the first in the days of the Sloboda. Come."

So I went with him. There was nothing else to be done, that I could see. I still do not think that there was anything else that could have been done.

They stood at attention, and I walked in front of them and saw not a formation of men, but each man's known face. There were the boys I'd ridden by and cheered up and drunk with and eaten rancid horse with, back in Astrakhan. There were others from the Baltic war. There were forced men and vagabonds and escaped serfs and born officers and common men with wives at home and sweethearts in camp, and I loved every one of them. I felt the tears run down my face and they were not the tears of grief for death, but as it had been at my coronation, a great moment, great . . . for whom? For the washerwoman. For Sheremetev's old whore, and Peter's widow. I'd suit them well enough, till better could be found; till young Peter Alexievich had had time to learn his lessons and be glad of his childhood and get to know his people freely as his grandfather had done. When it was time I'd name him my heir, if he needed naming. But now here were my own lads and I held out my arms to them, as their mothers might do, and their sweethearts and wives. Alexasha Menshikov stood behind me and took my arms and raised them to make the great double Imperial salute, and the men cheered me and I knew then that it would be all right, for as long as I lasted. After that, God knows. Again I hear the beating of the drums.

Alexasha may have thought that he had a pawn to use in me, but he is wrong. I have my own notions and they are not always his. Ah, my pieman, you will be of use, as always.

The first thing he and Tolstoy disagreed about was the bringing of the children home. I think Tolstoy fears the revenge of young Peter Alexievich, in time, for the treatment of his father. We all have our fears. I had Peter and Natalia brought to me and at first they were like caught wild things, with fear at the backs of their eyes, and they kept a hand fast in one another's as if it would ward off the danger. Much cruelty and neglect has been the lot of those children. After they had been with me for a little I was better pleased. They lost their shyness and the scared look, and I swear young Peter grew taller in the first week. He should make a good Tsar and I have given Menshikov the post of tutor to him, though the work is of course done by others. I see the children a great deal and they give me pleasure, and Elizabeth is kind to them.

Anne still loves her Holsteiner and I hear there is to be a baby. I hope she will come safely through her childbirth and that the child will live.

My task is for the common people. They are the bones of Russia. I want to ease their taxes—in the last years of my husband's reign they were taxed cruelly—and if I can abolish tariffs and bribes, although I doubt that last, it will be something. Living with Peter for so many years I would be a fool if I had learned nothing at all, as Alexasha pointed out to me. But he was startled when I said the other day, "There must be an end to war. The country has had enough of it, and it costs too much." It mostly concerned that unpleasant George of England, who had made himself troublesome again in the Baltic. But it takes two sides to fight, and we will not do so. There are enough widows in Russia.

Yes, the Turks and the English and the Swedes all thought that because there is a woman on the throne, they can have their way. But I wear the Cap of Monomakh, the first Vladimir of the old dynasty, that all Tsars wear, and I will use it for peace. What if my husband won an empire as vast as Alexander's? It is made up of ordinary men and women who want to eat and drink and work and laugh and have children who will not have to be sold in the market-places for lack of bread. There is good black soil in

Russia and given the chance it will grow grain. It is my task to see it harvested.

I must look forward and not back. Yet sometimes the ghosts stay with me. I keep sending for wine to solace my loneliness and banish them to a distance if I can. There is comfort in wine.

The Empress Catherine I died of the bottle in the midst of her good intentions. She only reigned for two years. On her death, Alexis' son became Peter II at twelve years old. He distrusted Menshikov and had him exiled to Siberia, where the prince-pieman died. Catherine had left the young Tsar with enough prudent counsellors and the right tutors. His reign should have been a fine one. But at fifteen the boy Tsar died of smallpox on what was to have been his wedding day. His sister Natalia had died a year earlier. Thereafter, the Monomakh Crown went first to the unpleasant daughter of Tsar Ivan the Tongue-Tied. Anna of Courland's reign was one of the worst in Russian history. After that the succession passed to the grandson of Anna's sister Catherine, who had married the Duke of Mecklenburg. This infant Tsar, Ivan VI, was never told what had happened to him. Elizabeth Petrovna, the daughter of Peter and Catherine, threw off her lazy ways and, in an overnight coup d'état with the aid of the guard, made herself Empress, and imprisoned her rival for life. Otherwise Elizabeth made a good ruler, and she reigned for twenty years. On her death, the crown passed to the son of her sister Anne of Holstein, the degenerate Peter III. Shortly he was deposed and murdered by order of his wife, a German princess who then took the title of Catherine II of Russia and is known to the world as Catherine the Great.